With Friends Like That

Peace
&
Blessings

A Novel By

Ty Goode

1

Copyright © 2007 Ty Goode

Library of Congress Control Number: 2007902122
ISBN: 0-9758602-2-4
First Edition-April 2007

Text formation by Marlene
Cover design concept: Ty Goode
Book design layout: Jeff Harrington
Cover models: Sameerah Stokes, Carlton Easton and Yvette Stokes
Cover photograph © by Ty Goode

Request for permission to make copies or any part of the work should be mailed to

Tytam Publishing
PO Box 1903
Newark, NJ 07101
E-Mail: Tygoode1@aol.com
Website:www.freewebs.com/tygoodeonline

Dedication

This book is dedicated to the woman who gave me life,
Ms. Diane Goode.
You had a choice to make and you chose me.
Thanks,
I Love You

In Loving Memory of
Nevine "Hakeemah" Stokes
July 27, 1961-March 4, 2007
RIP Auntie

Acknowledgements

First and foremost, I'd like to thank my higher power, Jesus Christ, with whom all things are possible

Where do I begin?

Tamirah, my shining star, I can't thank you enough for the understanding. You are amazing! I'm so blessed to have you in my life. You are always reminding me that I'm a mother first; without making me feel guilty about writing. I love you baby.

Carlton, thank you for all of your encouraging words, for ignoring the attitudes and for believing in me as much as I believe in myself. Your love is a lifesaver. (smile)

Felecia, my personal hairstylist- thanks for keeping my hair tight. Shakirah, thank you for helping me to escape every now and then. Thanks for always, always being there for me guys.

Zanasea and Al-fuquan, thanks for the times you kept Tamirah company so that I can do this!

Big Hak, good looking on everything! You know exactly how to be there without physically being there-1 LUV. My God brother Eric and family, (of Flawless Too Hair Salon) thanks for all of the support and love and for pushing the books. Nan and Jimmy Buchanan, thanks for the love. I'm ready for that book Nan. (smile)

To all of my aunties, uncles, cousins, friends and family, Thanks for spreading the word and showing Ty the love!

Endy-thank you for all of your continued support and those late night calls when I just needed someone to listen. (what's going on in your 'Hood?).

JM Benjamin-I see you doing your thing- Holla at ya girl!

Marlene Ricketts- You are one of those people who were sent into my life for a reason. I look forward to a great friendship! Thank you! Thank you! Thank you! For everything!

4

Fellow authors: You know who you are. You all may not realize it but, you all have been such a big help in making this that much easier for me. The things I ask of you all may seem small to you, but I'm so lucky to have had the opportunity to meet people who don't mind helping the next person reach a higher level.

Special thanks go out to my cover models. I really appreciate you taking the time and expressing the patience to help me make my vision a reality.

I would like to thank all of the loyal readers who provided feedback and suggestions to each of my books. It is and always will be greatly appreciated! A big shout out to all of the bookstores and bookclubs who read and reviewed my work. I can't thank you enough.

Thanks to all of my fans-without you spreading the word there would be no need for this book. Thanks for hanging in there with me. As always, let me know what you think.

Peace!

Chapter 1

Simone and Kareem sat side by side on one of the pews. Simone continually cried on his shoulders. She never meant for anyone to get hurt. When an officer stood in front of them for questioning, he informed them that the entire guest list agreed that Simone caused a scene. He told them that they could answer questions now or they can wait to have an attorney present.

Mrs. Hobbs went to Simone and told her not to say anything without a lawyer.

"But moms, we don't have anything to hide," Kareem said.

"Moms, I didn't mean for any of this to happen."

"I know baby but that's not the case. That chile was shot and all fingers are pointing at you. I don't know what happened back there but this does not look good for you. Kareem, y'all keep your mouths shut!" The officer asked Mrs. Hobbs not to discuss any more details with Simone and Kareem. He moved them to the back of the church where there were officers guarding the door. Simone held Kareem's hand and squeezed as tight as she could. Kareem looked around the church to see if anyone was in earshot before he spoke.

"Simone, we're gonna be ok. We just won't say anything until we get a lawyer." She continued to cry.

"Kareem, I'm scared. I don't wanna go to jail. I feel so bad for Melissa. I...I...didn't mean for this to happen," she said between sniffles.

"I know baby." He looked around again. He shook her and made her face him. "Simone, we can't be sure who shot Melissa. We both had our hands on the gun and it just went off. No one can prove that either of us shot her. But, if it comes down to that, I'll take the blame." She looked up at Kareem.

"What? Kareem I don't want you to go to jail either. We're not going to lie."

"Simone, please trust me on this. We are going to be fine. It was an accident. Even if I take the fall for this, there's not too much they can do to me." She shook her head no. She reached into her purse and grabbed some tissues. She used it to wipe her face dry. She squeezed Kareem's hands a little tighter.

"Kareem I can't let you take the fall for something that I did. I'm going to have to face my responsibilities for a change."

"What you mean by that?"

"I mean that it's time for me to take some blame in this whole fiasco. I went too far."

"Simone, where did you get that gun anyway?"

"I bought it from a shop a few weeks ago."

"Why would you buy a gun if you wasn't planning to use it?" She looked at him and wiped more tears from her face.

"Hey," Shelly said as she touched Simone's shoulder.

"Hi Shelly."

"Are you ok?"

Simone shook her head yes.

"The officer said that I could talk to you for five minutes." Kareem looked at Shelly with rage in his eyes. He was trying to figure out how they knew each other. Simone turned her body slightly away from Kareem and faced Shelly.

"I'm sorry Shelly. Things got a little out of control. I would never have invited you if I would have known all of this was gonna happen."

"I know sweetie."

"Invite her? What the hell are you talking about Simone? How do y'all know each other?" he asked as he stood up in front of Simone.

"I could ask you the same thing, couldn't I?" She said in a sarcastic tone.

Shelly looked at Kareem and revealed a wicked smile.

Chapter 2

Melissa opened her eyes and wondered where she was. She lifted her head and looked around the room suspiciously. A sharp pain shot through her stomach and caused her to yell out. Within seconds, a nurse was by her side.

"What's wrong Mrs. Monroe?"

Melissa spoke softly as she grabbed her stomach.

"I'm in pain. My stomach is killing me."

"Well, that's going to happen for a while after what you've been through."

"What does that mean? Mrs....? I'm sorry, I didn't get your name."

"Oh, I'm Nurse Gordon. I'll get the doctor in here to explain things to you." Nurse Gordon proceeded to put pain medication through Melissa's IV then left the room. Melissa tried to sit up but quickly realized that she didn't have the strength. She fumbled around until she found the bed button. She raised her head. She touched her stomach and tried to rub the pain away. Just as she closed her eyes, Dr. Michael Carter entered the room.

"How's it going, Lissa?" She pulled the sheets above her breasts and smiled in embarrassment.

"You tell me. I'm in so much pain." Dr. Carter pulled a chair up and sat next to Melissa.

"Do you remember being shot?"

"No, I was shot? When, who did it?" She couldn't get all of the questions out fast enough.

"Lissa, do you remember anything within the past twenty four hours?" She frowned her forehead and closed her eyes.

"I remember I was standing next to Tricia, at the wedding." Images of the wedding were coming back to her. "I remember Simone caused a lot of confusion. Oh my goodness, did she shoot me?"

"Calm down Melissa!" Dr. Carter said as he forced her to lie down. Melissa lay back on the bed. She began to replay the events in her head. She looked at Michael.

"What happened to Tricia and Tarik?"

"I need you to relax. Everyone is out front waiting to see you." She smiled then asked if they could come in.

"I have to discuss some things with you before I let them back here."

"Ok. I'm listening. How much damage was done?" She asked in pain.

He sat back in the chair and wrote something in her chart.

"Obviously, you were shot in the stomach. You've lost a lot of blood, but you will be ok." She sighed in relief. She looked at him with tears in her eyes. She couldn't believe that she'd been shot.

"There's more, Melissa."

"How much worse can this get?"

He fidgeted with her chart for a moment before he spoke.

"Melissa, you're pregnant. You're very lucky that your body didn't abort the fetus. Normally, in this kind of situation you would have lost the baby." There was a pause before he spoke again.

"I recommend that you see an OB/GYN immediately. You are a high risk pregnancy." Dr. Carter noticed that Melissa didn't respond.

"Are you ok, Melissa?"

"Mike, this is the happiest day in my life. Phil and I have been trying to have a baby for months. We are finally going to have the family that we've been working for." Dr. Carter stared at Melissa before he spoke again.

"I told your husband already. He and your friends have known for a few hours now. I thought they knew already. I hope you don't mind me telling them before I told you."

"Please Mike, don't be silly. They're my family. I'm going to send out notices as soon as I can." She laughed so hard that she made her stomach hurt. Michael Carter half smiled.

"When am I getting out of here?"

"Well, you are going to have to stay for a few more days for observation but we'll talk on Thursday." She smiled and thanked him.

"Now let me go get your husband in here." He walked towards the door and turned to face her. "Let me be the first to congratulate you on the good news." Melissa couldn't control her excitement. She had the biggest cheese smile on her face. "I'll be back to talk with you later, but if you need me before then, just call."

"Will do." She said as she patted her stomach.

* * *

Tricia tapped carefully on the door before pushing it open. She went to Melissa and grabbed both of her hands. Melissa squeezed Tricia's hands and began to cry.

"I'm so sorry that the wedding didn't go as planned, Trish."

Tricia sat on the side of the bed.

"Lissa, it wasn't your fault. You did everything right. I'm sorry for what happened to you."

Melissa wiped her eyes. "No. Simone did this, not you. I would never blame you for what she did. How is she anyway?"

Tricia looked away with tears in her eyes. Melissa changed the subject.

"Well, at least you still get to be an auntie." She sang as she rubbed her belly.

"Mike told me how lucky I am to still have the baby."

"Yeah, that is amazing. Mr. Hammond and I are truly happy for you and Phil."

"I don't remember you guys saying I do."

11

Tricia raised an eyebrow. "I told you that nothing was going to stop me from becoming Mrs. Tarik Hammond." Melissa frowned from the pain in her stomach.

"Are you okay? You need me to get a doctor?"

"No. I'll be ok. It's just that I'm trying to turn on my side." Tricia helped Melissa turn on her side.

"Tricia, where's Phil?" Tricia walked over to the window. She sighed and kept her back to Melissa.

"Well, when Dr. Carter came out and told us that you were pregnant, Phil walked out of the room. Tarik has had him paged twice but he hasn't responded. Tarik went to the cafeteria to see if he was there, but he wasn't."

Melissa had a confused look on her face. "I guess the news that we're having a baby shocked him." Tricia returned to Melissa bedside. Melissa tried to conceal her disappointment. She smiled at Tricia before she spoke. "He's probably out buying cigars or something." Tricia looked away and twirled her fingers in her hair.

Tarik opened the door carrying all kinds of balloons and teddy bears. Melissa smiled when she saw him.

"You are too silly Tarik." She managed a smile. Tarik knelt down to give her a hug. "Hey hon, how you feel?"

"I'm told I'll survive."

"Good!" You had us all scared for a minute there."

"Yeah, imagine how I felt." Everyone laughed. Tarik went over and kissed Tricia on the lips.

"Hey Boo, how are you doing?"

"I'm fine." She stood and allowed him to sit down so that she could sit on his lap. She tried to be enthusiastic when she spoke. She was trying hard to cheer up Melissa. "I was just telling Lissa how great it is that she and Phil are having a baby."

Melissa looked up with a grin on her face. "I'm so excited! I can't wait to be a mommy."

Tarik's whole attitude changed. "Well, I'm not so sure that now is a good time for you two to start a family." Tricia stood.

"Tarik, why would you say something like that?"

Melissa glared at him. "It's ok Tricia. That's his way of being subtle. He never could bite his tongue. I'm used to his shit!" Tarik and Tricia stared at each other. This was the first time since college he heard Melissa cuss. Tricia was just as shocked.

"Melissa calm down. I'm sure Tarik didn't mean it like that." Tarik sat on the side of the bed.

"Lissa, you know I love you and only want what's best for you. Look at the situation. You've just been shot! Where the hell is Phil? The only place he should be is right here by your side. He just found out that he's going to be a father and he's not here with you? Come on now. Stop making excuses for him!"

Tricia took Tarik by the arm and led him to the door. "Boo, go outside and cool off. Let me talk to Lissa alone for a minute." Tarik blocked the door with his arm. "I'm not going anywhere, Tricia. She needs to hear what I'm gonna say!"

Melissa pulled the cord for the nurse.

"Excuse me, please." Nurse Gordon said as she entered the room. "You called, is everything ok Mrs. Monroe?"

Melissa used a tissue to wipe her eyes and sniffed a few times. "I would like to be left alone, please. I don't want to see anyone except for my husband. Would you please escort my *friends* out of my room?" She lowered her bed and closed her eyes. The nurse asked Tricia and Tarik to follow her as she left the room.

"Melissa, please let me stay and talk to you," Tricia pleaded.

"We'll talk later Trish. I just want to rest right now." Melissa said with her face turned away from Tricia. Tricia backed out of the room and glared at Tarik.

Melissa tried to stop the tears from falling. The last thing she wanted was for Tarik not to be happy for her. This pregnancy was the one thing she's wanted for three years. She wondered why he wouldn't just accept the fact that she and Phil would be together for a long time. Sleep carried her away before she could complete all of her thoughts.

Chapter 3

Phil paced the living room of he and Melissa's home for what seemed like hours. He knew he should've been at the hospital with his wife but he couldn't get past the shock of her being pregnant. He tried to understand how it happened. He was very careful when they made love. He knew it was wrong but he only told Melissa they could start a family to shut her up. Now he is facing the fact that he's going to be a father at forty - five years old. He finally sat down on the sofa and picked up the phone. He called the hospital and asked for his wife's number. The operator transferred him to her room.

"Hello?" she asked unsure of who could be calling.

"Hey honey, how are you doing?"

Melissa raised the bed so that she could talk on the phone. "Hi sweetie, where are you?"

He re-positioned himself on the sofa. "I'm at home, baby. I'll be there in a little while."

She smiled, "Why aren't you here now? It would have been nice if my husband's face were the first I saw when I opened my eyes."

Phil sighed loudly. "Melissa, I'll be there in a few. I'm leaving now!" He waited for her to respond. "Ok. I'll see you when you get here." Phil hung up the phone and went into the kitchen and poured himself a double shot of Hennesy.

Melissa hung up the phone and tried to fight her tiredness. The pain medication had finally taken affect on her. She was asleep within minutes. She awakened twelve hours later with no sign of her husband.

Chapter 4

Tarik opened the door to their apartment. Tricia brushed past him and went straight to the bathroom. She turned on the water and ran a hot bubble bath. Tarik went into the bedroom and removed his tuxedo.

The phone rang as soon as Tricia entered the bedroom. She reached towards the nightstand and picked it up. Mrs. Hobbs was practically in tears as she told Tricia that Simone and Kareem had been taken to jail. Tricia listened to her mother vent. After about ten minutes, Mrs. Hobbs asked about Melissa. Tricia gave a brief report and told her mother she'd call her tomorrow.

Tricia removed her blood-soaked wedding gown and headed to the bathroom. Tarik was sitting in the tub with his hands folded behind his head. Tricia joined her husband in the water and put her arms around him.

"Trish, I'm so sorry about the wedding. I know how much you wanted it to be perfect."

"Hey," Tricia said as she lifted Tarik's face, "there's nothing we could have done differently. It wasn't our fault. I'm just so sorry for Melissa."

"I know Boo. She's gonna be alright, though," Tarik said as he shook his head up and down.

Tricia tried not to cry but the tears flowed like a river. Tarik scooted over and put her head on his shoulder. She sobbed for another five minutes before she broke his embrace.

"Tarik, how could you be so cold towards Melissa? You know how much she wants a child; couldn't you just pretend to be happy for her?"

"No! I'm not happy for her and I'm not going to pretend I am just to spare anybody's feelings!"

"Baby, she's just been shot! The last thing she needed was for her best friend to go off on her like that."

"Tricia, Melissa and I have been friends for a long time. I know her and she knows me. You just don't know how we deal with each other!"

"Excuse me?" Tricia said, "whatchu mean by that?"

"I'm saying that you shouldn't get in the middle of me and my friend. I know what I'm doing!" he snapped.

"I guess you forgot that you put me in the middle of it when you asked me to baby-sit her and her husband's marriage. And just in case you missed something, Melissa is my friend too!"

Tricia stood and got out of the tub. She grabbed a towel and went to the bedroom. Tarik sat back and cursed himself for making his wife upset. He stepped out of the bathtub and joined Tricia in the bedroom. She was lying across the bed crying.

"Boo, I'm sorry. I didn't mean to yell at you. It's been a long day and night. The last thing we need is to spend our first night mad with each other."

Tricia sat up and looked at Tarik. "I know baby. I'm still trying to make sense out of all of this. I can't believe that Simone would do something like this."

Tarik pushed himself to the head of the bed. Tricia climbed towards him and lay across his chest.

"Trish, don't you think it's time for you to talk to Simone?"

"Please, I definitely don't have anything to say to her now. That Bitch invaded our wedding and shot Melissa. Tarik, Melissa could have lost the baby! I don't have shit to say to Simone!" Tricia rolled over onto her back.

Tarik sighed, "I know how you feel Trish, but I still think you need to talk to her. Just promise me that you'll think about it." Tricia didn't want to argue with Tarik. Her mind was on Melissa and she didn't want to think about Simone right now.

"Fine, I'll think about it. But I'm not making any promises." She rolled over on top of her husband and went to sleep on his chest.

Chapter 5

Mrs. Hobbs hung up her cell phone after she heard that Melissa was ok. Her face was filled with worry. She sat on the bench as she waited for the lawyer that she called to represent Simone and Kareem.

Mr. Woodsby spotted Mrs. Hobbs on the bench and went towards her. She stood to greet him. "Hi Marvin, thanks for coming. I'm so glad you could come down on such short notice."

"It's ok Maryanne. My caseload has just died down so I'm available. Let me just talk to someone in charge so that I can get started."

Maryanne Hobbs met forty-nine year old Marvin Woodsby a year after she buried her husband. He approached her one day as she walked through the courthouse. She was getting a copy of her husband's death certificate. Marvin looked into her eyes and smiled as she swayed past him. When she came out of a room, she noticed him pretending to look for something in his briefcase. He looked up as she walked past him. Marvin cleared his throat and followed Mrs. Hobbs. He asked her name and continued to follow. She stopped and faced him. "Do you always go around following widows through the courthouse?"

This caught Marvin off guard. "Uhm...no...I...I...just wanted to...you are..."

Mrs. Hobbs smiled and patted her hair. "I'm sorry. I'm really in a hurry." As she tried to walk away, he handed her a card and asked if she'd call him. Mrs. Hobbs took the card and told him her name.

She stopped when she was out of his sight. She closed her eyes and found the mental picture she'd just taken of him. He was about five feet ten inches with deep jet black eyes. He wore his hair cut very close to his head, almost bald but not quite, with his edges having just a touch of gray. The beige suit he wore hung well on his body. She was able to see the cuts in his arms and the pecks in his chest. The only man she remembered being more handsome was her late husband Fred Hobbs. She would definitely give him a call. She and Marvin had dinner a few times but she let him know that she wasn't interested in a romantic relationship. She felt guilty just having dinner with him. Marvin was satisfied to have Maryanne as a friend.

* * *

Mrs. Hobbs sat on the bench and smiled. She was a little more relaxed. She tried to convince herself that everything would be ok. She waited for another twenty minutes until Marvin Woodsby touched her shoulder.

"Marvin, what happened?" she asked anxiously. Marvin sighed and asked her if she was up for a cup of coffee. Mrs. Hobbs grabbed her purse and started towards the door. She asked Marvin if he drove his car. He informed her that he took a taxi. Maryanne led him towards her car.

They went to a twenty-four hour Dunkin Donuts in Union, NJ. Marvin went to the counter as Mrs. Hobbs found a table near the back of the store. She wanted to talk with a little privacy.

Marvin returned to the table with a tray of coffee and donuts. He placed the tray in the center of the table and removed his jacket. He looked at Maryanne and shook his head.

"It's that bad huh?"

"Well it's bad but it's not a lost cause." He poured cream in his coffee.

"Are they going to set bail tonight?" Maryanne asked.

"Well it is Sunday so there's no court being held today but I called in a few favors and we have to wait it out. I talked to the clerk and she said she'd call the judge and request a night court hearing. She's going to call me and let me know what happens," he said as he sat back in the chair.

"How were they doing back there, Marv? Are they hungry?" Mrs. Hobbs asked questions a mile a minute. Marvin put his hands on top of hers and told her to calm down.

"Maryanne, they're fine. Simone is a little shaken up but she's ok. Kareem is a little more relaxed." Maryanne sighed loudly and put her hand against her forehead.

"I'm sure they'll be able to get bailed out tonight. I didn't get too many details but I plan to meet with them first thing in the morning," Marvin said.

"I would like to be there. What time are we meeting?" Mrs. Hobbs asked.

"Maryanne, it's up to them if they want you present or not. If they're not comfortable, then I can't include you."

"Oh, I forgot about that. I'm sure they won't object." There was a pause before Marvin's cell phone began to vibrate. He stepped to the side and flipped open his phone. He spoke for a few minutes then told the caller that he was on his way.

Marvin and Maryanne stepped inside of the courtroom and saw Kareem and Simone in handcuffs at a table. Marvin stood next to them while Maryanne took a seat in the first row behind them. The judge heard the arguments and ordered Simone and Kareem to surrender any passports and he set bail at twenty-five thousand dollars each cash or bond.

As Kareem and Simone were escorted back to their holding cells, Mrs. Hobbs told them that she'd post bail tonight. She pulled Marvin into the hallway and ducked in a corner. She told him that she was going to be paying his bill. She informed him that she didn't have that kind of money in her possession at the moment so she was going to call a bails bondsman.

Marvin hushed her and told her that Simone and Kareem said they could afford to bail themselves out and that whatever was spent would be reimbursed tomorrow. Mrs. Hobbs shook her head and agreed. They went to pay bail and wait.

Chapter 6

Simone was in tears when she was finally let out of the holding cell. She hugged Mrs. Hobbs tight and held on for a few minutes. Mrs. Hobbs walked her to a nearby chair. Simone immediately thanked her for calling an attorney.

"Hush baby, I don't want you to worry about that right now. I need you to concentrate on helping Mr. Woodsby keep you a free woman." Simone shook her head up and down and asked where Kareem was. Mrs. Hobbs told her that they were processing the paperwork so that he could be released. A few minutes later, Kareem and Mr. Woodsby walked through the double doors. Simone jumped up and hugged him.

"You ok?" Kareem asked as he stepped back to look at her.

"I'm ok, how about you?"

"I'm good." Kareem walked towards Mrs. Hobbs.

"Moms, I don't know how to thank you. We'll give you the bail money back first thing in the morning."

"Don't worry about that. Mr. Woodsby needs to meet with you two to discuss your defense. I've asked Marv…I mean Mr. Woodsby if it would be ok if I came along but I've changed my mind. I don't want to hear the details of what happened. I love you both but Tricia is my daughter." Mrs. Hobbs noticed Simone put her head down in embarrassment so she tried to reassure her that she still considered her a daughter.

"Simone you know that I'll stand by you 'til death, but I'm still not going to get in the middle of you and Trishs' fight. I'll do anything that I can to help you without compromising my relationship with Tricia." Simone reached out and hugged Mrs. Hobbs.

"Mom's I understand. I wouldn't ask you to do anything like that. I appreciate everything you've done for us already."

Marvin touched Mrs. Hobbs on the shoulder to break the embrace. "I want you two to get some rest. We have a lot of work to do." He handed Kareem a business card. "I would like for you two to meet me in my office at ten in the morning." Kareem took the card and assured him they'd be there.

Mrs. Hobbs told everyone to pile into the minivan and took them home. She dropped Simone and Kareem off first. She told them that they could call her if they needed anything or just wanted to talk. She pulled off as Simone unlocked the front door to their building.

* * *

Kareem sat on the bed and exhaled. He looked up and saw Simone walking in the bathroom.

"Simone, before you even bother to take a shower, we need to talk!" She froze in her tracks. She was trying to get out of discussing anything tonight. She slowly turned to face Kareem. He was not going to back off. She could almost see the smoke coming from his nose.

"What the fuck happened, Simone? Did you go to the wedding to shoot Trish?"

"Kareem I…I…it just all happened so fast. I didn't intend to hurt anyone." She stood in front of her vanity. Kareem shook his head side to side like he was trying to wake from dreaming.

"Again I ask you, why would you bring a gun to the wedding if you weren't going to use it? You know the rules about picking up weapons." Simone took a seat and started to sob.

"Don't start that crying shit again because it's not going to help us get out of this fucked up situation you put us in!"

"Kareem, I'm so sorry for getting you involved. I swear I never meant for it to get this out of control," she sobbed.

"Ok, now you need to start talkin'. I need to know what this whole thing with Tricia is about. Why did you two have a fight?" he demanded.

Simone looked at him and fidgeted with her dress. She patted her hair and sighed a few times. She was trying to waste time to think of something to say. As soon as Kareem opened his mouth to speak, the phone rang. He jumped up before Simone got a chance to answer it.

"Yeah?" he yelled through the receiver. A few seconds later Simone saw him cringe his face. "Shelly? Don't call my fucking house no more!" He slammed the phone and turned to Simone. "Better yet, how the fuck do you know Shelly?"

Simone thought she would pass out any second. She was worried about telling Kareem about her and Tricia. Now she had a few seconds to decide which fucked-up shit she wanted to tell first. She realized that there was no getting around it. She would have to tell him everything but she would buy as much time as she could. Of course, she flipped the script.

"How the hell do you know Shelly?" she asked.

Chapter 7

Melissa opened her eyes and looked around the room. She had been dozing off all morning. She tried to call Phil but she was getting no answer. She patted her stomach and felt that the pain was subsiding. She was able to sit up on her own. She reached for the tray that was placed in front of her and removed the cover. She opened the container of apple juice and took a sip. She buttered the toast and ate that. Afterwards, she pushed the tray aside.

Melissa picked up the phone and dialed Tricia's cell phone, "Mrs. Hammond?"

"Hey Lissa, is everything ok?" Tricia blushed.

"Yeah, everything's fine. I called to apologize to you. I would never intentionally hurt you. Tarik just pissed me off and I needed to be alone."

"It's ok Melissa, I understand. Tarik was out of line."

"Would you mind coming up to the hospital today? Alone?" Melissa asked.

"Of course, are you sure everything's ok? Do you need anything?"

"Some real food would be nice." Melissa chuckled as she hung up the phone.

Dr. Michael Carter tapped lightly on the door to Melissa's room. She put on her robe and told him to come in. He pulled a chair next to the bed and sat down.

"Hey Mike."

"Hello Melissa. How are you feeling this morning?"

"I'm feeling much better. I am not in as much pain as I was the last time we spoke."

"I'm glad to hear that. I wanted to come by to tell you that I've had my assistant schedule you an appointment with Dr.

Hazel Watters. She's one of the best OB/GYN's I know," Dr. Carter said.

"Mike, I would've done that. You didn't have to go through the trouble."

"It was no trouble at all. I told you that you needed to get started with pre-natal care immediately. Melissa, can I talk to you for a minute? As a friend?" Melissa sat up on the bed and gave him her undivided attention.

"Sure Mike. Am I ok?" she asked with concern.

"No, it's nothing like that," he paused, "remember when I told you that you could always call me if you needed to talk?"

"I sure do," Melissa said.

"I don't mean to step out of line but I just figured that with a baby coming, you'd want to be very careful," he fidgeted.

"Mike, I'm not following."

"Well, I would hate to see anything like what happened before happen to you again."

Melissa frowned her face in offense. "Mike, I think you're way out of line. I told you that was something that would never happen again."

"Hold on Melissa, I'm only saying. You are a high risk pregnancy and I'm only looking out for a friend. I would hate to see anything happen to you. I know how much you want this baby," Dr. Carter said in defense.

"Yes, you do know how much I want my baby, so why would you think I would let something like that happen again?"

"I don't think you *let* it happen the last time. It was something that you couldn't control."

"Dr. Carter, I'm not in the mood to discuss this with you, especially not right now. So would you please drop it?" It was more of a statement than a question. Dr. Carter shook his head and stood. He placed the chair back in the corner of the room. "Dr. Carter huh? Lissa, it's me you're talking to. We've worked together for years. It's time you stopped walking around trying to convince yourself that everything's ok with you. It's no secret that your husband abuses you. But maybe I am overstepping my bounds. My offer still stands. Call me if ever you want to talk!" With that said, he walked out of the room and closed the door. Melissa was fired up. She tried to hold back her tears as the reality of her secret being exposed smacked her in the face. She rubbed her stomach and shook her head in disgust. She lay back in the bed still wondering where Phil was.

Chapter 8

Phil woke and looked around his bedroom. He squinted as an attempt to adjust his eyes. He felt the other side of the bed and remembered that Melissa wasn't there. He jumped out of the bed and cursed himself for not being at the hospital with his wife. He had every intention of going back there last night.

He picked up the phone and called his wife's hospital room.

"Melissa?"

"Oh, hi Phil," she said unenthusiastically.

"How do you feel honey?" Phil asked.

"I feel better," Melissa said. She could hear him fidgeting on the other side of the phone. There was an awkward pause.

"Baby, I'm sorry I didn't make it last night. I'll be there in an hour."

"Take your time. I'll be here for a few more days. I won't wait up!" She slammed the phone in its cradle.

Phil stared at the phone with rage. He tried to stay calm by telling himself it was her hormones that made her act that way.

Phil went to the bathroom and took a shower. He turned off the hot water and stood under the cold for ten minutes after he washed. This was an attempt to sober him a little. After he finished showering, he got dressed. He sat on the edge of the bed and wondered how Melissa could possibly be pregnant. He fumbled through some papers and found the number he was searching for. He dialed and left a voice message. He told the recipient that he would call one day during the week.

On the drive to the hospital, Phil had time to think. He thought about how much Melissa meant to him. He'd promised himself and her that he'd do right by her. He remembered her attitude when he'd come home a few weeks ago. Her words echoed in his head. *'This is the last time you'll ever put your hands on me. I will not let you do this to me again. You'll never hurt me like this again.'* He shook the image of her face and continued to drive.

Once he arrived at the hospital, he went straight to the patient waiting area. He went to one of the payphones and opened the phonebook. He looked under counseling and wrote down a few numbers. Phil placed the numbers in his wallet and headed up to Melissa's room.

He tapped on the door as he entered. Melissa looked over at him with red eyes.

"Oh, you made it today?" She turned her face away from him.

"I told you I was on my way baby," he stepped inside of the room.

"Yes you did. But I really thought you were going to do what you always do and put your needs first." Phil sat on the edge of her bed and grabbed her hand.

"Melissa, I'm so sorry I wasn't here for you. I realize that you needed me to be here with you and I should have been. The initial shock of you being pregnant has worn off. I'm here now and I'm not going anywhere." He squeezed her hands to get a response. "Did you hear me, baby?"

"I heard you Phil, but I'm not going to get my hopes up high just so you could shoot them down. I'm carrying a baby inside of me. I am not going to let myself get all stressed out over you and risk anything happening to this baby!" She snatched her hand away.

"I understand how you feel, Melissa. I really do. I know you don't believe anything I'm saying to you but I mean every word." He reached into his pocket and pulled out his wallet. "I even took the first step by writing down the names of these marriage counselors. I'm going to call and see which one can see us first." Melissa's face softened. She reached out and hugged him.

"I really appreciate that Phil. I want us to be ok by the time the baby is born."

"Don't worry honey, we'll be fine." He moved closer to her and kissed her forehead.

"Dr. Carter came in this morning and told me that he's scheduled an appointment with an OB/GYN for us."

"That's great honey. But you do know that you can pick your own doctor."

"I know Phil. But Mike is a colleague and I trust his opinion. I'm sure he wouldn't send us to just anyone. We'll check her out and if we're not satisfied, we'll choose someone else."

"That's fine with me. As long as you're happy, I'm happy."

Phil helped her to the shower and helped her get dressed. He changed the bedding and went to get her fresh ice and water.

Phil and Melissa engaged in conversation for the next few hours. He apologized constantly for not being there when she needed him.

Dr. Carter entered the room. He glanced at Phil and gave him a nod. Phil responded the same. Dr. Carter checked Melissa's vitals and asked her a few questions. She responded with one word answers and didn't look him in the eyes. Dr. Carter kept his face buried in her chart and never looked at Melissa or Phil. He told them that he would be leaving for the night and gave them the name of the on call physician. He told them that they could have one of the nurses page him in case of an emergency. He exited the room without looking back.

"What was that all about?" Phil asked.

"Don't pay him any mind. We had words earlier and he's a little…"

"Words? What kind of words? Is everything ok with you?" Phil asked.

"Everything's fine Phil. He got a little personal and I had to put him in his place. That's all."

"Personal? Do you want me to talk to him? You wanna change doctors?" he asked.

"No Phil, it's not that serious. You know Dr. Carter and I work together. He just got a little carried away that's all."

"You're sure?"

"Positive, it's nothing," Melissa half smiled.

Chapter 9

Tricia hung up the phone and told Tarik that Melissa was ok. She told him that Melissa asked her to come to the hospital.

"What time are we leaving?" he asked.

"Um...*we* are not going. She asked me to come alone," Tricia said.

"You crazy as hell! I'm going!" Tarik sat up on the bed.

"Tarik, she doesn't want to see you right now. And I really don't blame her."

"What?"

"I just think you should let her cool off a little bit. It's only natural for her to feel like that after what you said. If anyone else would have said that to her, she probably wouldn't be as upset. But to hear that from her brother? Give her some space baby." Tarik looked defeated. He tried to convince Tricia that he was going to the hospital. Tricia cut him short by jumping on the bed and caressed his dick through his pants. He looked up and smiled.

"We haven't officially consummated our marriage." Tricia licked her lips. Tarik smiled and pulled her on top of him. She sat up on top of him and pulled her shirt over her head. Tarik's eyes widened as she squeezed her breasts together. She rubbed her nipples making them stand at attention. He reached out to grab her breasts but she jumped off the bed.

"No, this is my show. I'm doing all the work."

"Do yo thang baby!" He sat upright on the bed. Tricia put on a show like he'd never seen before. She got in front of the mirror and continued to play with her breast. Tarik became more excited as she did her tease. She removed her pajamas and turned her body towards the mirror. Tarik saw her front reflection through the mirror. She danced to an imaginary tune and continued to play with herself. She took both her nipples and licked them one by one. Tarik's dick was standing at attention. Tricia moved to the bed and reached under. She pulled out her ten inch dildo. She handed it to Tarik and lay back with her legs open.

Tarik turned the speed to medium and rubbed it against Tricia's nipples. He seduced her with the dildo from head to toe. She shivered and squirmed for twenty minutes. Trish undid his pants and tugged at his dick. She pulled him closer and took him in her mouth. Tarik didn't lose focus on what he was doing. He positioned himself in the sixty-nine position. His dick was in her mouth while he slipped the dildo in and out of her pussy. Tricia was in another world as she sucked and slurped on Tarik like he was ice cream melting in the sun. He finally tossed the dildo aside and put his mouth on her wetness. She guided his head and pumped his face. Tarik grabbed her ass and lifted her off the bed. Tricia kept pace as she never took her mouth off of him.

After another fifteen minutes of this, Tarik turned Tricia on her stomach and fucked her doggystyle. He moved to a slow pace and enjoyed every minute with his wife. She grabbed the sheets and moaned as she reached her orgasm. Tarik's pace became faster. Trish stuck her ass out to make it more pleasurable. He grabbed her hair and rode her ass like she was a horse. He slowed down and kissed her neck. She moaned as she reached another orgasm. This made Tarik move faster and reach his. He collapsed on top of her and nibbled on her ear. Tricia and Tarik went to sleep with smiles on their faces.

Tricia woke and went straight to the shower. She tried to wash away the images of her nightmare wedding. She scrubbed her legs until they were almost raw. She held her head down and stood under the water. This was the first time she'd thought about her wedding. She was in shock all over again. Her sniffles became louder as she lost control.

Tarik stood at the bathroom door and listened to her. He didn't know how to console her. He knew she needed to let out her frustrations so he stood there a few minutes longer. After he realized she wasn't stopping, he went to the shower and turned off the water. He placed the towel over her shoulders and led her to the bedroom. She sat on the bed and cried.

"Tarik, this entire weekend has been a fiasco. Melissa got shot and Simone and Kareem are in jail. I just feel like I'm responsible for everything."

"Just like you told me, we couldn't have done anything differently," he said.

"Maybe if I would have talked to Simone, she would not have invaded the wedding and Melissa wouldn't have gotten shot." Tricia stopped sniffling and looked up at Tarik with a confused expression. "Do you think that bullet was meant for me? I've been wondering about that. Melissa never did anything to her. That bullet was meant for me." Tarik saw Tricia's mood change from upset to rage. She paced the floor and mumbled to herself.

"Boo, just calm down. Now, you've known Simone for a very long time. There's no way she meant for anything like this to happen."

"Tarik please, she brought a gun to our wedding and fired it. She meant to shoot somebody!"

"How do you know that she brought the gun to the wedding?" Tarik asked.

"You don't think Kareem would do that? Do you? We never really got along but…"

"I'm not saying that either. I'm just saying anything to convince you and myself for that matter that Simone wouldn't do anything like that." Tricia looked relieved. She didn't know why Simone pulled that stunt but she did intend to find out.

"Tarik, I'm going to the hospital to see Melissa. If Moms call, tell her to call my cell." He leaned up for a kiss and watched Tricia walk away. She turned back once she opened the door. "I love you, baby."

"I love you too, Boo. See ya later." Tricia locked the door behind her.

Chapter 10

Mrs. Hobbs picked up the phone and called Tricia.
"Hi Tarik, how are you doing?"

"Hi Moms, you just missed Trish. She's on her way to the hospital to see Melissa."

"How is Melissa doing baby?"

"She called Trish this morning to say she was doing fine."

"I'm glad to hear that she's ok. How are you two doing? Were you able to get any sleep last night?" she asked.

"A little but Trish is not doing too well. She's blaming herself for everything. She's really pissed with Simone. I asked her to think about talking to her to get to the bottom of this," Tarik said.

"What'd she say?"

"She said that she'll think about it. Moms, I don't know what went on between those two but Tricia is not going to be able to move forward until she settles things with Simone. I think she realized this morning that she needs to talk to Simone. She's beginning to think that Simone meant to shoot her."

"Oh goodness. I was hoping they would have gotten past this by now. I'm going to talk to Simone and find out what exactly was she planning. I'll take care of Trish too." Tarik didn't say anything. There was a pause. He relayed Tricia's message to Mrs. Hobbs. She said she'd call Tricia later. Tarik said goodbye then hung up the phone.

Mrs. Hobbs sat on her sofa and wondered why Tarik's attitude changed. She replayed the conversation in her head and exhaled. She picked up the phone and dialed the number again.

"Tarik, I'm so sorry."

"Moms? What do you mean?" he asked confused.

"I'm sorry for taking over. I stepped in and told you that I'd take care of Tricia. I know that's your job now and I'm sorry. I'm going to have to pass the responsibility to you. I didn't mean to imply that you couldn't..."

"Moms, it's ok. I understand. I know letting go is not easy. I know she's your baby and I respect the relationship that the two of you have. It's ok," Tarik said.

"Thank you sugar," Mrs. Hobbs responded before hanging up the phone.

Maryanne Hobbs went to the kitchen and made herself some breakfast. She sat at the table and ate her sausages and French toast. She poured herself a glass of orange juice to wash down the food. After she cleaned the kitchen, she took a hot shower.

The phone was ringing when she stepped out. She ran over and answered.

"Yes?"

"Hi Maryanne, I know its short notice, but I was wondering if I could come over this morning? I wanted to talk to you about something." Maryanne Hobbs was thrown off guard. This is the last person she expected to hear from on a Sunday.

"Marvin, of course you can come by. Just give me about an hour to straighten up."

"That's fine. I haven't left my house yet. I need to finish up some paperwork before I leave. Would you like for me to bring anything?" he asked.

"Just yourself unless you can think of something else I may need." Marvin chuckled and then told Maryanne he'd see her in a little while. She hung up the phone and began clearing the dishes. She placed them in the dishwasher and went to get dressed. She was a little anxious about what Marvin wanted to talk to her about. She decided to call Simone while she waited.

"Simone?"

"Yes."

"How are you doing baby?" Mrs. Hobbs asked.

"I'm scared Moms. Last night was the first chance I got to really think about what happened. Kareem has been trying to reassure me all night that it's going to be ok. But I'm not so sure. I messed up big time," Simone sobbed.

"Simone, you have to calm down. I'm sure that it's all going to work out," Mrs. Hobbs said not sounding completely sure.

"Moms, someone got shot because of me. There's no way I'm going to get out of paying for it."

"Just wait and see what Mr. Woodsby says. He is a really good lawyer and he may find a way for you and Kareem to get out of this. Try not to worry too much," Mrs. Hobbs said. She heard Simone crying on the other end. "Simone? Did you hear me?"

"Yes Moms. I'll try. Thanks for calling."

"Simone, I'd like for you to come over to the house after you and Kareem meet with Marvin in the morning. Is that ok?"

"Kareem and I are going to the bank to get the money we owe you then I can come over," Simone said.

"Ok. I'll see you then. Give my love to Kareem."

"Ok, thanks Moms."

Chapter 11

Maryanne Hobbs went to the door and opened it for Marvin Woodsby. He hugged her gently.

"Hi Marvin, come on in," she said as she closed the door.

"How have you been Maryanne?" he smiled. She led him to the sofa and sat down.

"Marvin, Simone and Kareem are really scared. Please do everything that you can to help them," she said worriedly.

"Maryanne, don't worry about them. I'm going to do everything in my power for them. I know how much they mean to you. But if you don't mind, that's not what I wanted to talk about."

"Oh. I'm sorry. I just went on and on. What's on your mind?" she asked. "Would you like something to drink before you start?"

"No, I'm fine," he said as he adjusted himself on the sofa. "Maryanne, I am more than happy to take this case for you. I know you are like a mother to my clients so that means that we'll be spending a lot of time together." He cleared his throat. "I really would like to know if you'll reconsider us being more than friends?"

Mrs. Hobbs raised her eyes. This wasn't totally unexpected because she knew how Marvin felt about her.

"Marvin, I don't know what to say," she blushed.

"Maryanne, I know you have feelings for me also. We've been on several dates and have so much in common. We are getting too old to play these games." She was getting ready to speak but he put up his hands to protest. "I remember what you said about still missing your husband. I can respect that. You deserve to be happy and I know I make you happy." He looked at her with serious eyes. Mrs. Hobbs smiled. She was almost at a lost for words. She took one of Marvin's hands as she looked him in the eyes.

"Marvin, you know how I feel about you. I've never denied that you make me happy. I don't think that now is the best time for us to get involved with all of this mess going on. It wouldn't be fair to you or me. If we are going to stand a chance, we have to do it on a clean slate. This trial is going to take a lot out of all of us. And there's so much going on with my family right now. I just don't want to overwhelm you."

"I understand that you have things going on right now. I want to be with you and I'm willing to wait until things settle down. I just want to be sure you're willing to go that extra step with me."

She smiled and revealed several teeth. "Ok Marvin, you've won my heart. I would love to give us a shot." Marvin Woodsby smiled and hugged her. He reached for her and planted a passionate kiss on her lips. Maryanne responded by tilting her head and returning his kiss. Marvin grabbed her face with both hands and kissed her deeper. Maryanne could feel something stirring between her legs. She backed away from Marvin and excused herself to the restroom.

Maryanne ran cold water on her face and sat on the toilet stool. She held her head down and thought about what she wanted to happen between her and Marvin. She tried to shake the thought away. She thought of every reason to ask Marvin to leave. She couldn't think of anything. Then she held her head up. *'Hell, we're two consenting adults and I've been needing and wanting this for some time. I'm only forty six; I can still get my groove on. Why not?'* Maryanne went back out to the living room with Marvin.

"Are you ok?" he asked, "I'm sorry if I rushed things. I just…"

"Marvin, it's ok. I don't feel rushed." She picked up where she left off by nibbling on his ear. Marvin lay her down on the sofa and fondled her breasts. Maryanne could feel her wetness dripping in her panties. She felt between Marvin's legs as he moaned in her ear. She stood and grabbed his hands. Marvin followed Maryanne to the bedroom. She gently pushed him onto the bed and straddled him. He reached under her blouse and unhooked her bra. She smiled as she looked directly in his eyes.

"Maryanne, are you sure about this?"

"I've never been surer in my life," she smiled. Marvin continued to undress Maryanne and then lay her on the bed as he undressed himself. She slipped under the comforter and held back a corner for him to join her. Marvin began kissing and fondling her. Maryanne moaned and whispered for more.

Marvin got on top of her and they made slow passionate love. To her surprise, Maryanne's body responded better than she expected. She closed her eyes and held on for the ride. Marvin was as gentle as possible with her. He took his time and made sure they both were satisfied. Marvin rolled over just after they reached their climax. Maryanne rolled on top of him and exhaled. She smiled to herself as she dozed off. She couldn't help but smile as she'd just relieved years' worth of pent up energy.

Chapter 12

Tricia tapped on Melissa's hospital room door and eased inside. She saw Phil sitting on the bed next to Melissa.

"I'm sorry. Did I come at a bad time?"

"No, it's ok," Melissa responded, "Phil, would you mind if Tricia and I talked alone for a few? I asked her to come this morning before I knew what time you were coming."

Phil got off the bed and fixed the blankets. "It's ok baby. I'll go for a walk or something. Would either of you like something to eat or drink?" Both women said no in unison. Phil excused himself and walked out of the room. Melissa turned her face away from Tricia in embarrassment. She shook her head before she spoke.

"Tricia, I'm so sorry about last night. I…I just…"

"Melissa, there's no need to apologize. I understand your actions. I can't even say that I blame you."

"Yeah, Tarik just really pissed me off. Its one thing for him to feel the way he does about Phil. But for him to come at me the way he did is inexcusable!"

Tricia went to the bed and held Melissa's hand. "Lissa, I know what Tarik said was messed up. You know how he feels about you. I'm sure he didn't mean it the way it came out."

Melissa looked at Trish and shook her head. "Tricia did you come here to make excuses for him. I just told you how I feel and you're standing here telling me that he didn't mean it. You saw his face last night when he said that to me. How could you even fix your face to defend him?" Melissa asked.

"Melissa, Tarik is my husband and I think I know him well enough to know that he was talking out of anger."

"Well he's *my* friend and I think we know each other well enough to know how our words are going to affect one another. He was trying to hurt me and he succeeded!"

Tricia backed away from the bed. She looked at Melissa and raised her eyes. "Whoa, what was that about?" She threw her hands in the air. "You know, Tarik did the same thing to me earlier. He brought it to my attention that y'all are friends. I know that and I haven't forgotten! But if you and I are going to continue with any kind of friendship, you will not throw that up in my face again. I know you've just been shot and are going through some things but I haven't done anything to you so please don't take it out on me!" Tricia rolled her eyes as she walked towards the door.

"Trish wait, don't leave. I didn't mean anything by that." Melissa motioned for Trish to sit next to her on the bed. Tricia reluctantly sat on the bed next to Melissa.

"Trish, I'm not taking anything out on you. It's just that Tarik and I have been through so much together. The thought of him not being here for me now is unbearable."

"Melissa, Tarik is just upset. He's going to always be there for you. I've known for some time that you two are close but it wasn't until you got shot that I realized just how close you are. Tarik loves you. I've learned to respect that now that I know it's platonic. Trust me, he'll come around. He's not going to see anything bad happen to you." Tricia kissed Melissa on the forehead. Melissa closed her eyes and thought back to the night of Tarik's bachelor party. She felt guilty about what happened. She looked at Trish and shook her head. "I don't know what I did to deserve friends like Tarik and you but I'm glad that I have you two in my life."

Tricia smiled, "I'm glad you feel that way. I'm glad that you and I were able to become friends despite my feelings in the beginning. So, how are you doing?"

Melissa asked Tricia to lock the door.

"Tricia, Mike and I had it out this morning." Melissa proceeded to tell Tricia everything about her conversation with Dr. Carter. Tricia stretched her eyes in amazement after hearing Melissa's story.

"And Trish, the worse part is that he said it's no secret that I'm being abused. That insinuates that everyone knows," Melissa cried.

"Lissa, don't cry. I don't think people know. Mike knows because the two of you are friends. People who don't know you won't suspect a thing." Tricia tried to comfort her friend. "It's no use getting yourself all upset. You need to stay healthy for the baby. Stop worrying about what people think of you. Only one person has to live your life and that's you! You hear me?" Tricia rubbed Melissa's hand. Melissa shook her head up and down and wiped her tears away. She thanked Tricia for the comforting words then decided to change the subject. "Besides all of that mess, Mike says I'm fine. He says that I should be released in about a week or so. I need to take it easy for a while."

"Yes you do. Are you going to take an early leave from your job?" Trish asked.

"You know, this is funny because Phil asked me to take some time off from work so we could start working on a family. I told him that I'd think about it but I guess there's nothing to think about now. I'm going to call my Director of Nursing and talk to her on Monday."

"Good, I think that's a great idea."

"How are Simone and Kareem?" Melissa asked. Tricia turned her face away from Melissa. "Lissa, I really don't know. I haven't spoken to my mother today so I haven't heard anything yet."

Melissa sensed that there was more to be said. "Trish, I hope you don't still feel bad about what happened."

"I do regret not talking to Simone. Maybe this could have been avoided if I'd have spoken to her. I just can't help to think that I should have handled things with her differently."

"Stop stressing yourself out over it. It's still not too late to talk to her. I'm sure she could really use a friend right now."

Tricia looked at Melissa. "How can you be so nonchalant about this whole thing? You were shot because of the ruckus she caused. You could have lost the baby or even your own life. I'd think you'd be pissed at her."

"It could have been a lot worse than it was. I'm glad that I am alive. But let me ask you something. You and Simone were like sisters until a few months ago. How do you think she feels as she watched you become this friendly with me?" Melissa asked.

"That doesn't give her any right to hurt you!"

"You and I both know that this was an accident. Don't use this as an excuse for not making up with your friend." Tricia didn't want to hear anyone else tell her about her friendship with Simone. She was getting tired of hearing the same thing over and over again. "Melissa lets just drop it please. I don't want to talk about Simone anymore."

"Sorry, I didn't mean to push. Trish, it's getting hot in here. Would you open the door now?" Tricia stood and unlocked the door. Just as she was getting ready to turn the knob, Phil walked through the door.

"Am I interrupting?

"No, Melissa and I were just saying goodbye. Lissa, I'll call you tomorrow. If you wanna talk, call me anytime."

Melissa smiled, "yeah right Mrs. Hammond. I didn't forget how newlyweds do things." Tricia chuckled then said goodbye to Phil. He responded and then set up a tray for Melissa to eat dinner.

Chapter 13

Simone stopped the alarm clock from ringing. She and Kareem had been up half the night arguing about Shelly. She managed to take his attention off of Shelly by bringing up their case. He insisted that if it came to that, he was going to take the gun charge and whatever else came along with it.

"Kareem," she gently shook him, "It's time for us to get up. We need to hit the bank then go and see Mr. Woodsby." Simone had no idea that Kareem had been up all night.

"Yeah, I'm up," he grunted. Simone looked at him in confusion and went to the bathroom. Kareem followed her and stood in the doorway.

"Whatchu doin'? I'm tryna use the bathroom," she said.

"Oh, now I can't stand here? You never had a problem wit it before?"

"Kareem, please don't start. It's too early and I'm not in the mood. With all the shit going on right now, the last thing I need is for you to be getting on my nerves!" She pushed him out of the doorway and closed the door. Kareem stepped away from the bathroom and sat on the bed.

He looked at the clock and saw that it read seven-thirty two. He picked up the phone and dialed Shelly's number.

"Hello?" she asked in a groggy voice.

"What the fuck is going on wit you and my girl?"

"Who's this? Kareem?"

"Yea, who you think it is?" he yelled over the shower water.

"Kareem I don't have time for you. It's fucking seven-thirty in the morning. I'm still sleep!" She hung up the phone. He dialed her number again. This time she went off on him. "Kareem I don't know who you think you are, calling my house talking to me like you own me. I'm not your girlfriend! If you wanna know anything about her, then you'd better ask her. Don't be calling me with this bullshit this time of the morning!" *Click* The phone went dead in his ear.

"Fuckin' Bitch!" he said to himself. Simone was standing in the doorway when Kareem dialed Shelly the second time. She didn't hear what Shelly said but she did hear Kareem call her a bitch. She walked into the bedroom after he'd hung up the phone. He turned around with a surprised look on his face.

"Who are you talking to this early? And why she gotta be a Bitch?" Simone asked. Kareem rolled his eyes and went to take a shower. Simone smiled. She picked up the phone and hit redial to retrieve the last number. She saw the phone dialing Shelly's number so she hung up. She proceeded to get dressed while Kareem was in the shower. She made a mental not to call Shelly later.

Kareem and Simone arrived at Mr. Woodsby's office at 9 o'clock sharp. The receptionist told them to go right in. Simone walked into the office first while Kareem gawked at the long-haired beauty. He made eye contact and smiled. The receptionist returned the smile and winked at him.

"Come on in," Mr. Woodsby said, "Please, have a seat."

"Thank you," they said in unison. Simone was almost shaking. She looked around the office and noticed the degrees and awards on the wall to her right. Mr. Woodsby had at least twelve different certificates on his wall. Simone breathed a sigh of relief. She figured with all of those certificates, he must know his stuff.

"How are you guys holding up?"

"Nervous," Simone said.

"Well, let me get right to the point. The D.A. had to charge you both with weapons possession because both of your handprints were found on the gun. When they took you into custody, they found gun powder residue on the both of you as well. They're not sure which of you actually fired the gun. But believe me they will try to make a case against one or both of you. They're also charging you both with endangering the welfare of minors, and assault with a deadly weapon among other things."

"How can they charge both of us for one crime?" Simone asked.

"Well they'll make a case against one of you first, if by chance, they don't get a conviction, they'll go after the other and one of you will do some time." Simone shook her head in disbelief. She wiped a tear from her cheek. Kareem looked over and reached for her hand. He could not stand to see Simone this scared.

"Don't worry about it baby. We gonna be ok. Mr. Woodsby, what can you do to help us? This was an accident. We didn't mean for anyone to get hurt. Simone and Melissa are friends."

"First of all, we need to establish some trust. I'm going to need to know exactly what happened from the beginning. You need to tell me everything so that there are no surprises later. I'm here to help you and if you leave anything out, I can't defend you to the best of my ability. So now is the time to start talking."

Kareem looked at Simone while she tried to compose herself. She was more worried about she and Tricia's secret being exposed than anything else. She looked at Mr. Woodsby, "I'll tell you everything."

"Before you start Simone, I'd like to inform you that this conversation will be recorded for my records. I'm going to need to refer to this initial conversation every now and then to keep good notes. Is that ok?"

Simone and Kareem agreed that it was ok. Simone began telling Mr. Woodsby everything that happened the morning of the wedding. Kareem jumped in when she got to the shooting. He told Mr. Woodsby exactly what happened. Mr. Woodsby took notes as he listened to their story. He asked a few questions and then asked them if they had any questions for him.

"Mr. Woodsby, if one of us is going to be charged with anything, it's going to be me. I am not going to let my girl go to jail for nothing!" Simone squeezed his hand. Mr. Woodsby wrote more notes on the paper before he looked up. "I understand and I'm going to try my best to avoid anything like that. With any luck we can plea to something of a lesser charge." Kareem reached over to Mr. Woodsby's desk and handed Simone a few tissues. She thanked him and wiped her face dry.

"You say the woman that was shot and you are friends, Simone?"

"Yes, we're friends."

"Hmm, she's going to be the state's star witness. Is there anyway she won't testify? Without her testimony to which of you actually shot her, their case against either of you will be tough to prove."

"I don't know. I haven't spoken to her. I'll talk to her and see what she's planning to do."

"If you two are friends, no one can stop you from talking to her. Although, I would advise you to be very careful with what you discuss with her. The last thing we need is the state claiming that you tried to intimidate her," Mr. Woodsby warned. "Now if there's nothing else, I'm going to get started on the paperwork."

"Mr. Woodsby, how much is your fee?" Simone asked.

"Don't worry about that. It's all taken care of."

"How? We didn't give you a retainer," she asked.

"Maryanne Hobbs will be paying my fee."

"Moms? Oh no! She's done enough for us already. We can't let her pay our legal fees," Kareem said.

"Well, she was pretty adamant about paying. She's already given me a deposit."

"We need to talk to her. We'll let you know if anything changes with how you'll be getting paid," Simone said. She and Kareem stood and shook Mr. Woodsby's hand and thanked him. He said he'd be in touch and asked them not to discuss their case with anyone. They agreed then left.

Simone walked a couple feet ahead of Kareem. That's all the time he needed to slip his name and number to the receptionist. Simone was none the wiser since she never looked back.

Chapter 14

Melissa sat on the side of the bed and slipped into her robe. Phil had gone to work. She was able to move around much better on her own. She had been going to rehab/ therapy to strengthen her legs for the past week. She stood up and walked towards the bathroom. She glanced at the calendar on the wall and smiled at the big red circle. She would be discharged in two days and she couldn't wait to go home to her own bed.

She stepped into the bathroom and closed the door behind her. She brushed her teeth and washed her face. When she stepped out, she saw Simone standing in her doorway. She nearly fell to the floor. Simone rushed over to keep her from falling. Simone helped her to the bed and helped her sit.

Melissa stared at Simone for what seemed like an eternity. Simone stood back and held her head down. She searched through her pockets and found a tissue. She wiped her eyes before she came towards Melissa.

"Melissa, please just hear me out." Melissa took a deep breath and motioned for her to take a seat in the chair. She grabbed a napkin and wiped her own eyes.

"I'm here to apologize, Lissa. I'm so sorry this happened to you. I never meant for anyone to get hurt."

"Simone I could have lost my baby! Hell, I could have lost my life!" How could you be so careless?" Melissa cried. Simone looked at Melissa and tried her best to control her sobs.

"Melissa, I didn't know you were pregnant. That's not to excuse what happened, but I'm really sorry. I didn't mean to cause this kind of drama and pain to anyone." Melissa looked at Simone and her heart went out to her.

"Simone, when we first met, we clicked. I thought we were friends but I look at you now and see a different woman." Simone went to Melissa and grabbed her hands.

WITH FRIENDS LIKE THAT

"Melissa I can't say that I blame you. I'm here to let you know that if I could change anything that happened I would. I told you before that I love you like a sister and I still do. I'm hurting just like everyone else. I can't even think about the wedding without breaking down. I'm sorry. Honestly, I am. If I could trade places with you, I would do so in a heartbeat." There was an awkward silence. Simone let go of Melissa's hands and went to the door. She looked backed just before she walked out.

"This may be inappropriate for me to be here but I had to come and see you myself and apologize in person. Congratulations on the baby and take care." Simone walked out of the door.

"Simone, wait." Melissa called after her. Simone stepped back into the room. She used what was left of her tissue and wiped her face again. Melissa stood and walked towards her. She reached out and gave her a hug. Simone returned the hug and they both cried on each other's shoulders.

"I know it was an accident, Simone. A lot of people got hurt and they may not see that. I know that you and Tricia are going through something right now and I just want to let you know that I'm still your friend. I'm not going to judge you because of that. Take care of yourself, girl." Melissa let go of Simone and walked back to the bed.

"I really appreciate this Lissa. Thank you." Simone walked out of the hospital room with a burden lifted off of her shoulders. She really wanted forgiveness. She would slowly but surely work her way down the list to apologize to everyone involved.

Melissa sat on the bed and thought about Simone. She knew in her heart that Simone would never hurt her. She hoped Tricia would understand her decision to continue a friendship with Simone. Melissa got up and stood in front of the window. She looked around the room she called home for the past ten days. She smelled all of the flowers that were on the windowsill. She looked over on her nightstand and saw the teddy bear that Tarik brought in when she came out of surgery. She walked over to it and picked it up. She took the card out and opened it up. She sat in the chair and read the card.

Hey baby sis,
Just wanted to give you something to cheer you up.
This is nothing! We've been through worse. You'll
recover and be back to normal in no time. Keep ya head
up! Congrats on the baby!!
Luv U,
Tarik

Melissa put the card in the envelope and placed it back with the bear. She shook her head and grunted. "Hmp...he got some nerves telling me what's best for me...I"

"Easy baby, I come in peace," Tarik said as he entered the room. He closed the door behind him and stood there for a minute, "how are you doing?"

"I'll survive. I'm getting out of here in a couple of days."

"Good," he said as he stepped towards her. He hugged her then took a seat on the bed. "Lissa, I'm sorry. I had no right to come at you like that at a time like this." Melissa shook her head again. She stared at Tarik like he was crazy.

"You still can't admit when you're wrong, huh?"

"What are you talking about? I came here to apologize," he said.

"No you didn't. You are only sorry about when you said that. You're not sorry that you said it. How dare you come in here and tell me what I should and shouldn't do!"

"You act like I'm doing something that I've never done before. I always tell you what I think. I just assumed that you were salty because you'd just been shot. I didn't think you would let it take over your mind!"

"Damn it Tarik! Don't do that! You act like you did nothing wrong and I'm overreacting," Melissa said.

"No, you just want me to apologize for being me. I'm not gonna say I'm sorry for saying what I feel. I still feel the same way! I just realize that it was insensitive to say it at a time like this!" Tarik shouted. He looked around the room, "Is he here now?"

"He's at work. And don't come in here getting me all worked up. I can not have this kind of stress going on right now. I'm already a high-risk pregnancy and I don't want to jeopardize the baby."

"I didn't come here to get you upset. Can we just call a truce for now? We both know how the other feels and it's not going to change anything. I'm not going to spend the next nine months arguing with you. After all these years, you know that no matter what you decide to do, I got your back. I always have and I always will. But that don't mean I have to agree with you." Melissa smiled. She knew that Tarik did always have her back. She knew that she could depend on him for anything.

"Fine, it's a truce. I don't have the energy to argue with you about it anyway."

"Good, cause I miss you," Tarik chuckled.

"So how is married life treating you?" Melissa asked.

"I'm enjoying every minute of it," he blushed. Melissa sat on the bed and they talked. Tarik confessed that he's been trying to get Tricia to talk to Simone. Melissa told him about Simone's visit earlier that day. They talked until it was time for him to leave.

Chapter 15

Tricia was enjoying her last day off work. She and Tarik were invited to her mother's house for dinner. They were in the midst of getting dressed when Tarik walked up behind her and caressed her ass. He kissed the back of her neck and turned her to face him.

"I wish we could baby but we have to get to Moms' for dinner," Tricia said.

"Come on Boo, we can make the time. Let's do a quickie," he said as he rubbed her breasts. He was taking off her blouse while she put up a fake fight. She begged him to stop but didn't try to stop him. A few minutes more, Tricia had her knees in the chair by the bed while Tarik fucked her doggystyle.

They arrived at Mrs. Hobbs house half an hour late. Tricia used her key and unlocked the door. Mrs. Hobbs was on the phone. Tricia and Tarik walked past her and waved. They went straight to the kitchen and set the table. Mrs. Hobbs walked in the kitchen seconds later with raised eyes. Everyone started laughing but didn't say a word.

After dinner, Mrs. Hobbs brought out beers and wine. The three of them sat in the living room and talked. Mrs. Hobbs asked them if they planned on going on their honeymoon or if they'd decided to cancel indefinitely.

"We really haven't thought about it Moms," Tarik said.

"Yeah, we're still trying to cope with the wedding fiasco," Tricia added.

"Trish, I was waiting for you to ask about Simone and Kareem. I know you two are not on good terms but, she's been in ours lives for so long. How could you not want to know how she's doing?" Mrs. Hobbs asked.

"Momma please, I have enough on my plate right now. Every time I think about Simone, I think about what she caused."

"I know you're upset about that honey. But you know that Simone would never intentially hurt anyone. I know deep inside you want to know what caused her to flip like that. Or you may already know what caused her to flip like that." Tricia sat in the chair and stared at her mother. She didn't want to admit that she did need to talk to Simone. Her pride wouldn't let her make the first move.

"Boo, I think Moms is right. You are not able to focus on anything. Simone's friendship is worth saving because if it weren't, you wouldn't be as upset as you are."

"Tarik, I don't want to talk about this right now."

"Well, when is the right time? You go back to work tomorrow. What are you going to say to people who ask you about your wedding?" Mrs. Hobbs asked. Tricia sighed and fought back the tears.

"Well, there is something else that I wanted to discuss with you both." Mrs. Hobbs poured herself another glass of wine. "I've been talking to Mr. Woodsby and he wants to know if there are any witnesses."

"Moms, everyone saw Simone pull out the gun," Tarik said.

"Tarik, no one actually saw who pulled out the gun, besides, with the evidence the police have, either of them could have pulled the trigger. They both had gun powder on their hands." Tricia and Tarik just stared at each other.

"Do you mean she's going to get away with this Momma?"

"Trish, it sounds like you want her to go to jail."

"Momma, are you condoning what she did? Just about everyone at the wedding knew Simone and I were not on good terms. Anybody can come to court and say that she had every reason to cause a scene."

Tarik looked at Mrs. Hobbs with concern. "Moms, I love Simone too but, Melissa is like my sister. She's been shot and someone is gonna pay for it!"

"Will you both calm down? I just want to know if you two can find it in your hearts to forgive Simone. She really could use her friends. Besides, the way I understand it, Melissa has already forgiven her." Tarik put his head down and looked away. He knew Tricia didn't know about that.

"What?! She's not going to forgive Simone for shooting her," Tricia said as she looked at Tarik for support. When he never made eye contact Tricia snapped.

"Tarik, you knew about this?!" Tarik wiped his forehead with his hand. He tried his best to calm her down, but Tricia did not want to hear anything he had to say.

"Let's go, we're going to see Melissa right now!"

Chapter 16

Simone sat on the edge of the bed. Kareem had an appointment with his boss to see if he would be able to return to work. He was still asleep. Simone had taken a family medical leave of absence. She was too stressed about her legal worries to concentrate on work. She intended to fill out the required paperwork this afternoon. She looked over at Kareem while he slept. She knew she'd have to wake him within the next few minutes. She stepped into the living room and called Shelly from her cell phone.

"Hey Shelly," Simone smiled.

"Simone?" she asked, "how are you doing?"

"I'm ok. I can only talk for a minute. Kareem is in the other room."

"You know that fool called me the other day?"

"I know. I heard him. That's what I wanted to talk to you about. You think I can come over a little later this afternoon?"

"Sure. I can't wait to see you," Shelly smiled.

"I wanna see you too," Simone blushed.

Kareem had sat up in the bed and heard Simone on the phone. Since she was on her cell phone, there was no way for him to know who she was talking to. He hurried to lie down and pretend he was still asleep when Simone came back into the room.

"Kareem, time to get up." Simone gently tugged at his arm. It's time for you to get up, honey."

Kareem rolled over on his back and wiped his eyes so that he could see the time. "Damn, I'm tired as hell. I been going back and forth with this company to see if I still have a job all week. They supposed to have an answer for me today."

"I hope they let you stay. I would hate for you to lose your job on the count of me," she said.

"It'll be ok. My union rep. says I got a good chance to keep my job. It's not like I've been convicted of murder or anything." He sat next to Simone on the bed. "It's time for us to talk. I need you to keep it real with me Simone. I've been doing a lot of thinking since the wedding and I need some answers!" Simone knew this day would come. She did a good job stringing him along so far, but she had to tell him something.

"We do need to talk. Let's go into the kitchen so I can cook breakfast." She stood to walk out of the room.

"No, let's stay right here. I don't want any distractions. If you keep it real, this won't take long." Simone was disappointed. She would rather be in the kitchen where she could be close to the weapons if necessary.

"Fine, let's get this over with. What do you wanna know?" she asked.

"I was thinking about that surprise you said you had for me at the wedding. Was it Shelly?"

Simone looked nervous as she shook her head yes.

"How the hell do you know her anyway?"

"How the hell do you know her?" Simone retorted.

"Don't play games with me Simone. You know the deal with me and Shelly that's why you tried to surprise me!"

"*Tried* to surprise you? I saw the look on your face when she walked in with me. So Yes, I do know the deal with you two."

"Stop trying to change the subject. How do you know her?" he asked.

"She accidentally ran into me at the gym on purpose. She came to tell me all about my cheating man. It just so happened that we became cool before she had the chance."

"That Bitch!"

"Don't call her a bitch because you got caught cheating again," Simone said defending Shelly. Kareem noticed her reaction and raised his eyes. He knew Simone was pissed because Shelly made her look like a fool.

"That ain't why I called her a bitch! She knew about you from day one! She started getting serious, wanting me to leave you so I kicked her ass to the curb!" he said as an attempt to soften her mood.

"Don't even try it! That shit ain't gonna work this time. You didn't have enough respect to keep me from finding out. She showed me all types of cards you gave her and pictures of y'all! You were as serious with her as she was with you!" Simone yelled.

"No, I wasn't. She was just somebody I fucked."

"You don't just fuck somebody for more than a year Kareem! You took her places and spent quality time with her! So don't run that bullshit on me!" Simone got up in his face. She pointed a finger into his forehead to get her point across.

Kareem shook his head and grunted. "This shit is crazy. Shelly just played you and you fell right into it. She want what you got and since she couldn't have me, she told you about us. That shit ain't mean nothing!"

"For once in your life why don't you be a man and admit your shit? Keep it gangsta! You cheated right? Just fess up to it. It ain't the first time I caught you out there! She just saved me the trouble of finding out later!" Simone began to tremble. She was so upset she walked up to him and hit him in the face. She was going for a second hit but he grabbed her hands.

"Yo, keep ya fuckin' hands to yourself. We got enough problems going on right now to have to deal with this bullshit! I'm trying to keep you out of jail and you gonna come at me with this Shelly shit?" That hit a sore spot with Simone. She never thought he would use that to his advantage. Kareem knew what he was doing. He had a trump card that would last him almost a lifetime. Simone pulled away from him and sat on the bed. She put her head in her hands. She was speechless. Did she really want to say anything to keep him from taking the fall if it came to that? She shook her head and silently cried. Kareem hated to throw the incident in her face but she gave him no choice. He was backed into a corner and he had to come out swinging. He

58

sat down and hugged her. Simone kept her face buried into his chest. She couldn't bear to look in his face.

Kareem caressed her arms and legs. He wiped the tears from her eyes. He looked down at her and lifted her face to his.

"I'm sorry baby. I know I told you this before but I only wanna be with you. That's why I kicked Shelly to the curb. The thought of not being with you just made me snap on her. I love you baby. I'm sorry. I'm through wit' all that other shit. You're the only woman I need. Let's concentrate on what we gotta do for us instead of holding on to something that happened a long time ago." Kareem was very persuasive. Simone didn't say anything. She was upset with herself because she actually thought what he just said made some sense. She thought, *He must really want to be with me if he dumped Shelly after a year. He could've just stayed with her.*

Kareem kissed her on the mouth. Simone's body perked up. This was a reaction she hadn't experienced in a while with Kareem. Lately, her body didn't respond to him in this way. She became aroused as he put his hands between her legs. She began to pull down his boxers. His dick was standing at attention. She rubbed it until Kareem jerked away. He slid down to his knees and spread her legs. He put his face between her legs and licked her in a slow motion. She held on to his head and rocked back and forth. He came up and got on top of her. He kissed her nipple and made his way to her neck. He got in her ear and talked dirty.

"Baby, I want you to suck it for me. I miss those big lips wrapped around me. Put it in your mouth baby. Please."
Simone pushed him off of her and slid to the bottom of the bed. She played with him for a little longer before she took his entire dick in her mouth. She sucked him off for ten minutes until he couldn't take anymore. He pulled her on top of him and let her ride him until their volcano erupted. Kareem moaned so loud that Simone put her fingers in his mouth to keep the noise down. Just as he finished his first orgasm, she rocked faster and he lost control again. She leaned down and kissed him in the mouth. She sucked his tongue as he sucked her lips. She bounced up and

down as she called his name. They lay there for an hour then took a shower together.

Kareem got dressed and told Simone he'd be back before six o'clock. Simone told him that she had some errands to run and she would see him later.

Chapter 17

Phil went to the door and peeked through the peephole. He opened the door when he saw Tarik, Tricia and Mrs. Hobbs standing at the threshold.

"Hi Phil, we're sorry to drop by unannounced but we need to talk to Melissa. Is she here?" Tricia asked.

Phil stepped aside and invited them into the living room. He offered them drinks then went to get Melissa.

Melissa came downstairs in her pajamas. She tightened her robe when she saw Tarik. Everyone stood and greeted her. She hugged each one and then sat on an ottoman.

"What's up? Everything ok?" she asked.

"Melissa, is it true that you've talked to Simone and forgave her for shooting you?" Tricia asked.

Melissa took a deep breath. She didn't think the news would spread so quickly. She looked at Tarik before she spoke. "Trish, Simone came to see me the other day. She apologized and I accepted."

"But Moms says you forgive her for shooting you. Why? She could have killed you," Tricia said.

"I know that I was not shot intentially. I'm lucky to be alive and to still have the baby. Simone would never hurt anyone, you know that."

"Melissa, how could you forgive her? She put all of us at risk when she showed up at the wedding with a gun."

"Tricia, stop saying that. I told you no one actually saw Simone pull out a gun. Everyone was focused on the ceremony," Mrs. Hobbs said.

"Momma, would you stop! Everybody knows she pulled out that gun!"

"Maybe it was Kareem," Mrs. Hobbs said playing devil's advocate.

"What reason does he have to shoot me or anyone else at the wedding?" Tricia asked.

"What reason does Simone have to shoot anyone?" Tarik asked. Everyone paused and looked at him in surprise.

"What? You and her are going through something that no one knows about. For all we know she told Kareem what happened and he was trying to defend his girl," Tarik added.

"Don't go there, Tarik. Don't do that reverse psychology shit with me. She would never tell Kareem what happened."

"Don't be so sure about that Tricia. Simone may have the sense to realize that she needs to talk about what happened. She may have confided in Kareem," Mrs. Hobbs said.

Tricia looked at her mother with rage. She shook her head and sighed. She turned and faced her mother. "You act like you want everybody to forgive her and act like she did nothing wrong. You are going through a lot to keep her out of jail. What about what she did to me? What about the fact that Melissa and her baby could have died!"

"I know that you'll never forget your wedding day. But Simone spending time in jail isn't going to change that. You need to get off yo behind and go talk to her! She could really use a friend right now!" Mrs. Hobbs said.

"Yeah well, I could really use a mother right now!"
Tarik stood in front of Tricia and grabbed her. He hugged her and led her back to the sofa. Tricia was furious. She couldn't believe her mother.

"Trish, calm down baby," Tarik said.

Phil walked into the room and could cut the tension with a knife. He cautiously walked up to Melissa's side.

"Is everything alright in here? I could hear the yelling all the way upstairs."

Tarik didn't like the way Phil sounded.

"We alright man. Don't come down here trying to intimidate anybody," Tarik said.

Melissa looked at Tarik with pleading eyes.

trying to find out what time they get up in the middle of the night to have sex! I need you to do some digging. Be careful because I don't want to jeopardize my case."

"This must be serious if you want me to get grimy," Brian said as he looked over the file. He put them inside his briefcase and asked Marvin how soon he needed the info. Marvin told him to get as much info as soon as possible. He told him that the trial was set for early spring. Marvin went into his desk and wrote a check for one third of Brian's fee and handed it to him. Brian grabbed his belongings and left.

Marvin continued to do research for the case. He attempted to look up similar cases to find other options. He heard his cell phone vibrate and retrieved it from his jacket pocket.

"Hello?" he asked in a business tone.

"Hi Marv, are you busy?"

"Maryanne, how are you? I could use a break. What's up?" he blushed.

"Good, are you up to having lunch with me?" she asked.

"I don't see why not. Did you have some place in mind?"

"Actually, I wanted to bring the food to your office while I talked to you about something."

"That's fine. I'll be here."

"Good, I'll see you in half an hour."

Marvin placed the files inside his file cabinet. He continued to surf the internet until Maryann arrived. Arlene buzzed him and told him that Mrs. Hobbs was waiting. He went out to the waiting area and escorted her inside his office. He hugged her and kissed her on the cheek after he closed the door.

"How you doing Marv?" she smiled as she reminisced about their love making.

"I'm good. How are you?" He sat down behind his desk. Maryanne set up the food on the empty desk to her left. Marvin went over and began to eat the Chinese food she brought.

"So you wanted to talk?" he asked.

"Yeah, I hate to ask but I think we should keep our relationship to ourselves until the trial is over. I just want to keep my personal life personal until the time is right for everybody to know."

"You want to put off our relationship until after the trial?"

"No, we'll still see each other I just don't want anyone to know. Let's keep it between you and me," she pleaded.

Marvin hesitated before he spoke. "Maryanne, I have strong feelings for you. I don't feel comfortable pretending we're not together. But, if you think its best, then I'll agree to it."

Maryanne smiled and walked over to him. She kissed him on the lips and he returned the passion she expressed. They cleaned up the food and left out of the office. Marvin told Arlene that he'd be back in an hour. He grabbed Maryanne by the hand and escorted her out of the building.

Chapter 19

Shelly opened the door and welcomed Simone into her apartment. Simone walked past her and sat on the sofa.

"Simone, how have you been?" Shelly sat next to her.

"I'm hanging on. Everything is so hectic right now," Simone said, "I know we need to discuss some things but please, I'm so stressed right now. Just give me a few minutes to get myself together."

"Would you like something to drink? I have cranberry juice," Shelly asked.

"Yeah, that would be nice." Shelly returned with the juice and sat it on a coaster in front of Simone. She pulled Simone up and gave her a hug.

"I missed you," Shelly said. Simone felt that urge she feels around Shelly. She pulled away to keep from going where her body was headed.

"I missed you too. I'm sorry I wasn't able to get to you before now. I've been trying to cope with everything. This upcoming trial is taking so much out of me." She took her seat on the sofa. Shelly followed suit. She sat Indian-style on the sofa.

"Shelly, I just wanted to apologize for getting you in the middle of all of this. No one was supposed to get hurt. It all happened so fast."

Shelly sat back and nodded. "What's up with Kareem? You had a change of heart? You were all set to dump his ass a few weeks ago."

"I know, Shelly. There's no way I can go through with that now. Kareem has been so supportive of me. I just can't let him go at a time like this."

"What? We talked about this Simone. You said you were going through with it. I thought we were trying to build a relationship. Did you change your mind about that too?"

"Calm down Shells, you know I love being with you. It's just too much going on right now." Shelly sighed and looked away. She shook her head in defeat. She never dreamed she'd fall so hard and fast for another woman. Simone held out her hand and motioned for Shelly to come closer. Shelly put her head on Simone's shoulder. She rested for a minute while Simone held her. Shelly began to rub up and down Simone's back.

"I'm sorry that you are going through all of this Simone. I wish there were something I could do to make this easier."

"There is something... You can try to be a little more understanding. I can't dump Kareem right now."

"Are you sure you still want to dump him? You sound like you still want to be with him and I'm not just saying that because of us. Remember, we met because I wanted to expose his cheating ass. You said you'd had enough of him!" Shelly reasoned. Simone didn't say anything. Shelly looked up and kissed Simone on the lips. Simone pulled away. She didn't want to get anything started since she and Kareem was having sex again. Shelly wrinkled her face. "What's wrong?"

"Nothing, we need to finish our conversation. I wanted to ask you what Kareem said that day he called you."

Shelly raised her eyes at Simone. "Just like I told him, if you wanna know something about your man, you ask him! I'm not your girl!" Shelly said as she walked out of the room. Simone followed her to the bedroom.

"Whoa, don't even go there! I know you are pissed about this whole thing but don't be screamin' on me! Kareem is my problem and I will deal with him. We have over twelve years and I need to do this the right way! You got some nerves! You were fuckin' my man until he told you that he wouldn't leave me for you!" Simone yelled.

Shelly turned around to face her. "That's what he told you? Hmp, anything to keep you from dumping his ass, and it looks like it's working."

"I'm confused, why are you so upset about my relationship with Kareem? Do you still want him or something?" Simone questioned.

Shelly slightly cut her eyes away from Simone. "I'm the one who broke it off with him. If I wanted him we'd still be together. I don't know what I want anymore," Shelly said as she sat on the bed. Simone joined her. Shelly put her head in her hands and sobbed.

Simone comforted her until she felt herself getting wet. She tried to ignore the feeling but it took over. She turned Shelly towards her and kissed her on the lips. It was a peck at first. Shelly added the passion and Simone didn't pull away. Simone put her hands between Shelly's legs and massaged her. Shelly repositioned herself so Simone could feel more. Simone's hands explored Shelly's body until they were both naked. Shelly pulled the comforter back and she and Simone slid between the sheets. Shelly was in control the entire time. She had her way with Simone. She tried to make Simone see what she'd be missing if she didn't get rid of Kareem. They made love for two hours. Shelly hadn't had sex since the last time she was with Simone. She made up for lost time.

They sat in the bed and talked for another hour. Simone told Shelly that she'd take care of the situation with Kareem. Shelly asked Simone what she told Kareem about their relationship. Simone explained that Kareem thinks they are only girlfriends. She assured her that he doesn't know about their sexual relationship. Shelly was satisfied after their conversation and agreed to let Simone handle her business. Simone took a shower and left.

Chapter 20

Phil walked up to the receptionist and demanded to speak with Dr. Herbert Marrows. Dr. Marrows told the receptionist he'd be out momentarily. Phil paced the waiting area for ten minutes. Dr. Marrows walked out and escorted Phil to his office. Phil stood in front of Dr. Marrows' desk with rage in his eyes.

"Herb, My wife is pregnant!"

"Phil, there's always a chance that something can go wrong. We discussed all of the side effects and consequences of this procedure before you had the operation. You knew the risks."

Phil sat in a chair and took a deep breath, "what can we do to see if the procedure worked or not?" Phil asked.

"Well, I can take a sample of your sperm and see if it's active or not. How soon do you want to find out?"

"As soon as possible! I've waited long enough. Melissa is three months pregnant. I need to know if I'm going to be a father or not."

"Phil, come with me." He followed Dr. Marrows to the back of the office. Dr. Marrows handed Phil a sterile sealed cup. He walked him into one of the private rooms and told him to give a sample of sperm. Phil hesitated but finally closed the door behind him. He returned half an hour later with a full cup. Dr Marrows took the cup and told Phil to have a seat in the waiting area.

Phil flipped open his phone and called Melissa.

"Hey honey, how is the trip going?" she asked.

"It's business as usual, how are you doing? Are you staying off your feet?"

"I'm fine, Phil. Tricia's here with me now. She's almost worse than you. She won't let me do anything," Melissa laughed.

"Good. I'm glad she's there with you. I'll be home tomorrow. Do you need me to bring you anything?"

"Just yourself," she blushed.

"I'll see you tomorrow. Good night," he said.

Phil was pissed. He asked Melissa not to have her friends in his house. She argued that they all were upset and she continues to stand up for Tarik. He got tired of going back and forth with her. She was not backing down this time and he couldn't make her. He was sort of glad that Tricia was with his wife. He didn't want her doing too much on her own. He talked to her about hiring a nurse but Melissa insisted that she didn't need one.

"Phil, I have your results. Come into my office."

"Just tell me what you found Herb."

Herbert shuffled some papers in front of him. He didn't know quite how to read Phil. He wasn't sure if Phil wanted to be the father of his wife's child or not.

"Herb, tell me."

"There's no way you could have fathered a child. I ran the test twice and turned up the same results." Phil was shocked. He was unresponsive for a few minutes. He looked at Dr. Marrows with tears in the corners of his eyes.

"I'm sorry Phil. Is there anything that I can do?"

"I'll be fine. I just need to clear my head. Would you have your secretary call my car service please?"

"Sure." Herbert buzzed his secretary and gave her instructions. Phil shook Herbert's hand and walked out of the door.

Phil arrived at his hotel and made a detour to the bar. He ordered two double shots of Hennesy and a Corona beer. He sat at the bar half the night drinking. He finally went upstairs to his room. He opened his cell phone and dialed home. Just before the call connected, he hung up. He was so hurt he knew he couldn't talk to Melissa right now. Phil lay across the bed and sobbed like a baby. *Why Melissa? Why did you have to cheat on me? Whose baby are you carrying?*

WITH FRIENDS LIKE THAT

Phil woke up and analyzed his situation. He was furious. He wanted to remain calm so that he could get answers from his wife. Phil sat on the side of the bed and sighed. He never thought in a million years that Melissa would ever cheat on him. He wasn't sure if he was more upset about the cheating or about the baby. In the back of his mind, he really wanted to know who is the father of that baby. He packed his bags and headed home to his wife.

Chapter 21

Tricia left for work an hour early. She was going to hold an in-service for the employees at the company and needed extra preparation time. Tricia was a Human Resources manager with Macy's department store. She was responsible for the entire metropolitan area. She had to travel to New York for the rest of the week. She left early to beat traffic.

Tarik finished getting dressed and sat on the sofa in the living room. He thought about Melissa. He had the strangest feeling that she needed him. He picked up the phone and dialed her number.

"Hey Lissa, what's up?"

"Hi Tarik, how are you?" she responded.

"I'm just calling to check on you. Is everything ok? You need anything?" he asked.

"Everything's good. Phil will be home this afternoon. Are you ok? What's going on? And don't tell me nothing because I know you too well."

Tarik laughed and shook his head. "How is the baby?"

Melissa patted her stomach and smiled, "I'm getting big. I'm just a little over three months but I see my stomach growing right in front of my eyes and it's amazing," she smiled.

"Well, I'm on my way to work but I'm taking you to lunch tomorrow so be ready at about twelve-thirty."

"What's the occasion?"

"Can't a man just want to have lunch with his little sister?" Melissa laughed and said goodbye. Tarik hung up the phone and stared at it. Melissa sounded fine to him but he still had this gut feeling that something was wrong. He'd be able to tell when they had lunch and she was right in his face.

* * *

Phil entered his house and dropped his bags on the floor by the door. He called out to Melissa and got no response. He walked into the kitchen and didn't find her there. He went to the pantry and took out one of the many bottles of Hennessy he kept hidden behind the trash bags. He took out a glass from the cupboard and filled it to the top. He sat at the table and drank until the glass was empty. He continued to do this until the bottle was empty.

Phil went into the living room and walked up the stairs. He peeked into his bedroom and didn't see Melissa. He walked over to the bathroom and knocked on the door. When he didn't get an answer, he went to the telephone and called Melissa on her cell phone. He heard the cell phone ring and followed the sound. He walked into one of the guest bedrooms and found her asleep on the bed. He stood over her and stared. He sat down on the bed and gently shook her. She didn't respond until he shook her a little harder.

"Oh, hi Phil, when did you get here?" She sat up on the bed.

"I've been here for about half an hour. We need to talk. Now!"

Melissa rolled onto her back. She tried to open her eyes. "Could it wait baby? I'm so tired. I just want to get a little more sleep."

"NO! We need to talk right now! Get up!" Phil tugged at her robe.

"Phil, wait a minute. I'm getting up. Let go of my clothes. What's wrong with you anyway?" she asked as she sat up on the side of the bed. Phil moved over towards the foot of the bed so he wouldn't be too close to his wife.

"You have some explaining to do! I want you to tell me who in the hell is the father of that baby!" he said pointing to her stomach.

"What are you talking about? You are the father. Are you drunk?" she asked in confusion.

"I'm not the issue here! You better tell me the truth! Who did you cheat on me with?"

"Phil, I didn't cheat on you. What are you talking about? Why would you think I cheated on you?" Melissa got scared. She was careful not to let Phil see her reaction. "Phil, you've been drinking and you're not thinking straight. Why don't you come on in the bedroom and lay down?" She pulled Phil by the hands but he snatched away from her. Melissa was beginning to get scared of what her husband was going to do to her. She eased away from him and stood close to the door. She was trying to get out of the room before Phil attacked her.

"Where are you going Melissa? We are not finished talking. You didn't answer my question! Who were you cheating with? And don't tell me that you weren't because I know I'm not the father of your baby!"

"Of course you're the father, Phil. What makes you think I've cheated on you?" she asked in a cracking voice.

"DAMN IT, MELISSA! STOP LYING!" He headed towards her. Melissa backed out of the room and walked backwards until she reached the top of the stairs. Phil grabbed her and shoved her into the wall. Melissa grabbed her stomach and bent over.

"Phil, please. Think about the baby," Melissa pleaded.

"The baby? Think about the baby? Whose baby should I think about? It sure as hell ain't mine!" He stepped closer to his wife. Melissa was desperate. She tried to reason with Phil but for some reason, his mind was made up that he wasn't the father of the baby.

"Phil, I'll prove it to you. We can take a paternity test. Please just don't do anything that you're going to regret. Think about this innocent baby. Don't hurt me or this baby, Phil." Melissa walked down the steps as she continued to plead with her husband. Phil looked into her eyes and backed away. The demon inside of him was pleading to come out. He didn't want to hurt his wife or the baby. Phil looked at Melissa with tears in his eyes. He wanted to hold her. He wanted to make everything ok.

Every time he looked at her, he saw an image of her with another man. He went back into the guest bedroom and slammed the door.

Melissa went and sat on the sofa. She balled up in a knot and rubbed her stomach. She cried out of fear. She didn't know what to expect from Phil but as long as he was up in the room, she felt a little safer. She didn't know where Phil got the idea that she cheated on him.

She stayed on the sofa crying. She was terrified to go up to the bedroom. She stayed on the sofa shaking until he came down with red eyes. Melissa sat up as soon as she heard him open the door. Phil came down the steps slowly. He stood at the bottom of the steps and stared at Melissa. He didn't know how to approach her. He was still pissed about the baby but he couldn't understand why Melissa kept denying she cheated. He went to the sofa and sat down. Melissa held her head down and sobbed. Phil wiped the tears from the corners of his eyes and shook his head.

"Melissa, please just tell me the truth. I already know that I'm not the father of your baby."

"Phil, why do you keep saying that?" She looked at him for answers.

"Melissa, I went to see my doctor for a check up and he informed me that I can't have any children. I know that you've been with someone else. I want to know who!" Phil hadn't meant to yell but he was getting sick of Melissa denying the truth.

"Phil, it's the liquor you've been drinking. You aren't thinking straight. We are getting ready to have a beautiful baby. Why…why…don't…just go upstairs and sober up." Phil looked at Melissa with rage in his eyes. He stood up to leave out of the house but Melissa grabbed his arm.

"Phil, where are you going? Don't go out driving while you're drunk!" Phil shoved Melissa down on the sofa and left out of the house. She cried after him for what seemed like forever.

Chapter 22

K areem walked into the apartment and saw Simone hang up the phone quickly. He walked up to her and pretended that he didn't notice.

"Hey baby. How was your day?" she asked.

"It's all good. Have you heard anything from Mr. Woodsby?" he asked.

"Not yet. He said he'd call sometime this week so I'm expecting to hear from him any day now."

"Good. I'm tired of waiting. I want to get this whole thing over with as soon as possible," Kareem said as he sat on the bed next to Simone.

"Kareem, I never did thank you for insisting that I don't do any jail time. I really want you to know that I appreciate it."

"You don't have to thank me, Simone. I love you. Besides, you my girl. I know I fucked up and cheated and all that other stuff but, I'm not gonna see nothing bad happen to you. I know you wouldn't intentionally hurt nobody," he said as he faced her on the bed.

"I love you too Kareem," she said as she kissed him. Kareem was trying to avoid any intimacy with Simone. He had been with Mr. Woodsby's receptionist, Arlene only hours ago. He pulled away from Simone and went into the bathroom. Simone knew this routine all too well but she refused to believe that Kareem would be with another woman when they were in the situation that they were. She shook off her intuition and lay across the bed.

Kareem came out of the bathroom about forty minutes later. He plopped down on the bed. Simone crawled to him and rubbed between his legs. He felt himself getting a hard on and got off the bed.

"What's wrong with you?" Simone asked.

"Nothing, I just got a lot on my mind. I'ma go out for a little bit." He went to the drawer and pulled out a pair of jeans. He quickly got dressed and left.

Kareem got into his car and headed across town. He ended up at Shelly's apartment. He rang the intercom and waited for her to buzz him in. She protested at first. Kareem assured her that he came in peace. She was skeptical but she let him up.

"Hey," she said as she stepped aside to let him in.

"How you doing?" he asked with a turned up face. Shelly's heart melted as soon as she saw Kareem. She had been in love with him for over a year and she couldn't deny that she still felt the same way. Even after all of the drama.

"What's up with you and Simone, Shelly? Why are you hanging around her trying to be her friend? What kind of shit is that?" Kareem yelled.

"Kareem, don't come in here yelling and shit! You don't even know the whole story. Simone and I hit it off and we just kick it every now and then. What's the big deal?" she asked.

"The big deal is that she's my girl! How the hell you look runnin' round wit my girl?"

"Why are you coming at me like that? She's the one you should be talking to. She's the one who have to be around the woman her man cheated with. She calls me to hang out! I don't call her." Shelly tried her best to convince Kareem that she and Simone were only friends.

"You just doing this shit to get back at me! That's fucked up Shelly. You knew about Simone from the start!" Shelly shook her head and sighed. She stared at Kareem.

"You really think it's all about you don't you? Why everybody gotta be sitting around with you on their mind? Simone ain't thinking about you anymore. Do you really think she's gonna stay with you? Don't you realize that her hanging with me only gives her motivation to leave you? What do you think she's thinking every time she sees me?" Shelly felt good inside. She really thought she made Kareem hurt. Kareem shook his head at Shelly.

"You think it's that easy, huh? Simone ain't gonna let you or anyone else keep us apart. She assures me on a regular basis that she's not going anywhere," he said as he grabbed his dick.

"Whatever! That's between you and your girl!" Shelly tried to conceal the disappointment in her voice. She didn't want to believe that Simone was still having sex with Kareem. She knew Kareem had no reason to lie to her since she was no longer seeing him and since he didn't know about her and Simone. Her heart melted at the thought. Kareem read defeat on Shelly's face, or so he thought it was defeat. "Shelly, just stay away from my girl!"

"Kareem, stop frontin' like it's all about Simone. You and I both know you're just doing all of this because she found out about us. It's only a matter of time before you're on to the next chick!"

"Whateva! I gotta use the bathroom." Kareem got up and went to the bathroom. Shelly's mind began to race. She knew Kareem would walk out the door when he came out of the bathroom. She had to do something to get him to stay.

Kareem came out of the bathroom and headed back to the sofa. He saw Shelly sitting in the nude. She had her legs swung over the arm of the chair so Kareem could see her pussy. He stopped in his tracks and smiled. She patted the empty space next to her and motioned for him to sit. Kareem kept the smile on his face as he sat next to Shelly. She swung her legs around and sat up.

"So you think this gonna get me to leave Simone? I ain't feeling you like that anymore, Shelly."

Shelly jumped up and sat on Kareem's lap. "You sure you're not feeling me? I think your little friend has something to say about that," she smirked. Kareem eased his hands on her ass and kissed her neck. Shelly lifted her head and kissed him on the lips. Kareem returned the kiss with full force. Shelly pushed him on the sofa and inched her way up to his face. She sat on his chest and let him have dinner.

She squeezed her nipples as he pleasured her. She moaned as he slid her down to his lap. Shelly undid Kareem's pants and helped herself to a licking. She got down on her knees and made Kareem squirm and moan. Shelly got up and sat on his lap. She bounced up and down until she reached her orgasm. Kareem flipped her on her knees and rammed into her doggystyle. Shelly looked back and began to talk dirty. *"I knew you wanted some of this pussy baby."* Kareem moaned and talked back. *"You know I wanted some of this pussy. I missed you so much. Come on and help me bust this nut."* She raised her ass as far as she could. Kareem smacked her butt cheek and rode her faster. He was sweating uncontrollably. Shelly began to pump in and out to help him with his orgasm. It only took another three minutes for Kareem to explode on her ass. He breathed heavily and kissed her back. "Damn baby, that was aiight," he said.

"You missed me, huh?" Shelly asked.

"You know I missed this ass. Stop acting like you don't want no more of this dick. You know you love me baby. Don't you?"

"I love you baby. You know I do," she said as her body shook from another orgasm. Kareem played with her clitoris until she finished.

He went to the bathroom to wash off the evidence. Shelly followed him to the bedroom and grabbed her robe. She turned on the shower. "You not gonna join me?"

"Nah, baby, I gotta go. You know how it is."

"Yeah, I know how it is." Shelly kissed him on the lips then followed him to the door. Kareem turned around and smiled at her. "I'll call you." He closed the door behind him.

"I'm sure you will." She smiled. Shelly was the queen of games and she intended to have her cake and eat it too since she found out the truth about Simone and Kareem.

Chapter 23

B rian Castro sat opposite Marvin Woodsby in a café in Montclair, NJ. Brian always wanted to meet where there was no chance of a client popping up. He slid a folder over to Marvin and folded his hands. Marvin read the top page and raised his eyes. He looked up at Brian and smiled.

"Are you sure this is true? How did you find this?"

"It was tough. I'm positive that every bit of it is true!" Brian said.

"I'll be damned! My clients may not have to do a day in jail." Marvin shook Brian's hand and stood. He thanked Brian for the information and told him to keep looking.

Marvin sat behind the wheel of his black BMW. He shook his head up and down and then flipped open his cell phone. He said Maryanne and his phone dialed her number.

"Hi sweetheart, are you up for dinner? Fine, I'll pick you up in an hour." He closed his phone and headed to his office. He carefully placed the file in a locked cabinet then turned on his computer. He popped in a disk and typed in a few notes. He smiled to himself and wrote a reminder to call the prosecutor in the morning.

Mrs. Hobbs smiled as Marvin opened the car door for her. She stepped inside and buckled her seatbelt. Marvin got in the car and leaned over and kissed her on the cheek.

"So what would you like to eat?" he asked.

"How about Italian? Olive Garden?"

"That's fine." He said as he headed up Route 280 towards West Orange, NJ.

After dinner, Marvin ordered a bottle of Chardonnay. He poured two glasses and handed one to Maryanne. He held up his glass and toasted to their one month celebration.

"Maryanne, this past month has been wonderful. I enjoy every minute we spend together. I'm glad you decided to let me make you happy," he smiled.

"Oh Marvin," she blushed, "I also enjoy the time we spend together. I can't wait until it's safe for us not to hide our relationship." They clinked glasses then drank their wine.

Marvin opened the door to his car and helped Maryanne get in. Once he was in, he turned to face her.

"Maryanne, do you have any plans for tomorrow?"

"Just some errands, why?"

"Well, I was wondering if you would mind spending the night at my place tonight. You could take me to work in the morning and use my car to do what you need to do. I'll just need you to pick me up in the evening." Maryanne was speechless. She didn't expect Marvin to ask her to spend the night out. She thought about Tricia. What would she say if Tricia called or came by the house and she wasn't there? The thought of her spending the night with Marvin overrode her thoughts of Tricia.

"Let's just swing by my place so I can grab my overnight bag," she said.

"No problem," Marvin smiled. He didn't know what to expect but he was ecstatic that she said yes. They headed to her house and she went inside to pack a bag. Twenty minutes later, she returned. Marvin drove the speed limit to his suburban condo in Woodbridge, NJ.

When they walked into his house, he placed her overnight bag on the floor by the door. He gave her a tour of his place. She complemented his taste and admired his paintings. He told her to make herself comfortable.

Maryanne came downstairs after a hot shower and joined Marvin in the den. He put on a Nina Simone CD and held Maryanne in his arms. They sat and talked into the late hours of the night. Marvin escorted Maryanne up to the bedroom and turned down the bed. He pulled her into his arms and they fell asleep in that position.

Chapter 24

Tarik rolled over and kissed Tricia on the neck. It was almost time for her to get up to get ready for work. She rubbed his back and smiled.

"Hey baby. What are you doing up so early?" she asked.

"I didn't have a say in the matter," he said as he guided her hand between his legs.

"Oh I see," she said as Tarik climbed on top of her. He caressed her breasts and rubbed between her legs. Tricia responded accordingly. She wrapped her legs around his waist and sucked his neck. Tarik placed two fingers between her legs as she moved to his rhythm. Tricia was enjoying the foreplay.

Tarik sucked on her nipples until they were rock hard. She slid from under him and got on top of him. It was her turn to seduce him. She used her tongue to locate his nipples. She sucked them as he moaned underneath her. The reaction from Tarik made her want him more. She put her hands between his legs and rubbed until he couldn't get any larger. Tarik moved back and forth as he practically forced Tricia on top of him. She slid down on his shaft and rode it very slow. Tarik wanted fast movement so he tried to guide her to move faster. Tricia placed one of her fingers in his mouth to distract him for a minute. Tarik sucked her fingers until she almost had her whole hand in his mouth. She leaned close to him so he could suck her nipples.

Tarik thrust deep into Tricia. She jerked from the welcomed pain and bounced a little higher with each ride. She moaned his name as she reached her peak of enjoyment. Tarik placed his hands under her ass and bounced her faster. Tricia moaned louder with each thrust. Tarik sat up and let Tricia ride him to paradise. He held onto her back and pumped until he released all of himself.

Tricia jumped off of him and went to the shower. Tarik lay in bed basking in the glow. He didn't have to get up for another hour. When Tricia got dressed, she told Tarik to tell Lissa to call her and kissed her husband on the lips. She walked out of the door and Tarik rolled over until his alarm clock woke him.

He got out of the bed and went to his closet to find a suit. He felt energized after his shower and looked forward to lunch with Melissa. He worried about her and wanted to see for himself that she was alright. He picked up the phone and called her to remind her about lunch. She told him that she'd be ready and hung up the phone.

Tarik stared at the phone and thought about calling Melissa back. He shook his head and realized that she may be groggy because it was still early. He grabbed his car keys and headed out the door.

Tarik finished up some paperwork and headed out of his office. He told a colleague that he'd be back in about an hour and to call him on his cell if he's needed.

He jumped in his truck and headed to Melissa's. She was waiting in the foyer when he pulled up. She held out one finger to indicate that she'd be right out. Tarik got out of the truck and helped her to step inside.

"Hey hon, what's up?" she asked.

"You, how have you been?" he asked.

"I'm surviving, you know me," she nervously laughed.

"What do you have a taste for today?"

"Uhm, I don't know. My appetite is not too bad these days. I still eat just about everything. Let's go to the diner."

"Cool." Tarik said as he kept his thoughts to himself about the last time they went to the diner.

They walked inside and requested a table for two in the non-smoking section. Tarik pulled out the chair for Melissa and helped her to sit. She smiled and kept her head buried in the menu.

"Melissa, what's going on with you? I can see that everything is not ok, so talk to me. Is Phil acting up again? Did that muthafucka put his hands on you?" Tarik yelled. Some patrons turned their way while Melissa grabbed his arm to hush him.

"Tarik calm down. You are embarrassing me! Sit down!" Melissa pleaded through clenched teeth.

"Well tell me what's going on. You're definitely not fine." Melissa drank a sip of water then fiddled with her napkin. She wanted to tell Tarik about Phil but she didn't want Tarik to go off. She knew for the sake of her child that she had to tell Tarik so that he could have her back.

"Talk, Melissa!"

"I'm going to tell you but you have to promise to hear the entire story before you respond." The waitress walked to the table and they ordered lunch. Tarik looked into Melissa's eyes and saw pain. He wanted to protect her from the world. He'd always been over-protective of her and never could explain why. He didn't think it was possible for him to love her more until they had the affair. He wasn't in love with her romantically but their friendship was made even stronger. "Go head. I'm listening." Tarik sat back and watched her facial expressions. He knew that whatever she had to say would be difficult. She let a teardrop escape her eye then quickly wiped it away. Tarik was getting frustrated. He knew Melissa was hurting and he grew tired of waiting for her to tell him the problem. She looked up at him and saw that he was getting impatient.

"Tarik, I'm scared. Phil and I had an argument last night and he walked out of the house. I haven't heard from him since he left. I don't know where he could be," she blurted.

"You're all upset over an argument? What did y'all argue about?" Tarik folded his hands together and waited for her answer.

"He went away for a business trip last week. He came home last night and started going off about the baby."

"What did he say about the baby?" Tarik demanded. Melissa began to cry uncontrollably. Tarik went by her side and hugged her.

"He came home and said that the baby wasn't his."

"The fuck he say that for?"

"Tarik, calm down. You said you'd hear the entire story."

"Well tell me! And stop beating around the bush." He didn't mean to yell. He knew between Phil and her hormones she was upset, the last thing he wanted to do was make it worse.

"He had been drinking again and started claiming that he couldn't possibly be the father of my baby. I tried to keep him calm and reason with him but he was out of control. I was scared, Tarik. He had that look in his eyes again."

"Did he put his hands on you Melissa?" She looked away. "Melissa! Did he hit you?" Tarik asked with rage in his eyes and voice. The waitress brought their food as Melissa was about to answer. Tarik told the waitress if they needed anything else, he'd send for her. She excused herself and left. "Did he hit you?" he asked again.

"He shoved me against the wall," she said between sniffles.

"That muthafucka! He don't give a fuck about you or that baby! I told you to rethink this whole baby idea!"

"Tarik, I do not need you to throw this up in my face. I'm only telling you this because I'm scared for my baby! Do not start with the I told you so's!"

"That fuckin' bastard! He better pray I don't find his ass! Ima show him what the fuck it feels like to be shoved into a muthafuckin wall!" Tarik pounded his fist to the table and clenched his jaw. "Did you get hurt? Is the baby alright? You not in any pain are you?"

"No Tarik. I feel fine. It was just a little shove," Melissa said.

"A little shove! He could have made you lose the baby and you're sitting here defending him? Get up! Call that Dr. Mike and tell him we're coming for him to check you out!"

"Tarik, we can't just demand that Mike check me out. He may be busy," Melissa procrastinated.

"Well, we'll wait until he's available."

"We could just call my OB/GYN. I'm sure she'll see me because she knows I'm a high risk pregnancy." She fumbled with her cell phone.

"Well call her." Tarik opened his own phone and called his job. He told them that he'd be out for the rest of the day. He then called Tricia and told her that he may be home late. He told her that he was running Melissa to the hospital. He calmed Tricia and told her not to worry. He promised to call her later and fill her in on the details.

"Well, Dr. Watters is out, she's delivering a baby right now." Tarik left money on the table and grabbed Melissa's hand. They headed off to St. Barnabas where she worked.

Chapter 25

D r. Carter extended his arm and invited Tarik and Melissa into his office. Tarik shook his hand.

"Thanks for seeing us on such short notice, man."

"That's ok. Melissa knows she can always count on me." He looked into her eyes. "So what's the problem? Are you having complications?" he asked as he took a seat behind his desk.

"She says she's fine but I'll feel much better once I hear that from you," Tarik said.

"Did something happen, Melissa?"

She looked away in embarrassment.

"She fell last night and I just want to make sure she and the baby are ok," Tarik said.

"I see." He wrote notes in her chart. "Dr. Watters wouldn't squeeze you in?" he asked in disbelief.

"She's delivering a baby today," Melissa added.

"I see. Just step into the exam room and we can check you out. Tarik you're welcome to stay here until we're done. This won't take long." Dr. Carter escorted Melissa out of the room.

"You fell, Melissa?" he asked as he put the gel on her stomach to give her an ultrasound.

"I'm not in the mood, Mike. Please don't start with me." Dr. Carter shook his head. He proceeded to listen to the baby's heartbeat.

"The baby's heart sounds normal. There's no sign of weakness and it's moving around as expected. I don't see anything unusual." He handed her a wipe and wrote more notes in her chart. "Melissa, I told you that you could talk to me anytime you needed. It's not just you anymore. You have to think about your baby. If he can knock you down while you're pregnant, how much further is he willing to go?" Melissa sighed and wiped her eyes. She knew Mike and Tarik made a lot of sense. Phil is her husband and she knows he's just still shocked about the baby. She didn't want to believe that he'd hurt her while she carried his baby. But she was scared because Phil truly believed that the baby wasn't his.

"I really appreciate this, Mike. Thank you so much." She struggled to put on her shoes. Dr. Carter leaned on one knee and put her shoes on her feet then tied them. She looked into his eyes and turned away. She got off the exam table and sat in the chair.

"Mike, I know your concerns, but I'm fine. I have it all under control. I have friends who care and they aren't going to let anything happen to me."

"Tarik really believes you fell doesn't he?" Dr. Carter asked.

"He knows what happened," Melissa retorted.

"Lissa, how can you expect anyone to help you when you won't even help yourself? Tarik doesn't sleep in the house with you and your husband. What happens when it's too late by the time someone finds you?"

"Please Mike! I have to hear all of this from Tarik on the ride home. I don't need to hear it from you too!" she frowned.

"We need to talk Melissa," he said sincerely.

"I'll call you Mike."

Dr. Carter shook his head. He knew Melissa was just saying that to keep him off her back.

"Melissa, you know that it's my duty by law to report any signs of abuse towards a patient. Don't make me go there! We need to talk!" Melissa shook her head and headed out of the exam room. She couldn't believe that Mike was going there with her. She opened the door and stepped out.

"Melissa?" Dr. Carter called after her.

"How dare you threaten me!"

"It's not a threat. I'm worried about you. You're leaving me no choice," he said.

"Hmp. I'll call you as soon as things settle down a little."

He looked skeptical.

"I promise."

He followed her back into his office where Tarik was waiting. Tarik stood and rushed towards Melissa. "How is she?"

"Melissa and the baby are fine. She really needs to take it easy. Melissa, I want you to make an emergency appointment with Dr. Watters so she can give you a vaginal exam. But as far as I can see, everything is ok."

Tarik shook Dr. Carter's hand and escorted Melissa out of the office. "We appreciate this Doc."

"Anytime. Uhm, Melissa, don't forget." She looked back and shook her head in agreement.

Tarik helped her in the truck and drove her home. They sat in the truck and talked for a while. Melissa begged Tarik not to do anything to Phil. She asked him for the opportunity to work this out on her own. He insisted that he was going to kick Phil's ass when he saw him. Melissa would not get out of his car until he agreed to let her handle the situation. Tarik made her promise that she would call if she couldn't handle things on her own. Melissa agreed then thanked Tarik for everything. She finally stepped out of the truck and went inside her house. Tarik drove off once she waived to him from the foyer.

Chapter 26

Kareem walked into the apartment and found Simone laying on the bed. He bent down and kissed her on the cheek. Simone instantly got aroused. She hadn't found Kareem this irresistible in a long while. She assumed it was the excitement of fucking one of his chics on the side. She could almost understand what Kareem felt when he cheated on her.

Lately she was the one making all of the advances and initiating the sex. Today was no different. She jumped on him as he removed his jacket.

"Simone, chill. I'm tired as hell. I just wanna take a shower and lay down." Simone wrinkled her forehead. Just a few months ago, he was the one begging for sex. Simone was horny as ever. She was going to get sex from someone tonight.

The phone rang as Kareem walked into the bedroom wrapped in a towel. He answered, "Hello? Hi Mr. Woodsby. Yes, we'll be there. Thanks." He hung up the phone and called out to Simone.

"Simone, Mr. Woodsby wants to meet with us tonight. He said he has some news about the case."

"What time?" Simone asked.

"He said about seven. He wants us to come into his office. I guess I won't be getting no rest now." He went to the closet and pulled out a sweat suit. He laced up his sneakers and walked into the kitchen. Simone was making hamburgers. She sliced tomatoes as Kareem sat at the table.

"Kareem, do me a favor and get the lettuce out of the fridge." Kareem got up and did what Simone asked. She got up and flipped the burgers and checked the French fries.

"So have you talked to Trish yet?"

"No, I'm giving her some more time. Moms told me how she acted when she found out I spoke to Melissa. I think I need to wait a little bit longer."

"You're gonna have to face her sometime. Might as well get it over with," Kareem suggested. Simone shook her head no. She continued to check the food.

"I'll have a better response from Tarik than Tricia. I'm going to stop by his job one day this week."

"How about I go with you to talk to him? We could invite him out for drinks or something," Kareem said.

"No baby, I appreciate what you're doing but I need to do this on my own. I have to do this my way." They sat at the table and ate their hamburgers.

Simone volunteered to drive. She grabbed the car keys and headed in front of Kareem out the door.

Kareem walked up to the receptionist and asked if Mr. Woodsby was available.

"Is he expecting you?" Arlene asked as she flirted with her eyes. Simone cleared her throat and rolled her eyes before she spoke, "yes he is. Please tell him that we're here."

Arlene buzzed Mr. Woodsby and he told her to escort his clients into his office. She stood and led the way. Kareem followed close behind so that his hand can accidentally brush against her ass. Simone grabbed Kareem's hand as soon as they stood in the office doorway. Arlene took notice and chuckled to herself. She thought about the time she spent with Kareem and smiled. She totally understood why Simone latched onto Kareem a little tighter. She said goodnight to her boss and closed the door behind her. She went to her desk and mumbled, *"If only you knew."*

Mr. Woodsby shook their hands and asked them to sit. "Have you found out who all will testify against you in court?"

"We don't have to worry about Melissa but her husband is another story. He keeps trying to force her to testify. He said he's going to do whatever he can to see that someone pays for what happened to her," Simone said.

"Well, I wouldn't worry too much about Mr. Monroe. I don't think he'll be testifying to anything once his little secret is exposed."

"What secret?" Kareem asked.

"I don't intend to share that information until necessary. But you don't have to worry about him," Marvin smiled.

"I don't get it Mr. Woodsby," Simone said.

"Well it's my job to do all I can to make sure you get the best representation. I've had my detective do some digging to reassure the case. He gave me some information we could definitely use for the case. I don't want you two to worry about it. I'm doing everything in my power but, there can't be any other witnesses."

Both Simone and Kareem stood and shook hands with Mr. Woodsby. They said goodbye then parted ways.

Simone felt inside her jacket to remove her cell phone. She read the number then sent it to voicemail. She smiled at Kareem then asked if he wanted to go and have a drink.

"Yeah, why not? I could use a drink."

They rode to a bar in Bloomfield, NJ. Kareem found a parking spot right in front of the bar.

They walked in and looked around. There was a long bar in the middle of the room. The lights were dimmed and a DJ booth was in the back. It was jumping with people. Simone looked around to see if she knew anyone. Kareem walked up to the bar and ordered their drinks. There was a table next to the DJ booth filled with food. It was happy hour with free food. Kareem walked back to Simone and handed her the drink. She sipped it and shook her head in approval. They sat at a table to their right.

"So, what do you think Mr. Woodsby have on Phil?" she asked.

"Shit, I don't know. You're the one friends with his wife. Whatchu know about him?"

"Not much. But whatever it is, I hope Melissa doesn't get hurt," Simone said.

"You need to be worrying about us and not her feelings," Kareem stated.

"She's still my friend Kareem. I don't want to put her through anything else." Simone grabbed Kareem's hand and led him to the dance floor. The DJ was playing old school club and Simone couldn't resist. They danced for half an hour before Kareem had had enough. He sat down while Simone continued to dance. A guy about 6'2" strolled up behind Simone and began dancing with her. She turned to face him and stepped to his rhythm.

Kareem ordered another round of drinks as Simone kept dancing. The guy she danced with tried to dance close to her ass. Simone pushed him off of her twice. He continued to move in close to her. He went behind her and started to grind on her ass. Simone faced him and danced in front of him. He grabbed her waist and pulled her close to him. She finally had enough and tried to walk away. He grabbed her arm and she snatched away. Kareem walked out to the dance floor.

"It's a problem my man? Why you gripping my girl like that, yo?" Kareem said as he stepped in front of Simone.

"Chill man, we just dancing," the guy said.

"Fall back nicca, go dance wit somebody else," Kareem said as he pushed Simone away from the commotion.

"Yo, you need to relax partner. It's not that serious."

"Yeah aiight. Go head man," Kareem said.

"Punk muthafucka, don't nobody want yo girl."

Kareem walked up to the guy and punched him in the nose. Simone stepped in front of Kareem and pushed him back.

"Kareem no! We don't need this kind of trouble." The guy got to his feet and headed towards Kareem. Kareem pushed Simone aside and swung a right jab. The guy ducked the jab and came back with a jab of his own. He landed on the side of Kareem's head. Kareem shook it off and came back with an uppercut to the guy's chin. The guy fell and the security guards rushed Kareem to the floor. They pushed him out of the bar while Simone followed closely behind.

Simone joined Kareem in the shower. "You ok baby?"

"I'm aiight. But the next time I'm in a fight, don't jump yo ass in my way!"

"I was trying to be the reasonable one. We are awaiting trial and the last thing we need is more trouble. My bad, I didn't mean to jump in yo way," she said as she hugged him.

"I know baby. I got so pissed when I saw him all over you like that." He rubbed her back and gave her a passionate kiss. She stood on her toes to reach him. He scooped her up so that her legs were wrapped around his waist. They had sex right in that position. Kareem confessed his love for her by talking during the entire episode. Simone found this strange because Kareem always expressed his feelings afterwards. She enjoyed every minute of it.

They climbed out of the shower and continued in the bed. Simone lay in Kareem's arms happy. She was beginning to feel like he was ready to be the man she wanted him to be.

Chapter 27

Tricia had just finished her aerobics class at the gym. As she headed to the showers, her cell phone rang. She took the call and told the caller that she'd be there in an hour. Tricia got dressed and went to the mall. She needed to get a few autumn suits.

She went to Lord & Taylor and tried on a few outfits. She asked her sales associate to alter the suits to fit her. Tricia liked her clothes to fit her body to accentuate her shape. She picked up a few pounds just recently. Her clothes were a bit snug and she didn't feel comfortable. The associate returned just as Tricia was putting on her sneakers. She told Tricia that the suits would be ready in two weeks. Tricia thanked her and went to the register to pay.

Trish headed to the shoe department and picked out three pairs of shoe boots. She paid for them then headed to her car. She called Tarik at their apartment and told him that she'd bring dinner when she returned.

Tricia walked up the steps and rang the doorbell. Melissa hurried to the door and let Tricia inside. She was in tears as she practically jumped in Tricia's arms.

"Whoa...what's the matter?" Tricia asked as she helped Melissa to the sofa, "Is Phil here? Did he do something to you?" Tricia looked around the room.

"No, he's not here. I don't know where he is. He left a couple days ago and I haven't heard from him," Melissa cried.

"Calm down and tell me what happened Lissa. Do you need some water?" Melissa grabbed her stomach and leaned forward. She had a look of pain on her face.

"Are you ok?" Tricia asked, "Do you need me to call an ambulance?"

"No, I'll be ok. I just need to relax a little." Melissa took a few deep breaths and put her feet up on the sofa. Tricia covered her with the throw blanket. She went into the kitchen and grabbed a bottle of water. She rushed back into the living room to Melissa.

"You feel better, sweetie? You really need to stay calm for the baby."

"I know. I'm just pissed! That Phil!"

"What happened, Melissa?" Tricia sat back on the sofa and prepared to hear what Melissa had to say.

"Ok, first of all, when Phil came back from his business trip. He was drunk."

"Damn, he's starting that shit again? I thought he was going to meetings and trying to quit," Tricia added.

"That's not the worst part. Out of nowhere, he started yelling talking about he's not the father of my baby." Melissa began to cry again, "he said that he was positive that he wasn't the father of my baby."

Tricia was stunned. She had a confused look on her face. "What! Why would he say something like that? What else did he say?"

"Well, I tried to ask him why he thought he wasn't the father but he kept cutting me off calling me a liar. He was drunk so I assume it was the alcohol talking," Melissa sniffed, "he called me a liar and told me that there was no way he could be the father of my baby. I was scared. He had that look in his eyes and I thought he was going to hit me. But he didn't."

"Wait, Melissa, why would Phil say something like that? What makes him think he's not the father? There has to be something else. If he's that adamant about not being the father, he's not telling you something. What reason could he possibly believe that he didn't father your baby?" Tricia asked.

"Well...he did accuse me of cheating on him. He kept asking me why I cheated on him and who I cheated with." Melissa wiped her eyes and looked at Tricia. Through all of the drama, Melissa never thought about it like that. "But what would give him the idea that I cheated on him?" Melissa began to cry harder. She kept her head low and didn't look at Trish. She continued to rub her stomach and sob. Tricia hugged her and tried to calm her with soothing words. "Phil is trippin'. He knows that you would never cheat on him. Was he against the idea of having a baby that much?"

"I'm a little scared, Trish. I thought he was going to hurt me and the baby."

"What did Tarik say?" Trish asked.

"I told him everything I told you and he wanted to search for Phil. He made all kinds of verbal threats but I talked him out of doing anything. I begged him to let me try and work it out on my own."

"Why would you do something like that if you're scared?"

"Because I don't want Tarik to hurt my husband. I at least want to find out what's going on. I want to know what possessed Phil to say those things to me." Tricia looked at Melissa and shook her head. She wanted to slap some sense into her. If she thought she could do it without hurting the baby, she would have.

Melissa and Tricia sat on the sofa and talked for a few more hours. Melissa called her husband several times. She kept leaving messages on his voicemail. Tricia called Tarik to tell him she was on her way. They discussed what to eat for dinner then she hung up the phone. "Lissa, I gotta go. But if you need me to stay here with you, I will."

"No no, I'll be ok."

"How do you feel? Is the baby moving around more than usual?" Tricia asked.

"I'm fine Trish. Get on home to your husband," she smiled.

"Don't hesitate to call us if you need us. I don't care what time." Tricia walked towards the door. As she was about to turn the handle, Phil opened the door. Tricia stared at him with an icy glare and then turned to Melissa.

"I need to talk to my wife," he said as he looked at Tricia.

"I'm not going anywhere! Melissa, I'm calling Tarik."

"Tricia, I can promise you that I'm not here to hurt anyone. I just need to talk to my wife," Phil pleaded. Tricia looked back at Melissa for an answer.

"It's ok Trish. I promise to call you later. Please? It's ok."

"You don't have to worry about Melissa. She's safe with me. Trust me. Please?" Phil begged. Tricia went to Melissa and whispered something in her ear. She kissed her on the cheek and walked past Phil. She glanced one more time at Melissa, shook her head then left.

Chapter 28

Melissa sat up on the sofa as Phil plopped down next to her. "Where have you been?" she asked.

"I've been doing some thinking. I love you Melissa. I told you before that I would do anything to keep this marriage together and I meant it. You are too important to me to let this come between us."

Melissa looked confused, "what are you talking about? Let what come between us?"

"This baby."

"My goodness Phil, I thought that since you are sober, you'd stop this nonsense."

"Nonsense? You are going to sit here and still deny that you cheated on me? Even after I told you that it doesn't matter?" he screamed.

Melissa jumped. She eased away from him and sighed deeply. "Phil, where would you get the idea that I cheated on you?" I told you that we can take a paternity test and you still insist that I cheated."

"Because I know you did! All I want is for you to admit it and we can move forward with our lives. I'll raise this child like my own with no regrets. Just admit to me that you had an affair. I don't even want to know who you were with."

Melissa began to cry. She looked at Phil and searched his face for answers. She couldn't believe what Phil was suggesting. She held her head in her hands and cried while Phil went into the kitchen. He returned with a bottle of Hennessy. He sat on the chair opposite his wife. He stared at her for a minute then took a gulp of the alcohol. Melissa looked up at him and shook her head in disbelief.

"You promised me you would stop. What happened to you going to the meetings?" she sobbed.

"You promised me for better or for worse. You promised to be faithful. What happened to that?" he slurred.

Melissa continued to cry. She rubbed her stomach to keep the baby calm. "Phil, why are you doing this? Are you that unhappy about us having a baby?"

Phil stood and got in Melissa's face. He swallowed another gulp of his drink before he spoke. "The baby I can deal with. It's the fact that you won't admit what you did! I know I'm not the father because I can't have kids!" he said in near tears.

Melissa looked up at her husband with stretched eyes. "What are you talking about?" Phil drank the rest of his drink and threw the empty bottle across the room. Melissa jumped at the shattered glass and looked back at her husband.

"I went to the doctor and took some tests. He assured me that there's no way I could have fathered any baby! So just admit to me that you had an affair!" Melissa turned her face away from Phil. She wasn't sure if he was telling the truth or not. She thought maybe he was testing her to see if she actually did have an affair. She didn't even try to conceal the tears. She asked Phil over and over why was he doing this to her.

Phil turned away from Melissa. His eyes were also filled with tears. He turned back around and looked Melissa directly in the eyes. "I know I haven't been the perfect husband and our marriage is not the best. But through all that we've been through, I've never cheated on you. I never thought in a million years that you'd cheat on me." He walked up the stairs to their bedroom. Melissa chased after him.

"Phil, don't walk away. Please listen to what I have to say." He opened their bedroom door and walked back inside to the bathroom. He started the shower then went to his closet.

"Sweetie, I don't know what's going on but I didn't have an affair. Maybe we should get a second opinion. You can see another doctor and you'll see that I didn't cheat on you." Her pleas and cries fell upon deaf ears. Phil walked about the room like she wasn't even there. He entered the bathroom and closed the door. Melissa went back downstairs and sat on the sofa. Phil was too calm for her. She'd never seen him like this before, especially after a drink. She grabbed a blanket out of the closet because she didn't feel safe sleeping in the same room with her husband. There was no telling what he was capable of with the attitude he displayed. She lay back on the sofa and for the first time since it happened, she thought about Tarik.

She cried even harder at the thought of her husband finding out about the meaningless escapade she had with Tarik.

Chapter 29

Simone waited for Kareem to leave the apartment before she called Shelly. Shelly was on her way to work and told Simone that she could only talk for a second.

"Shells, lets have lunch today. I need to see you about something."

"My place?" Shelly smiled to herself.

"No, at that little Deli around the corner from your job," Simone said.

"Ok. I'll meet you there about twelve-thirty."

"Cool, see ya later." Simone hung up the phone and started her day. She would go down to visit Tarik today. It was a meeting that was long overdue.

She parked her car in the visitor's parking lot and went into the building. She signed in the book and took the elevator to his floor. She wanted to run back inside the elevator as it opened but she knew she needed to face him. She walked to his office and the door was closed. She tapped lightly on the door and waited for a response. She could hear him ending a phone conversation before he invited her in.

Simone entered the office in what seemed like slow motion. Tarik stood to meet his visitor and got the shock of his life when Simone pushed open his door. They stood face to face staring at each other for the longest minute imaginable. Simone broke the stare by looking out of the window. Tarik backed into his chair and sat down. He sighed and threw his pen on the desk. "What are you doing here Simone?"

"I just wanna talk to you. I want to apologize for everything. Can I sit for a minute?" she asked as she reached towards a chair. Tarik motioned for her to sit and went to close his door. "I don't have much time so make it quick."

"I'm sorry to just pop up here like this but its time for me to get this off my chest," she took a deep breath, "I never got the chance to personally apologize for interrupting your wedding. I'm sorry Tarik. If I could take any of it back, I would. I love you and Tricia. I never meant for any of this to happen."

Tarik looked at her sympathetically. He believed that Simone was sincere with her apologies. "Simone, I don't know what to say."

She looked down nervously. "You don't really have to say anything. I just wanted you to know how I feel. I'm not asking you to forgive me today but I hope in time you will. I just wanted to say sorry." She stood up to leave. Tarik stood up and met her at the door.

"Simone, what happened? I'm still trying to understand. You and Tricia were so close. What could've possibly happened to break up a sisterhood like you two had?"

Simone looked away. She shook her head side to side. "It's complicated, Tarik. But I hope with time, Tricia and I would be able to get that sisterhood back." She turned the doorknob.

"I'm sure you will in time," he said. "And I want you to know that I don't think you meant for any of this to happen."

Simone smiled, "Thanks Tarik."

"That's all I can offer you right now. Tricia is my wife and I can't say that what happened is ok because I still look into her eyes and try to help her make sense of this. But I do know that you wouldn't hurt anyone."

"Thank you, Tarik. That means a lot to me." She walked out of his office.

"Hey, good luck with everything," he yelled behind her.

* * *

Simone sat at a booth and waited for Shelly. She looked over the menu to kill time. Shelly slid into the booth a few minutes later. "Sorry I'm late. Had to do some last minute reports. So what's up?" she smiled.

"I need to talk to you," Simone said.

"Well, you said that on the phone. What did you wanna talk about?"

"Us," Simone said quickly.

"What about us?" Shelly asked.

Simone took a deep breath and looked Shelly in the eyes. "I've been doing a lot of thinking about this whole situation."

"What kind of thinking?" Shelly inquired.

"Well, I know that when me and you first hooked up, we were both trying to get back at Kareem."

"That's why you got wit me? To get back at your man? Wow, that makes me feel good."

"I didn't mean it like that, Shells. We have fun together. I like you a lot."

"But?" Shelly asked.

"But I love Kareem. We are going through this trial and everything. We are getting to know each other all over again and he really loves me. We are doing so much better than before and I don't think he's cheating on me anymore."

Shelly shook her head at Simone. She realized how she must have sounded when she asked Kareem to leave Simone to be with her. "So you wanna stop seeing me and get back with your man?"

"I really wanna work it out with Kareem. We have too much invested to give up because of a fling."

"A fling, huh? You're still letting him confuse you. You can't even see what's in front of your eyes. He's a dog Simone! He's being a good boy for now because he has to gain your trust again!"

"Look Shelly! I know my man!"

Shelly cut her off. "I know him too! You can go back to him if you want to. You'll deserve everything he throws your way!" Shelly got up and left. She never looked back at Simone.

Simone sat at the table and thought about what Shelly said. It all made sense but she just had this gut feeling that

Kareem was changing for the better. No, she forced herself to believe that he was changing for the better.

Chapter 30

Mrs. Hobbs walked into her house and smiled when she saw Tricia. She went and gave her a hug.

"How you doing, baby?" she asked as she sat next to her.

"I don't know Momma. I haven't slept in months and I'm so worried about Melissa," she sighed.

"I ain't gonna pretend to know what you're going through. I do know that you need to take care of yourself before you try to take care of anyone else."

"I know Momma. I'm doing everything in my power to keep busy. I still have nightmares about my wedding. I just wanna put this behind me and move on."

"I know baby, you hungry?" she asked as she went into the kitchen, "I made spaghetti last night."

"Oohh. I want some," Trish said excitedly as she followed her mother. Mrs. Hobbs looked in the fridge and took out the pot of spaghetti. Tricia handed her two paper plates and she began to fill the plates.

"Momma, how are Kareem and Simone doing?" Mrs. Hobbs smiled on the inside. She wanted to talk about Simone but she didn't want to be the one to bring it up.

"They doing ok. Simone is so stressed about the trial. She so scared she's gonna go to jail." Tricia looked at her mother with saddened eyes. Mrs. Hobbs took advantage of Tricia's weakness. "I think if you talked to Simone, you'll feel a whole lot better."

"I don't have anything to say to her."

"Maybe you just need to hear what she has to say. And then if you wanna say something, you'll have the opportunity." Mrs. Hobbs removed one plate of food from the microwave and put the other inside. Tricia held her head down and grunted.

"I don't know Ma. I've really been giving some thought to what everyone keeps saying. But, it's hard for me to approach Simone. We've been through so much but we've never had a physical fight. I don't even know if I can look at her without wanting to fight again." The telephone rang and Tricia stood up to answer it. Mrs. Hobbs rushed past her and grabbed the phone off the wall. After she recognized the caller, she turned away from Tricia and whispered into the phone. She told the caller she couldn't talk at the moment.

Tricia went to the microwave and removed the food. She sat down to eat as her mother got them something to drink. "Momma, I'm so stressed out. I need a vacation."

"Have you and Tarik thought about going on your honeymoon? You know you all can go anytime you want. Maybe you two should consider getting away for a few days."

"We can't go anywhere right now. Melissa is having complications and even if I wanted to go somewhere, I couldn't drag Tarik away right now."

Mrs. Hobbs finished her food and cleaned the table. "Trish, grab our drinks and come in the room with me." Tricia did as she was told. She sat in the recliner while her mother propped up on the couch. "Trish, Simone wanna talk to you. She doesn't know how to approach you. And since you feel the same way, you really need to talk to her." Tricia tried to say something but her mother cut her off. "Now listen to me. You need to find out if the friendship is worth saving. There is that possibility that Simone will go to jail. How would you feel if that happened?"

"If Simone goes to jail, it's because of what she's done," Tricia said.

"That's not what I mean, what if she goes to jail before you had the chance to clear the air?" Tricia took a sip from her iced-tea and stared into space. She knew she needed to talk to Simone. She knew that was the reason she couldn't put the drama behind her. Simone was too close to her and she needed to confront her.

"I'ma do it," Tricia said as she looked at her mother, "It's time for us to get to the bottom of what happened." Mrs. Hobbs smiled. She waited so long to hear those words.

"I'm glad you decided to do this. You'll feel much better." Tricia went into the kitchen to refill their drinks. When she returned, she and her mother sat on the sofa and talked for another two hours.

Chapter 31

Marvin Woodsby sat in a meeting with Assistant District Attorney, Paula Stykes. Ms. Stykes suggested the meeting to discuss a plea bargain. Kareem and Simone sat next to their lawyer and listened to the A.D.A.

Ms. Stykes offered three to five on attempted murder charges for Simone. When Simone heard the offer, she burst into tears. Mr. Woodsby grabbed her hand and told her not to worry.

"Ms. Stykes, there's not enough evidence to charge my client with attempted murder. So please stop with this little scare tactic," Mr. Woodsby stated.

"Mr. Woodsby, this is the best deal your client is going to get. I suggest you advise her correctly. Does she really want to take her chances at trial?"

"How do you charge someone with attempted murder, when you not even sure if they tried to kill anyone in the first place?" Kareem asked.

"Don't worry, I did not forget about you Mr. Brown. You are being charged as a co-conspirator."

"Ms. Stykes, I don't see how you can prove that Ms. Benson pulled a trigger at anyone. You can't charge my client with attempted murder when you don't have anyone to corroborate that story," Mr. Woodsby smiled.

"Well that's for me to worry about. Isn't it? I can and will produce a witness to say that Ms. Benson indeed caused a scene. My witness will get on the stand and convince a jury to utilize common sense. Ms. Benson was irate and emotional. It doesn't take a genius to see that it was her who took the shot," Ms. Stykes said.

"I think my clients will take their chances in court, Ms. Stykes. You have a nice day." Mr. Woodsby, Kareem and Simone left the room.

Ms. Stykes called after them. "You're sure about that Mr. Woodsby? She smirked, "oh, did I tell you that my witness is Dr. Phil Monroe?"

"I'm positive. But thanks." He closed the door behind him and smiled. Mr. Woodsby invited Simone and Kareem to lunch. He explained his defense and why he didn't cut a deal with the prosecutor.

Chapter 32

It was a cold February 16th. Melissa tossed and turned in the bed. She glanced at the clock and it read nine-eighteen. She felt pressure on her bladder and got up to use the bathroom. She sat on the side of the bed and looked down at her stomach. She was well into her third trimester.

She protected her stomach as she felt a sharp pain in her side. Melissa walked to the bathroom and sat down. At the sight of blood-soaked underwear, she panicked. She jumped up as soon as she finished. She looked into the toilet and saw it was full of blood. Melissa felt another sharp pain and slid to the floor.

She crawled to her bed and reached for the phone. She dialed 911 and spoke to the operator. She was told that someone would be there momentarily. Melissa tried to stand up. She felt so much pain when she stood on her feet that she dropped back to the bed and held onto her stomach. Melissa cried out in pain. She reached for the phone again and called Phil's cell phone. She got the voicemail and hung up.

Melissa could hear the paramedics downstairs banging on the door. She couldn't move. She called 911 again and told them the situation. She heard a window break and hung up the phone. She cried louder so they could find her.

The paramedics burst into her bedroom and examined her. They took her temperature and pulse. They tried to keep her calm. One of the men started an IV in her arm. Melissa calmed down after a few minutes. They called the hospital and informed them of the situation. They placed Melissa on a stretcher and headed to St. Barnabas Hospital.

Dr. Carter stood in the emergency room signing paperwork when the ambulance pulled in. He heard the commotion and went to assist the paramedics. He assisted them with the stretcher and saw Melissa soaked in blood. She still held onto her stomach. Dr. Carter escorted the paramedics to an empty room and took over. He was briefed of her situation by one of the paramedics. He gave Melissa an ultrasound and yelled out instructions to the nursing staff.

Dr. Carter saw that Melissa had lost a lot of blood. He hurried to get her to an operating room. Melissa was still conscious and was in so much pain. Dr. Carter gave her a shot of morphine. He wasn't sure if Melissa was going to have the baby but he was positive that she was in labor. Her water broke about half hour ago and it was a pool of blood. Dr. Michael Carter did everything in his power to save Melissa and her baby.

He knew it was highly dangerous for her to deliver. He also knew that her cervix was weak due to the gunshot wound. He examined her just to make sure Dr. Watters stitched it up to make it strong enough to carry a baby full term. He sighed a sigh of relief when he felt the stitches. Dr. Carter left the room and pulled Melissa's chart. He picked up a phone and called Phil's cell. He left a message to the voicemail. He looked on her emergency contact and found Tarik's name and number. He called Tarik's cell phone and told him the news. Tarik told Dr. Carter that he was on his way.

Tarik arrived at the hospital twenty minutes later. He called Tricia at work to tell her what happened. He went to the desk and asked for Dr. Carter. He took a seat by the double doors. Dr. Carter rushed through the doors and looked around. Tarik rushed towards him with questions. Dr. Carter told Tarik to follow him and they disappeared behind the double doors. He took Tarik to a private room and sat down.

"Tarik, I really need someone to sign some paperwork on Melissa's behalf. I tried to call her husband but he's not answering his phone. Can you make a decision about her care?"

"Yeah man. What's the problem?" Tarik asked.

"Melissa is in labor."

"What? It's too soon!" Tarik stated hysterically.

"Calm down man. Let me finish. Her water broke a while ago but she's not dilating. She's seven months and if she dilates, it's possible that she can have a healthy baby. I've seen cases where babies were born and survived long before seven months."

"What do you need from me?" Tarik asked.

"I would like to give her an IV to stop her contractions. I don't want her to have this baby right now. There's a chance that the IV won't help stop the contractions but I'd like to try."

"I don't get it. You just said that she could have the baby and it would be fine. Why would you wanna stop her from having the baby?"

"I said that it's a possibility that the baby would be fine. The baby is not fully developed. Since Melissa was such a high risk, I'm not sure if it's a good idea to let her deliver right now. I need you to sign for me to do this."

Tarik thought about what Dr. Carter said. He stared at him with watery eyes. He knew how much this baby meant to Melissa. He didn't want to give permission and something went wrong. "Dr. Carter would this hurt the baby?"

"The baby won't be affected one way or the other."

"What about Melissa?" Tarik asked.

"Melissa would have the same risks if she gave birth right now. I need an answer Tarik. We don't have much time. The only thing that's in our advantage is the fact that she's not dilating. I need to inject her with this IV before that starts.

Tarik looked at Dr. Carter. "Well you're her friend and I don't think you'll do anything to put her in harms way. Where's the paper? I'll sign," Tarik said solemnly. Dr. Carter reached into Melissa's file and handed Tarik a copy of the paperwork. Tarik quickly read it over and signed the bottom line. Dr. Carter thanked him and asked him to sit out in the waiting room while he attends to Melissa. Tarik shook his hand. "Take care of my sister, man."

"I'll do my best," Dr. Carter replied.

Chapter 33

Tricia and Mrs. Hobbs ran into the emergency room and spotted Tarik.

"Tarik, how is she? What happened?" Tricia asked.

"Her water broke and she went into labor. Dr. Carter is in there with her now," he stated with tears in his eyes.

"It's ok Tarik, women have children all the time. Melissa will be fine," Mrs. Hobbs said as she rubbed his back.

"It's not that, Moms. There was a situation."

"What kind of situation?" Tricia asked. Tarik pulled both women outside of the emergency room and told them what Dr. Carter suggested. He looked on to Mrs. Hobbs for assurance that he made the right decision.

"Well Mike is her friend. If he thought that was best, I would have done the same thing. I'm sure everything will be ok," Tricia said as she hugged her husband.

"Has Dr. Carter come out to tell you if it worked?" Mrs. Hobbs asked.

"No Moms. He said it was gonna take some time. So all we can do now is wait. I know one thing. If Phil did anything to her to make her go into labor, I'ma kill his ass!" Tarik said and went back inside the emergency room. Tricia and Mrs. Hobbs followed closely. Tricia walked over to where Tarik stood. She hugged him from behind and pulled him off to the side. "Baby calm down. Don't jump to conclusions just yet. Hell, he already thinks she cheated on him so I'm not surprised he's not here"

"Whatchu mean he thinks she cheated on him?" Tarik asked.

"She didn't tell you? Remember when she was about three months and they had that argument? He told her that he was positive she cheated on him," Trish said.

"Still, why the fuck he ain't here? We all tried to call him and we keep getting the voicemail. Why he ain't here with his wife!? This is happening too many times. This better not be his fault!" Tarik warned.

"When is the last time you called him?" she asked.

"About an hour ago," he said.

"Give me the number. I'll try." Tarik handed her his cell phone and told her to look up Phil's cell number. Tricia walked over to her mother and asked her if she was hungry. She told her that she was staying until she knew Melissa would be ok. She told her mother that she could take her car and leave if she wanted. Mrs. Hobbs declined and went to use her cell phone. She called Marvin and told him that she wouldn't make it to his house tonight. She told him about the emergency and then she called Simone to let her know about Melissa.

Tarik sat in the chair and thought about his night with Melissa. He counted back in his head and thought about the night they were together. *Oh shit, this can't be right,* he thought.

Tricia called Phil's cell and got his voicemail. She left a message and then placed a call to information. She got the number to his clinic and tried to call him there. Phil's assistant, Alicia answered and told her that Dr. Monroe was with a patient. Tricia expressed the urgency of the call and was put through to Phil. Phil told her he was on his way and hung up the phone.

Tricia went back inside and sat next to Tarik and her mother. "Phil is on his way. Dr. Carter come out to let us know anything?" she asked. Tarik shook his head and looked towards the double doors. Dr. Carter came through the doors and they met him by the information desk.

"Guys, it looks like it worked. She is still bleeding but not as bad as she was. Hopefully, it'll stop once the medication starts to work."

"How is the baby?" Tricia asked.

"The baby seems to be fine." Dr. Carter smiled.

"Can we go in and see her?" Tricia asked.

"She's a little out of it right now. But I'll let you go back there for a few minutes. Follow me." Everyone went behind the double doors.

Simone and Kareem walked up to the desk and asked about Melissa. They were told that Mrs. Monroe was in stable condition. Mrs. Hobbs walked out just as Simone was about to speak.

"Simone? Over here." Mrs. Hobbs waved.

"How is she? Is the baby ok?" Simone asked.

"It was scary at first but she's ok. The baby is fine too." Mrs. Hobbs proceeded to tell them the situation.

Phil walked in and spotted Mrs. Hobbs.

"Where is she?" he asked.

"She's back here. Come on, I'll take you." The nurse buzzed the door and let them back.

Phil walked into Melissa's room and went by her side. "Baby, I'm here," he said as he held her hand.

"Where the fuck was you?" Tarik yelled. Tricia pulled his arm and asked him to be quiet.

"Whatchu do to her? Let me find out that this is all because of you!" he shouted as Tricia pulled him by the arm. She and Mrs. Hobbs pushed Tarik back to the waiting area. Tarik snatched away from them and headed outside to cool off. Tricia walked to the seats and saw Simone and Kareem sitting there. Simone walked over to her and reluctantly hugged her. Surprisingly Tricia hugged her back. Mrs. Hobbs smiled and took a seat next to Kareem.

"Tricia, how is Melissa?" Simone asked.

"She'll be ok. The baby is fine and she's resting now."

"Would you take a walk with me to the cafeteria?" Simone asked.

Yeah, it's time we talked," Tricia said.

Chapter 34

Tricia and Simone sat in a booth as they sipped on hot chocolate. Tricia kept her eyes in her cup and played with the stirrer. Simone was the first to speak up.

"Trish, there is so much that I need to say to you. I don't even know where to begin." She cleared her throat when Tricia didn't respond and continued talking. "I'd just like to start off by saying I'm sorry about your wedding. I know how much your wedding day meant to you." Simone then apologized for what happened to Melissa and her baby. "The thought of us not being friends anymore is really fuckin' me up. I know you must hate me but I have to get this off of my chest. I never planned to have sex with you, it just happened."

"What the fuck did you just say?" Tarik asked as he walked up on their conversation. Tricia jumped up and stood in front of him.

"Baby, it's not what you think. Don't take this the wrong way," she pleaded.

"She just said that y'all had sex. How many ways can I take that shit? You gay?" he asked with a face of disgust. Tricia reached out for his hand but he pulled it away. "Don't put yo fuckin' hands on me!"

"Tarik, calm down please," Tricia begged.

Simone stood in shock. Tricia grabbed the back of Tarik's jacket as he almost knocked her down to get away from her. Tricia stood in the middle of the café and cried like a baby. She attempted to go after him but a security guard walked up on her and asked if she were ok.

"We're fine," Simone said. She grabbed Tricia by the arm and pulled her to the elevator. "I'm so sorry Trish. I had no idea he was standing behind us." Tricia was in a trance. Simone had to literally drag her back to the emergency room waiting area.

"What happened? Tarik just flew out of here like he was on fire." Mrs. Hobbs asked, "did y'all hear some news about Melissa?"

"No Moms, that's not it," Simone said as she assisted Tricia to the chair.

"Well what then?" Mrs. Hobbs asked.

"I think Tricia needs to tell you about that." Mrs. Hobbs went to her daughter's side and hugged her. She gathered their things as a security officer told them they were keeping too much noise. Kareem grabbed Simone by the arm and pulled her to the side.

"What did you do?" he asked.

"I didn't do anything. Well not on purpose anyway." He grabbed her hand and told Moms they were leaving. They headed out the door.

Mrs. Hobbs continued to hold Tricia and ask her if she was ok. Tricia didn't respond to her mother. She just kept rocking back and forth in tears. Mrs. Hobbs told her that she was going to take her home.

Tricia shook her head no. She held on tighter to the chair. Mrs. Hobbs tried to pry her hands off the chair. Tricia looked at her mother and shook her head. "I'm staying here, Mommy. I can't leave Melissa right now. I don't know where Tarik is but I know he'll come back here. I'm gonna be right here so we can talk this thing out!"

Mrs. Hobbs' eyes became watery. She couldn't stand to see her daughter in this condition. "Trish, just come outside with me for a minute. Let's talk out there."

Tricia looked at her mother and put on her coat.

Mrs. Hobbs pulled Tricia to the side of the building. Tricia constantly wiped her eyes. She tried to keep her face dry as the wind blew.

"Baby, what's the matter? Why did Tarik run outta here like that?" Tricia looked at her mother and burst into tears again. Her mother held her and tried to comfort her.

"Momma, I...I...well he overheard me and Simone talking...and he..." Tricia tried to keep her composure but lost the battle. Mrs. Hobbs walked her to the parking lot. She put Tricia in on the passenger's side and jumped in on the driver's side. She didn't know what Tarik and Tricia were going through but she knew Tricia needed to get some rest. The only way that was going to happen would be if she slept in her old bedroom.

Chapter 35

Shelly opened the door and let Kareem inside. She was more than happy to see him. She had been out of town all week and needed to unwind. Kareem went straight to the bedroom and undressed.

"Well damn! Not wasting any time today, are we?" Shelly asked.

"It's cold as hell outside! I'm just trying to warm up. I ain't no good to you if I'm freezing. You know that," he said as he slid under the comforter. Shelly walked to the thermostat and turned the heat up to 80 degrees.

She sat on the bed next to him and slid her hand under the blankets. "Damn baby. I see you missed me as much as I missed you," she smiled.

"You know I did. You see how fast I got here, right? Now whatchu gonna do to show me how much you missed me?" he asked.

Shelly walked over to her dresser and turned on the radio. She put on a CD and did a strip tease. She removed each piece of clothing with her mouth. Kareem was so excited to see her sit on the floor and remove her panties. Shelly bent down and grabbed them with her teeth and ripped them off. She was wearing a thong so it didn't take much effort to tear them off. She got on the bed and continued to dance in Kareem's face.

Kareem caressed her nice sized yellow ass. She danced until he pulled her to his face. Kareem positioned Shelly to stand right in his face so he can lick her insides. She grooved to the rhythm and pumped his face. She moaned as he took her to ecstasy. Shelly dropped down to her knees while Kareem grabbed a handful of her hair. She devoured his entire dick in her mouth. She took her time and sucked him off. Kareem's eyes rolled to the back of his head. Shelly looked up at him and smiled as she saw the look of satisfaction on his face. He pent her down on her back and jumped on top of her. Shelly wrapped her legs around his neck and fucked him. Kareem couldn't control himself. He shook and jerked until his cream had exploded. He stayed inside of her for ten minutes.

Shelly wasn't finished. She hopped on top of Kareem and gyrated her hips until his soldier stood at attention again. She bounced up and down in a slow motion. Kareem closed his eyes and held onto her waist. Shelly began to feel her heartbeat fasten. She moved faster and faster until she exploded. She slowed her pace and kissed him on the neck. She reached inside her nightstand and grabbed her pink emotion lotion. She hopped off of Kareem and began to rub the lotion on his very erect soldier. The vigorous rubbing sent sensual heat throughout his body. Shelly got on her knees and rubbed a little lotion on her asshole. She looked at Kareem with raised eyes and tooted her ass up in the air.

"Word? It's like that?" Kareem asked.

"You don't want it?" she asked.

"Oh hell yeah! Been wanting it for a while," he said as he eased inside of her. Shelly arched up and took it like a trooper. Once Kareem was inside of her, she was able to move to his rhythm. He rode her ass for almost twenty minutes. He kept stopping to savor the moment. Finally, when he couldn't take it anymore, he shot semen all over her ass. Shelly moaned in pleasure and Kareem dozed off on top of her.

An hour later, Kareem got up to take a shower. He got dressed then reached inside his pocket and called Simone. He asked her if she needed him to bring anything home. He closed his phone and went into Shelly's bedroom after his conversation. He shook her gently. She turned on her side and faced him.

"I'm leaving baby," Kareem said.

"Ok, can you let yourself out? I'm too tired to get up. Call me," she said.

"Ok, later," he said as he kissed her on the forehead.

* * *

Kareem walked inside the dark apartment. He called out for Simone and put the ice cream in the freezer.

"I'm in the bedroom, baby," she called out. Kareem walked into the bedroom and saw the candles all around the room. Simone had a red light bulb in the lamp and she was wearing a black sheer teddy. She sat in the middle of the bed with a red rose in her hand.

He hesitated when Simone motioned for him to come to her. She got up and kissed him full on the lips. She was seductive and horny. She felt him up and moved him to the bed. Kareem tried to push away but Simone kept a grip on him. He returned her kisses as they rolled over the bed. Simone began caressing him to get him hard. Kareem's body did not respond. Simone thought she had to take the foreplay to the next level. She got up and went into the kitchen and came back with the ice cream. She removed Kareem's clothes and threw a white blanket over the bed. Kareem tried to get up but Simone wasn't taking no for an answer. She sat the bowl of ice cream next to him and got on her knees. She put a scoop in her mouth and sucked him off. She seduced him with the ice cream for about half an hour before she realized he wasn't responding.

"What's wrong?" she asked as she sat on the bed next to him.

"Nothing, I'm tired," he said.

"You're too tired for me? That's a first. You may say you're tired but I always manage to get you in the mood. What's up?" she asked.

"I don't know. It's cold as hell outside maybe I'm not warmed up yet."

Simone looked at him with disappointment. She accepted defeat and cleaned up the room.

Kareem went to take a shower to wash off the ice cream. He let the hot water sooth him. He stepped out of the bathroom in pajamas. He walked into the bedroom and found Simone on the bed with her dildo satisfying herself. He grunted and shook his head. It looked like Simone didn't care that he wasn't able to perform. He gathered a pillow and went to sleep on the sofa.

Chapter 36

Tarik drove around the city with no destination. His mind was cluttered with personal issues. He was worried about Melissa. He knew Phil was at the hospital and he knew it would not be a good encounter if he went back.

He looked down at his cell phone and saw Tricia's number. He sent the call to voicemail and kept driving. He drove by his apartment to see if Tricia was there. He didn't see her car outside and there were no lights on in the apartment. Tarik went inside the apartment to grab some clothes. He got a suitcase from the closet and grabbed some of his belongings. The telephone rang as he was leaving. He glanced at the caller ID and saw Mrs. Hobbs' number. He assumed that's where Tricia was. He turned out the lights and left the apartment.

Tarik rode around for another hour. He finally checked into a Marriott hotel. He sat on the bed and held his head. He couldn't believe what he overheard Tricia and Simone talking about. He grabbed his keys and left the hotel.

Tarik pulled in front of Mrs. Hobbs' house and looked at his watch. He got out of the car and slammed the door. He walked up the steps and Tricia swung open the door.

"Tarik, we need to talk. Baby, you didn't even give me a chance to explain," she cried.

Mrs. Hobbs came down the stairs to see what the commotion was about. She asked Tarik to come inside to talk but he declined.

"I'm not coming inside, Moms. I just want to talk to Tricia." He looked at Tricia. "Lets go Trish, come outside and talk to me," he yelled. Tricia's hair was matted down to her face. She had changed into a pair of sweats. Her face was swollen and red from crying. She went to Tarik and grabbed his arm. He snatched his arm away hard enough to make Tricia fall to the ground.

"Tarik, you need to calm down!" Mrs. Hobbs screamed. She went to Trish and helped her off the ground.

"I'm ok Mommy. Just leave us alone cause we have to talk," she pleaded.

"I'm not leaving you out here with Tarik and he's acting a fool."

"Mommy please? He's my husband. Let us work this out. I'm ok. I promise."

"Moms, we aiight. We just gonna talk. Trica, come on home with me," he stated, "Moms, we're ok. You don't have to worry," Tarik said.

"I don't like to see the two of you this upset. Please just stay here to talk?" Moms insisted. Tricia sniffed and looked at Tarik. She was shaking uncontrollably. Tarik hugged her then pushed her away.

"AAAAHHHH!!" he yelled as he stepped away from her. He sat on the bottom step and put his head in his hands. "DAMN IT! I can't believe this shit!!" he cried. Tricia hated to see her husband so upset, especially since she was the cause. She motioned for her mother to go inside. Mrs. Hobbs gave her an *'are you sure'* look and Tricia nodded her head. Mrs. Hobbs closed the door and sat on the sofa.

"Baby, come on. Lets go home and talk. Please?" Tricia begged.

"How could you, Trish? How could you do this to me? he yelled, "so that's the secret you and Simone have been hiding!"

"Baby, lets go home and talk about this. I really don't want my mother to hear this. Please?" Tarik looked up at her and blinked away the tears. He stood and went to the car. Tricia went inside the house and told her mother she was leaving. She told her she'd call her later.

Tricia jumped behind the wheel and drove off. They made it home in twenty minutes. Tarik slammed the door as he got out of the car. Tricia followed close behind him. Tarik broke the silence as soon as they walked into the apartment.

"What the fuck are you doing fuckin' Simone?" How long has it been going on? Are you two lovers?" He asked the questions before she had a chance to answer.

"Tarik let me explain baby. It's not like that...we just...it was an accident."

"Come on man, how the fuck do you accidentally fuck another woman?" He stared in her eyes as he spat the words.

"Tarik, listen to me. I'm telling you the truth. Calm down and give me a chance to explain."

"Tell me what happened!" he demanded.

Tricia sat at the kitchen table and held her head down. She hesitated and pulled on her hair.

"Tell me, Tricia! Don't sit here and act like you don't know where to begin. Tell me what the fuck happened!"

Tricia jumped as he slammed his fist on the table. She knew she had to say something. Through the crying and sniffing, she explained the incident to Tarik. She told him everything that happened with Simone. She even told him how Simone reacted when she called her Tarik.

Tarik listened to Tricia and shook his head. "It takes two people to have sex! Stop acting like this is all Simone's fault," he yelled. Tricia tried to cut him off and make him see it her way, but he over talked her. "If this was so fuckin' innocent, then why not tell me before we got married. How could you keep something like this from me? You know you can tell me anything."

"Tarik please, it wasn't like that. I didn't know how to tell you. I was embarrassed!"

"I gave you every opportunity to tell me what happened. I asked you over and over again about that fight. You kept blowing me off telling me that you didn't want to talk about it!"

"Baby, I just..."

"No! If I wouldn't have overheard you and Simone, I still wouldn't know! It just seems to me like you had something to hide by not telling me!" He pounded his fists to the table. Tricia cried harder. She pleaded with him to believe her story. She did all she could to convince him. Tarik didn't want to hear anything she had to say.

"I can't even look at you right now! You betrayed me Trish! I love you but I don't like you right now!" He grabbed his car keys and walked out the door. Tricia went behind him and called his name. He never looked back as he sped away.

Chapter 37

Melissa had been in the hospital for almost two weeks. Dr. Watters informed her that she was on complete bed rest. She told her that she was not going to be released until after the baby was born.

Phil sat on the edge of the bed next to Melissa. He looked into her eyes and smiled. He and Melissa had been discussing their situation for the past week. Melissa insisted that she never cheated on him. She continued to ask Phil to get a second opinion.

"Melissa, I think maybe I should go and prepare for the baby. I need to get the room together and everything. I can bring you some magazines and you can tell me what you like. How does that sound?" He intended to raise the child as his own. He gave up on trying to get Melissa to confess. She would not even suggest that there could have been someone else.

"That sounds good. I guess we should start preparing for our baby. It could be any day now. You see the doctors are surprised I didn't deliver yet," she smiled.

"Ok. I'll stop by a few baby stores and pick up some things. I'll see you a little later, ok?"

"Ok sweetie, I'll be right here," she smiled. He kissed her on the lips then walked out of the room.

Tarik walked into the hospital room as Phil walked out. Phil mumbled hello but Tarik ignored him. Phil looked back at Melissa and shook his head. He told Melissa he'd be back and left.

"Damn, it seems like every time I come here, he's not here or he's just leaving. When does he spend time with you?" Tarik asked.

"Don't start, Tarik. Where have you been? I've been calling you all week. Why haven't you returned my calls? I wasn't able to reach Tricia either," Melissa said.

"Tricia and I are going through something right now. I haven't been staying at the apartment."

"What happened?" Melissa asked as she sat up.

"Whoa, calm down! You don't need to be getting upset. Anyway, we have bigger fish to fry!" he spoke.

"What does that mean?

""Why didn't you tell me that Phil thinks you cheated on him?" Melissa was shocked and speechless. She didn't know how to respond.

"Tarik, he was just drunk and talking mess. He didn't mean that," she stuttered.

Tarik sat down next to her. "Look Melissa, I blocked it out of my mind too. But if Phil knows something then we need to consider the possibility that you are carrying my baby."

"I'm not carrying your baby, Tarik! My husband and I are getting ready to have a baby!" she yelled.

"Well if that's true, why are you so hostile?" he asked.

"Because I've already dealt with Phil about this whole thing and I don't need to hear the same drama from you! You are supposed to be my friend, there's no reason you shouldn't trust what I say!" she cried.

"Don't get all excited with me! I just asked you a question. I don't know what's going on but I do intend to find out!" he yelled.

"Just because you and Tricia are going through something, don't come in here trying to cause problems in my marriage!" Melissa said.

"You definitely don't need my help in wrecking your marriage. Hell it was wrecked from day one!"

"Get the hell outta here, Tarik! I don't need this from you!" She pointed towards the door.

"I'm not going nowhere! You better come clean and tell me if there's a chance that I'm the father of that baby! Because one way or the other, I will find out. And if by some chance I am the father, your husband will never get the chance to play daddy to my child!" Melissa was pissed and it showed all over her face. She frowned her face in pain as she cried.

Tarik stood by the door and stared at her. He looked harder and noticed she was really in pain. She grabbed her stomach and screamed out. Tarik went to her bedside and pulled on the call bell. A nurse came into the room within seconds. She went to Melissa and read the monitor. It showed that Melissa was having contractions. The nurse ran out to get a doctor.

Tarik squeezed Melissa's hand and apologized for getting her upset. She squeezed back and begged for help. Tarik stroked her arm and stomach but Melissa continued to cry.

Dr. Watters entered the room and pushed Tarik aside. She raised Melissa's head and examined her. She looked at Tarik and said, "It's time. She's eight centimeters. She's going to deliver any minute." The nurse pulled Tarik out of the room and took him to get cleaned up. She gave him scrubs and helped him wash his hands.

Dr. Watters had a team of orderlies push Melissa to the Labor & Delivery section of the hospital. When Tarik came into her room, she was calmer.

"What happened to her?" he asked.

"I gave her morphine so she could relax a little. She was too excited to deliver and we don't need extra complications."

"Can she hear us?" he asked.

"She's awake. The medication makes her relax between contractions. She's fine. She's doing well. I'm going to check on another patient, I'll be right back." She exited the room.

Tarik grabbed Melissa's hand and rubbed it. He talked to her and told her that everything was going to be ok. She looked at him with sweat and tears all over her face. Her IV had come out of her arm and the contractions started to come more frequent. Tarik ran out the door and called for help. Dr. Watters ran into the room and looked under the sheets. "The baby's coming." She sat at the foot of the bed and assisted Melissa in giving birth. Tarik coached as best as he could.

"You're doing great Melissa. I need you to give me another big push," Dr. Watters said as Melissa screamed in pain.

"Uuuggghhh…uuuggghhh…uuuggghhh…Aahhhh!" Melissa screamed at the same time as her baby.

"It's a boy! I need to get him to the ICU right away. Nurse Gordon, see if there's another Dr. nearby," Dr. Watters demanded as she proceeded with the afterbirth.

Within minutes Dr. Carter walked into the room in scrubs and a mask. Nurse Gordon helped him with the gloves and he went to Dr. Watters. "What do you need doctor?" he asked.

"Would you please take over? I need to tend to the baby," She said as she left the room.

Dr. Carter did what was asked of him. Tarik stood next to Melissa and held her hand the entire time. He was amazed at seeing childbirth. He comforted Melissa while Dr. Carter did his job.

Dr. Carter looked up and told them he was done. He asked Melissa how she was feeling. Melissa asked about the baby. Dr. Carter told her he'd go check and walked out of the room.

"Tarik, call Phil?" Melissa asked. She was sleepy and groggy.

Without thinking about it, Tarik called her husband. Phil answered on the first ring.

"Yeah?"

"Phil, it's Tarik. Melissa just had the baby. She's asking for you, man."

"I'm on my way!"

Chapter 38

Dr. Carter and Dr. Watters walked into Melissa's hospital room. Dr. Carter went to Melissa and touched her hand. "How are you?"

"I'm better than yesterday. How is the baby? Can we see him now?" she asked.

"That's why we're here, Melissa," Dr. Watters said, "There are some complications with the baby."

"What happened?" Phil and Tarik asked in unison.

"Well the baby lost a lot of blood when your water broke. We ran some tests and it looks like your little guy is anemic," Dr. Watters said.

"What does that mean?" Melissa asked. Phil grabbed her hand tighter and stroked her back.

"When your placenta ruptured, the baby lost a lot of red blood cells. He's going to need a blood transfusion."

"Oh no," Melissa cried.

"Baby, this is normal in premature babies. You can give him some of your blood and he'll be fine," Phil said.

"Well, not exactly. Melissa can't donate blood right away," Dr. Carter responded.

"But what about the blood you took from her a couple of days ago?" Phil asked.

"Your guy should be better in no time," Dr. Carter said for reassurance.

"Good. Is there anything else wrong with him?" Phil asked."

"Well, his lungs are a little underdeveloped but we'll continue with the iron shots and they should develop normally."

"Are you sure doctor? Is there a chance that he won't be normal?" Melissa asked.

"Mrs. Monroe, he's just small. It's going to take him a little more time to reach the status of full-term babies but I don't see anything major," Dr. Watters reassured them.

"So when is he going to have the blood transfusion?" Tarik asked.

"Well, he needs to have it right away. Melissa's blood has already been screened so it can be done right away. I'll prep him for surgery and perform the procedure immediately," Dr. Carter said.

"Don't worry, he'll be fine," Dr. Watters said as she and Dr. Carter exited the room.

"I'll be back baby; I'm going to see if I can watch the surgery." Phil kissed his wife on the forehead then left.

Tarik moved closer to the bed. He took Melissa's hand and caressed it. "I'm sorry, Lissa. I didn't mean to get you all upset."

"It's not your fault, Tarik. Dr. Watters told me that my son was ready to enter this world. She said once the IV came out, it was just a matter of time before I delivered."

"But still…I shouldn't have gone off like that."

"Can we just put this behind us? Would you stop all this nonsense now?" Melissa asked.

"Melissa, I still wanna know if that's my son in there," Tarik said as he pointed towards the door. "Maybe we can ask your friend to do a paternity test while the baby's still here?"

"Tarik, I'm not going to ask Mike to do a paternity test! Are you crazy? This is me and Phil's son, accept it and move on!"

"Move on? What's that supposed to mean?"

"Tarik, are you trying to hold on to that night? We both agreed that it meant nothing! Now you come around talking about fathering my child? What's that all about?"

"Like I told you before Melissa, there were no feelings involved. Hell, I put that night out of my mind until Tricia told me that your husband accused you of cheating on him." Tarik froze for a moment, "And why didn't you tell me that Phil suspected you had an affair? I was just with you. You told me everything but that. Is it because deep inside you know there's a possibility?" Tarik asked.

"Even as Phil accused me of an affair, you never crossed my mind until you brought it up! So let's not go there! And I'm getting a headache."

Tarik backed off and felt Melissa's forehead. It was a little hot. "You want me to get a nurse?" he asked.

"No, I'll be fine."

Tarik went to the bathroom and wet a washcloth and placed it on her head.

"Have you told Trish about the baby?"

"Nah, I haven't spoken to her," Tarik mumbled.

"And by the way, what's going on with you two? Why are y'all not speaking?" Melissa asked.

Tarik walked to the window. He opened the blinds and peeked out.

"Tarik?"

He shook his head before he spoke, "I finally found out why she and Simone had the fight," he faced her.

"What was it about?"

"I don't want to talk about it!"

"Well at least do me a favor and think about how Tricia would feel if you find out this is your baby."

Tarik held his head down and cursed.

"Please call Mrs. Hobbs at least, and let them know I've had the baby."

"Yeah aiight. I'll be back later," he said and walked out of the room.

Chapter 39

Mrs. Hobbs pulled up in front of Tricia's apartment complex. She called Tricia from the car. When she didn't get an answer, she went up to the apartment. She didn't hear any movement so she banged on the door.

"Tricia, it's me, open this door!" Still no answer. She banged some more. "Trish? You better open this damn door!" Mrs. Hobbs yelled as continued to bang on the door.

Tricia walked to the door and snatched it open. "Mommy, do you have to be so loud?"

Mrs. Hobbs looked at her and shook her head.

"I know you are feeling bad right now, but you gotta pull yourself together. Tarik called me and told me that Melissa had the baby."

"What?" Tricia jumped up. "When? Oh my goodness!" She sat back down on the sofa as she quickly lost the enthusiasm.

"Uh uh, go get yourself together. You're going to the hospital. You will not spend another minute in here soaking in yo own misery! Go take a shower and get ready!" Mrs. Hobbs ordered.

Tricia wiped the tears from the corners of her eyes and did what her mother told her to do. Mrs. Hobbs looked around the apartment in disgust, *"This don't make no sense. She sittin' 'round here all depressed. I know we raised her better than that!"* She opened the windows to get some fresh air circulating then started cleaning the place until Tricia announced that she was ready.

They got into Mrs. Hobbs' minivan and she sped off. She turned to Tricia and asked her if she wanted to talk about what was going on. Tricia declined and changed the subject.

"Momma, did Tarik say how Melissa was doing?"

"All he said was that Melissa asked him to call us and that the baby had to have surgery."

"Surgery for what!?" Tricia looked alarmed.

"He didn't say."

"Well, is Tarik still at the hospital?" Tricia asked.

"I'm not sure. But, you are not going to the hospital to see him. I know y'all have unresolved issues but you need to concentrate on Melissa right now. Her baby is having surgery and she could use a friend!"

Tricia shook her head up and down and looked out the window. They parked the car and went to the desk and found out where Melissa was.

Tricia tapped on the door and walked inside with her mother close behind. "Hey sweetie." She went to give Melissa a hug. "How are you? How's the baby?"

Melissa smiled at the sight of her friend, "Quit fussing over me. It's my son who's just had surgery."

"What happened, baby?" Mrs. Hobbs asked.

Melissa sat up and explained the situation to them. She told them that her son had just had a successful blood transfusion.

"You had a boy, huh?"

Melissa smiled and shook her head, "he lost a lot of blood when my water broke and Dr. Watters said that he didn't have enough red blood cells. I was able to give him a pint of blood since we're the same type. She said that his being anemic will most likely wear off as he gets older."

"That's great honey! I'm so proud of you." Tricia leaned over and hugged Melissa. She stepped back and looked around the room. "Um…er…have you seen? Um…is Tarik around?" she stuttered.

"He left a little while ago. He said he'll be back later though," Melissa said through sad eyes.

Mrs. Hobbs looked at Tricia with an icy glare. "Melissa, I'm glad that you and the baby are going to be ok. I gotta go now so take care of yourself and that baby." She bent down and kissed Melissa on the forehead, "and congratulations!" She turned towards Trish. "Do you need me to drop you off at home or are you coming with me?"

"Momma, I'm going to stay here and keep Melissa company. If that's alright with you Melissa?" She asked as she faced her.

"That's fine. I need to talk to you about something anyway."

"No problem. Moms I'm staying," Tricia smiled.

Mrs. Hobbs knew Tricia was physically there with Melissa but she also knew that her heart and mind was racing trying to figure out a way to bump into Tarik before she left the hospital. "Ok. Call me on my cell if you need a ride, bye." She said as she walked out of the door.

"Tricia, this is so scary. My son is two months early and he had to have a blood transfusion right after birth. What else could go wrong?"

"It's not as bad as it seems. You and the baby made it through the delivery. That's enough to be thankful about. Dr. Watters said that this was normal for premature babies, right?" Tricia asked. Melissa shook her head yes.

"Then it's going to be fine! Have you seen him yet?"

"No. Phil says that he has to stay in the ICU until he's recovered. He said I could probably go around to see him tomorrow. I think he's seen him already. He went to watch the surgery so maybe he got a good look at him," she smiled.

Phil walked into the room and smiled, "he is adorable baby. I was able to see him as they took him back to the ICU. I couldn't see his face during the surgery but he's beautiful just like you." He kissed his wife passionately.

"Baby, you're just in time. I was getting ready to ask Trish right now," Melissa laughed.

"Ask her what?" Phil inquired.

Tricia looked at them with a puzzled expression. "Tricia, I want you and Tarik to be the Godparents."

Tricia froze at the mentioning of Tarik. Melissa turned to Phil and smiled, "Right sweetie?"

Phil was put on the spot. He kept his composure and put on a fake smile, "Of course, who else would we ask?" He continued to smile.

"I'm sure I can speak for Tarik and say we'd love to be the Godparents. Thank you." She hugged Melissa.

"No, thank you," Melissa said.

"What did you name him?" Tricia asked.

Phil and Melissa looked at each other. "We haven't thought about a name yet. We were so concerned with his health. I guess we'll let you know tomorrow?" She looked at Phil.

"Sure. We should come up with something by then. Baby, I'm going to go home and change. I need to get some things in order at the clinic, and then I'll be back." He kissed her on the cheek.

"Ok sweetie hurry back."

"Dr Watters will be in to speak with you shortly. Oh, make sure you look over the books I left on the nightstand about the baby's room." Phil said goodbye to Tricia then left the room. He stood on the other side of the door and exhaled. He felt overwhelmed. He tried his best to get excited about the baby. He had a hard time pretending it didn't matter about the baby's father. He walked to the elevator with his head hung low.

Chapter 40

Mrs. Hobbs used her key to open the door to Marvin's house. She placed the grocery bags on the floor by the door and went to the car to get her overnight bag.

Marvin met her at the door as she was walking back inside. "Hi Marv, I didn't know you were going to be here. I was going to surprise you with dinner," she said.

"It's good to see you," he kissed her on the lips, "I was just on my way out so you can still surprise me," he smiled.

"Oh, ok. What time are you coming back?" she asked.

"I'm going to meet a colleague to discuss a little business. I shouldn't be long at all. Maybe two hours at most." He grabbed his briefcase and walked towards the door. He stopped in front of Maryanne and kissed her on the lips. She returned his passion and rubbed his back. Marvin broke loose and smiled, "Ok now, lets not start something we can't finish." He kissed her forehead and walked to the door.

"Well, we already started it so we may as well finish it as soon as you get back," she blushed. Marvin glanced back at her and smiled.

Marvin pulled up in front of the restaurant and the valet parked his car. He walked inside and spotted Brian and a very attractive woman waiting to be seated. He walked up and shook Brian's hand. The waitress told them their table was ready. They followed her to the table.

"Marvin Woodsby, I would like you to meet Ms. Belinda Chaste."

Marvin shook her hand. He couldn't help but notice her hazel-brown eyes. Her hair hung down to the middle of her back. She was about 5'7" with a muscular physic.

140

"Ms. Chaste, it's good to meet you. Thank you for meeting with us on such short notice. I really appreciate your help."

"The pleasure is all mines. Anything I could do to help," she said as she removed her coat. She revealed a black tight turtleneck sweater. Both men turned away as they caught themselves gawking at her breasts.

They ordered cocktails while Marvin explained exactly what he needed from Belinda. He told her all the information that concerned her.

"Mr. Woodsby, I'm going..."

"Please, call me Marvin."

"Ok, Marvin. I'm going to be staying at a hotel for the next month or so. Do you think you'll be able to wrap up this business by then?"

"I'm sure we'll have everything taken care of by then. I have a dinner appointment so I have to leave."

Belinda stood and reached for her coat. "Well thanks for everything."

"Oh, I insist that you and Brian have dinner. It's on me. I'll be in touch Ms. Chaste." Marvin walked over to Brian and shook his hand. Marvin excused himself and walked out the door. Once he sat in the car, he placed a call to his house.

"Hi sweetie, I'm on my way. Do you need me to bring anything? Just the wine? Ok, I'll see you in a bit," he said.

Marvin walked into his house and the lights were dimmed low. He hung his coat in the closet and followed the scent of food. He stepped into the kitchen to a candlelit dinner. Maryanne stood to greet him at the entrance. She was wearing a black sheer robe. She tightened the belt and kissed Marvin on the lips. She pulled him to a chair and fixed their plates. She and Marvin enjoyed the steak and potatoes.

"Maryanne, dinner was wonderful."

"Thank you. But you haven't had wonderful yet, follow me." She walked upstairs to the bathroom. She and Marvin took a shower together and washed each other down. They held hands and walked inside of the bedroom. Marvin removed Maryanne's towel and laid her on the bed. She smiled and rolled onto her side as he let his own towel drop to the floor.

"Maryanne, you are like a dream come true. I've waited so long for you to come into my life, I love you." He kissed her on the cheek. Maryanne smiled. She rolled on top of him and seduced him. She played with the few hairs on his chest and nibbled in his ear. He rubbed her breasts and ran his fingers through her hair. Maryanne lifted up and slid on top of him. She rocked back and forth in slow motion until she exploded on top of him. Marvin flipped her on her back and placed her left leg on his neck. He pumped in and out for several minutes. Just as he felt Maryanne getting ready to explode again, he put her other leg on his neck and cupped her ass with his hands. She softly called his name.

Marvin was so aroused by hearing his name that he moved faster and released himself inside his woman. Together they moaned until their voices put each other to sleep.

Chapter 41

Tricia walked to her door and looked through the peephole. She saw Simone standing on the other side of her door. She unlocked the door and opened it. Simone smiled and Tricia walked back into the apartment.

Simone walked inside of the apartment and looked around. It was a mess. Tricia was lounging around in pajamas and her hair was matted to her head.

"Trish, what's the matter?" Simone asked as she sat on the sofa.

"Simone, ever since Tarik overheard us, he hasn't been here. He just left and won't return my phone calls," she cried.

"He didn't even hear you out?"

"I tried to explain it to him but he wasn't trying to hear it. He told me that he didn't know if he could trust me again." Tricia shook her head and cried.

"I'm sorry, Trish. I didn't mean for this to happen. Tarik will come around. Do you want me to talk to him?" Simone asked.

"No, I think you're probably the last person he's gonna listen to."

"Yeah, you're right. Is there anything I could do to help?" Simone asked.

"No. But I'm glad you're here. We do need to finish the conversation we started."

"Yeah, that's why I'm here. I need to get some things off my chest." Simone exhaled and looked Tricia in the eyes. "Trish I'm really sorry about coming on to you. I didn't even know I had those kinds of feelings until it happened. I would never put you in that situation intentionally."

"Simone, what happened? I mean…why would you act on those feelings if you never thought about it? Have you ever been with a woman?"

Simone looked at Tricia and shook her head yes.

Tricia stared at her in disbelief. "I thought I knew everything about you. Why didn't you ever tell me?"

"Wait, it happened after you. I was never with a woman before you. Like I said, I didn't even know I had those feelings."

"So are you gay now? Bisexual? What's up?" Tricia asked.

"I'm so confused right now. I don't even know how to classify myself. I'm still with Kareem but I'm trying to fight these feelings I have for this woman."

"Damn Simone. I don't know what to say."

"You don't have to respond to that. I just hope that we can repair our friendship. I miss you so much, Trish."

"I really missed you, too. Melissa is cool as hell but no one can take your place." Tricia reached over and hugged Simone. "I just need to know that you won't ever come on to me like that again."

Simone broke the embrace. "Trish, I must admit. After that night, I thought about you in that way for a while. I lusted for you. But in time, I realized that it was just me trying to find myself. I know what it's like to be with a woman at her own will. I can promise you that I don't have those feelings for you anymore. I want our friendship back that's all. I know it's going to take you some time and I'm willing to wait," Simone revealed.

"Well these days, I've been so busy trying to make up with my husband, I can't even think straight."

Simone looked around the apartment. "I see. Lets say we get you decent again?" she smiled.

"Can I ask you a question?" Tricia asked.

"Sure."

"Does Kareem know?"

"Hell no! I was going to tell him right after the wedding but…" Tricia looked away. The thought of her wedding made her want to cry. "Gosh, I didn't get the chance to apologize for the wedding. I'm really sorry. I wish we can do this past year over again. I know how much your day meant to you. Please forgive me?" Simone asked.

"That's going to take a little time. But I'm going to take it one day at a time," she tried to smile.

Simone stood and began to remove clothes that were strewn all over the apartment. Tricia went to the kitchen and washed the dishes. Afterwards, she took a shower and got dressed. Simone was sitting on the sofa watching TV when Tricia walked into the living room.

They sat and talked for hours. Simone did her best to keep Tricia from thinking about Tarik. They talked about Melissa and then Simone told Tricia all about her relationship with Shelly. Tricia stared at her in amazement. As close as they were, she couldn't believe that there was something about Simone that she didn't know.

Chapter 42

Tarik walked into the hospital nursery and saw Melissa feeding the baby. She looked up and smiled. He went over and stared at the baby. He looked long and hard.

"It's too soon to tell. He doesn't look like anyone yet," Melissa whispered.

"Is Phil here?" Tarik asked.

"He's on his way. He's leaving work early so we can finish getting Christopher's room ready."

"How is little man doing anyway?" Tarik smiled.

"Dr. Watters says that he's gaining weight and he can drink from a bottle on his own. See? They took out the feeding tube."

"I see. That's good. He should be home soon, huh?"

"Hopefully," she smiled at her son.

"Lissa, have you told Phil about us?"

"No! Are you crazy? Have you told Tricia?" Melissa snapped.

"Well you better think about telling him! He already suspects you cheated so there's your way," Tarik said. Melissa shook her head and peeked towards the door before she spoke.

"Tarik, why are you doing this? I already told you that I'm not asking for a paternity test. Phil is my baby's father and that's that!"

"Lissa, how long have you known me?"

"Too long!"

"Exactly! You know I'm not going to sit around and do nothing while there's a chance I may have a son."

Melissa turned the baby on his stomach like she was taught. She rubbed his back so that he could burp.

"How are things with you and Tricia?" she asked as an attempt to change the subject.

146

"I'm still at the hotel."

"When are you going to stop this nonsense and make up with your wife? Tarik, she is miserable! Before I went home, she was up here everyday hoping to see you."

"That's what she said?" he asked.

"She didn't have to say it. Every time I talked, her mind and eyes went to that door to see if you were coming," Melissa said as she held Christopher to her chest.

"Let me hold him." Tarik grabbed a blanket and held out his hands.

Melissa hesitated for a second then placed her baby in Tarik's arms. She helped him support the head and he rocked little Christopher to sleep.

"Melissa, I don't know if I can ever forgive Tricia. The trust is gone! She did some fu…messed-up stuff!"

"You want to talk about it?" Melissa asked.

"I can't tell you what she did. You and her are too close now. It's up to her to tell you," he said.

"Was it enough to make you stop loving her?"

"I love Tricia. I love her to death. I just can't get past what happened."

Melissa was getting sick and tired of being left in the dark. There was no way she could comfort her friend if she didn't know what to comfort him about. "Tarik, since when have you not been able to tell me anything?"

"Since you and my wife became good friends."

"That doesn't mean you can't trust me with your secrets anymore. I'll always be a loyal friend to you no matter how close Trish and I become. I love her but you were my friend long before she was. If you need to talk, let's talk!"

Tarik placed the baby in the cradle. He stood by the window contemplating if he should tell Melissa what happened.

"It's complicated Lissa," he said as he walked back over to where she was standing. Melissa looked at her friend. She couldn't stand to see him in so much pain.

"I promise not to mention to Tricia anything we talk about. You don't have to worry about me telling her that I know about her and Simone's secret," she said.

Tarik blew into the air, "I guess I do need to talk about it. I've been holding it in since I found out a few weeks ago," He pulled Melissa to a secluded area of the nursery. "I walked into the cafeteria and overheard Trish and Simone talking. I heard Simone apologize for coming on to Trish." Melissa's eyes grew wide.

"I went over to them and snapped! To make a long story short, I finally spoke to Tricia to give her the chance to explain and she said that she and Simone had sex but Simone initiated it."

Melissa continued to stare at Tarik as tears streamed down his face. She didn't know what to say. She opened her mouth to speak but quickly decided to choose her words wisely.

"Do you think she's lying?"

"Melissa, I know Trish. She's not into women. I don't believe that she did that willingly. She said that they were drunk."

"I can't say I know how you feel about that but I do know how you feel about Trish. Why can't you get past that? She said it was an accident."

"If it were an accident, why didn't she just tell me what happened? I asked her over and over again to tell me but she refused. That's the part I can't get past!"

"Tarik, you are not being fair. Did you forget that we had a..."

"Hi sweetie, are you ready?" Phil asked as he walked into the room.

"Oh, what's up Tarik?" he asked dryly.

"Wassup?" Tarik responded. "Lissa, I need to get going anyway but I'll call you so you can help me make a decision about all of this." He picked up Christopher as he spoke to let Melissa know what he was referring to. He kissed him on the forehead and handed him to Melissa. Tarik said goodbye then left.

Chapter 43

Phil and Melissa arrived home at 10:06pm. They left the hospital shortly after Tarik left and went shopping for the baby's room. Melissa went up to the room and added the latest gadgets she'd found in Babies R Us. She looked around and smiled at her son's room. She turned off the light and closed the door behind her. She bumped into Phil as she started towards her bedroom.

"Ouch!" she said as she rubbed her head.

"We need to talk!" Phil said and pulled her by the arm into their bedroom. He pushed her on the bed. She looked up at her husband and frowned.

"What's the matter with you?" she asked.

"You are Melissa! I'm trying my best to pretend that everything is ok with us. But we're bringing that baby home in two days and you need to come clean with me. Who is that baby's father?" he demanded.

"Phil, please don't start with this again. I told you I wasn't with anyone else!"

"Did you hear me when I told you that my doctor assured me that I couldn't father any children? I'm not the father so stop lying!"

Melissa began to cry. She held her hands up to Phil to keep him from grabbing her. He smacked her hands down and grabbed her anyway. She pulled away and fell onto the bed. He snatched her up and smacked her across the face. "LIAR! Who were you with?" he screamed as he grabbed her by the neck. Melissa grabbed onto his leg and pulled herself up. Phil kicked her in her side as she was almost on her feet. He looked at her in disgust. He began punching her in her back.

Melissa begged for him to stop as she covered her face. He stopped for a brief second as she cried out in pain.

150

"Phil, you promised not to hit me anymore. Please stop. I can't move," she cried as she held on to her side.

"Who were you with Melissa!" Phil was out of control. He yelled over and over begging Melissa to tell him who she'd slept with. Melissa stuck to her story. She told Phil over and over that she was faithful.

"Tell me, Damn it!" He lifted her off the floor and threw her into the armoire. She screamed as loud as she could. Phil rushed to her and hit her in the mouth.

"How could you cheat on me? I gave you everything you ever wanted! You had a baby by another man and you sit here and try to convince me that it's mine!" He sat on the bed while Melissa cried out.

"Phil, p p plea please help...me. I'm hurt...hurting."

He looked at her and shook his head. Phil went to his briefcase and pulled out a pint of Hennesy. He removed the top and put the bottle to his mouth. Melissa moved close to the wall. She inched her way to the bedroom door. Phil put his head in his hands and made a loud noise.

Melissa sat up on the floor. She winced in pain. She never let go of her side while she wiped blood from her lip. Phil looked over and threw the empty bottle in her direction. The bottle broke against the wall and Melissa covered her face. There were tiny pieces of glass in her hair and face. She felt her face and started to scream. Phil walked over to her. "Tell me now! Who did you have an affair with?"

"Phil, I'm so...sor...sorry. Please forgive m me," she said as she shook her head.

"Why Melissa? Why?" Phil cried.

"I...I'm I didn't...mean it Phil." She sobbed as she rubbed her side. The more she rubbed, the more it hurt. "I...need help Phil." Melissa couldn't see out of her left eye. It was swollen and sore. There was blood all over her face. She slid to the floor to lie down. She wanted nothing more than to make the pain go away. She attempted to close her eyes but Phil stood over her and lightly kicked her to get her attention.

"Who was it, Melissa? And don't tell me that shit about a second opinion. I am a doctor remember?"

"T...Ta...rik, it was Ta...rik," she cried. The tears were beginning to sting her face.

"Tarik? That bastard! You had him in my fucking house and you were fucking him?" Phil was livid. He went to Melissa and lifted her to her feet. She begged for her life. She'd seen Phil upset before, but she'd never seen him like this. Melissa covered her face with her arm and Phil threw her across the room on the bed. She slid off the bed and fell to the floor. She rolled under the bed to get out of his reach. Phil cursed and called her every name under the sun. He bent down and looked under the bed. Melissa was balled up holding her side. He reached under the bed and pulled her out. He lifted her to the bed and threw her across. She cried as the pain in her side was unbearable.

After another ten minutes, Phil really looked at her and saw the excruciating pain she must be in. He picked up the phone and dialed 911. He kissed her on the forehead and stared at her.

"I need to get away from you. I love you Melissa and if I keep looking at you knowing you cheated on me, I will kill you. Help is on the way." Phil walked out and left the front door wide open.

Chapter 44

Melissa was barely awake when the paramedics arrived. She smiled on the inside when she saw the help. She wanted to go to sleep. She fought hard to stay awake. She'd tried to convince many a patient to stay awake at a critical time like this. She knew if she closed her eyes, she could easily slip off into a coma or worse.

The paramedics inserted the emergency IV and rushed her to the hospital. They did everything to keep her awake. She stayed awake right up until they hit the emergency room doors. She closed her eyes as a paramedic called out to her. Within minutes, Melissa was out cold.

She was rushed to a trauma unit. She was barely recognizable. There were two surgeons in the operating room. Her left leg was broken in two places and her eye was swollen shut. Her face was covered in blood and glass. She had a spleen on her right arm. There was a noticeable bruise on her side.

The head surgeon looked at the x-rays that the technician handed him. He called the other surgeon to make sure he was seeing clearly. The head surgeon shook his head and wiped his face with his hands. "Damn it, her ribs are broken! And it looks like they're barely healed from what looks like previous fractures."

"What the hell is going on?" The doctor asked the head surgeon. "What's her name? We need to get in touch with her physician."

The head surgeon shook his head. "Nurse, please check to see if she has ID or anything on her person maybe she has a chart with this hospital."

The nurse walked out of the room. She bumped into one of the paramedics. "How is Mrs. Monroe doing?"

"Oh, you know her? The doctor just asked me to find out who she is. Do you know her first name?" she asked.

"It's Melissa Monroe. That was what the 911 caller said."

"Melissa? Oh my goodness! I didn't even recognize her! Shit! I'll be back." She rushed back into the operating room.

"Doctor? Doctor?"

"What is it? Did you find anything?" the head surgeon asked.

"This is Nurse Monroe."

"Melissa? What in the hell happened to her? Look at her! I would never have known it was her if you wouldn't have said anything." He looked down at Melissa and shook his head. "Nurse, call Dr. Michael Carter, I think they're good friends. Maybe he can help."

Dr. Carter was in the nursery visiting with Christopher Monroe. He stood in front of the incubator and smiled at the baby. He was so tiny. The baby slept the entire time Dr. Carter was there. Dr. Carter stood to leave. He'd just finished his shift and was heading home. He walked out of the nursery and waited for the elevator. He heard his name over the intercom. He was being asked to call an extension in the emergency room. He walked back to the nurse's station and picked up the phone. The page came over the loud speaker again. This time it was Stat. Dr. Carter picked up the phone and dialed the extension. He hung up the phone and rushed to the stairwell.

Dr. Carter burst through the doors and looked at the patient. He walked past and went to the doctor in charge. "Well, where is she?" he asked as he looked around.

"This is Mrs. Monroe," the surgeon said as he pointed to Melissa.

"No! This can't...what happened? She's so...How did she get here?" Dr. Carter asked.

"She came in an ambulance. Mike, I need to talk to you. She's in pretty bad shape. Can you tell me anything about her medical history?"

154

Dr. Carter sighed and told the surgeon what he needed to know. He was almost in tears as he explained the injuries from the incident eight months ago.

"I'm going to get sterilized so that I can assist."

"No Mike! You are too close to Melissa. I'm not willing to risk it. You have to sit this one out."

Dr. Carters' eyes became watery. He sniffed then left the room. The doctor came behind him and asked him to contact Melissa's family.

Dr. Carter was furious. He knew somehow that Phil was responsible for Melissa's condition. He was thankful that he'd taken Melissa's friends numbers and stored them into his cell phone in case of an emergency. He went to his office and called Tarik. Tricia answered the phone hoping it was Tarik. Dr. Carter explained what happened to Melissa and asked Tricia to come to the hospital immediately.

Tricia called Tarik's cell and left a message. She then called her mother and told her what happened. She asked her mother to stay home and keep trying to call Tarik.

Dr. Carter called Tarik's cell. Tarik answered on the first ring. He cursed out loud as Dr. Carter told him that Melissa was in the emergency room. Dr. Carter told him it was pretty serious and asked him to come ASAP. Tarik closed his phone and rushed to the hospital.

Chapter 45

Dr. Carter met Tricia in front of the emergency entrance doors. Tricia was hysterical. She was in tears as she asked about Melissa.

"Tricia, I need to talk to you first. Lets go someplace quiet." He walked her inside and stopped at the desk. He left directions where to send Tarik when he arrived.

Once inside an empty office, Dr. Carter pulled a chair and asked Tricia to have a seat. She sat across from him as he handed her some tissues.

"How is she Mike?"

"I'm going to give it to you straight. She's worse than before. I saw her a little while ago and I didn't recognize her."

"Oh my goodness! That bastard!" she yelled.

"Phil?" Dr. Carter asked.

Tricia didn't want to put Melissa's business out there. She didn't want to volunteer any information.

"It's ok Trish, I understand your reservations but I know that Melissa is in an abusive marriage. I've seen her try to hide a black eye too many times," he said.

"What did she say happened?" Tricia asked.

"She's unconscious right now. They weren't able to get anything from her. The paramedics are saying that a male called in the emergency."

Tarik banged on the door. Dr. Carter swung it open and let him inside.

"Tarik, she's hurt really bad," Tricia said as she ran into her husband's arms. Tarik hugged his wife and tried to make sense of the situation. Dr. Carter explained to them both about Melissa's injuries. Tarik became angrier with each word the doctor spoke. Tricia held him tight so that he wouldn't walk out of the room.

156

"How did this happen to her?" Tarik asked.

"Hold on Tarik, I'm not done. Her ribs are broken."

"Damn I was just with her!" Tarik yelled.

"That's not the worse part. They were barely healed from the fracture several months ago. So it's going to take longer for them to heel this time around."

Tarik looked at Dr. Carter, "what happened several months ago?"

Dr. Carter looked at Tricia, "he didn't know?"

"Know what!" Tarik demanded.

"I'm sorry to be the one to break the news but I think it's time he knew the entire story, Tricia." Dr. Carter proceeded to tell Tarik about the previous incident. Tricia held on to her husband as tight as she could. She cried and tried to control her sniffling. When Dr. Carter revealed that he thought Phil was behind the last incident and said that it was likely he was the cause of this one, Tarik pushed Tricia away from him.

"You knew about that, Tricia?"

"Tarik, just wait a minute! Melissa asked me...well she told me..."

"Trish, I asked you to look out for her! I told you I had a feeling that she was in trouble and you keep something like this from me? How could you? The lies just flow off your tongue these days, huh?" he yelled.

"Will both of you please calm down!?" Dr. Carter asked, "Melissa is not doing well. She has serious injuries and she's going to need all of the support that you can give."

"He's right Tarik," Tricia said in a shaky voice.

Tarik didn't even try to stop the tears from falling. He covered his face with his hands as Tricia stood in front of him and rubbed his back. He buried his face in her stomach and cried. "When can we see her?" Tricia asked.

"I'm not sure. Her doctor is doing everything in his power for her. He's a colleague of ours so she's in good hands."

"Phil is a dead man. When I catch up to his ass, I'm going to show him how it feels to be beat the fuck up!" Tarik said as he walked out of the room.

"Tarik! Tarik!" Tricia yelled after him. Dr. Carter went to her to console her while she cried like a baby.

Dr. Carter escorted Tricia to the eighth floor where Melissa lay on the operating table. He told her to sit in the waiting area while he checked on Melissa.

Dr. Carter walked into Melissa's room and asked for a report on her progress. The head surgeon handed him a chart and escorted him to a corner of the room.

"Mike, she's in and out of consciousness. She's responsive so that's always a good sign. I repaired all of her injuries. Her ribs are pretty bad. She's going to be in pain for quite some time. She's out of it right now but I'm sure she'll survive."

"I can't believe this. I just spoke to Melissa."

"Mike, were you able to contact her family? I think it'll do her good to hear familiar voices."

"I called the closest people to family that she has. Is it ok if she had a visitor now?" Dr. Carter asked.

"Of course, I'm on call tonight so I'll be around. I'm going to leave my pager number at the nurse's station in case you need me," the surgeon said as he walked out.

Chapter 46

Dr. Carter stood over Melissa and stared at her for a few minutes. He shook his head as he looked at her face. He was hurting on the inside. The Melissa he was used to seeing was nowhere in sight. She looked as if she'd been in a fight with a stranger on the streets.

"Melissa, why didn't you call me? I told you I'm always here for you. I'm so sorry I wasn't there for you." Dr. Carter wiped his eyes and held Melissa's hand. He pulled a chair next to the bed and gently squeezed her hand. *"Lissa, I need you to wake up. I need to look into your eyes. I want you to look at me,"* he sniffed. *"And Tricia is out there waiting to see you. I know you wanna see her. Open your eyes Melissa. Just let me see that you're ok. Please?"* Dr. Carter begged.

He felt Melissa squeeze his hand. He looked at her face and saw that her eye was open. He gave a quick examination. Her vitals were normal and she was responsive. She wasn't able to talk because there was so much equipment hooked up to her. She moaned and grunted until Dr. Carter removed the oxygen mask. She parted her lips to speak.

Dr. Carter placed his fingers over her lips. "Me first, you were hurt pretty bad, but you'll be ok. You are in and out of consciousness and I just needed to know that you were still here with us."

"Mike, I…I just…I'm sorry. I planned to call you." Melissa spoke slowly as she was in pain.

"It's ok Melissa. You don't have to apologize for anything. I'm still here for you. We'll talk later ok? Right now, Tricia is outside waiting to see you. Ok?"

Melissa shook her head up and down. She tried to smile but winced in pain. Dr. Carter let go of her hand and went to get

Tricia. He handed Tricia a card with his numbers. He told her he'd be back soon but to call if they needed him.

"Hey sweetie, how are you feeling?" Trish asked as she entered the room.

"I'm in pain. Mike says I'll be ok," she said slowly.

"Where's Phil?"

"Don't know. He wasn't there when the ambulance came," Melissa mumbled.

"Melissa, I need to tell you something. Just listen ok?" Melissa shook her head up and down as Tricia sat in the chair. "Tarik knows about the last incident. Mike was explaining your injuries and it kind of came up."

"Oh no! Where is Tarik now?" She struggled to speak.

"He stormed out. He's going to find Phil." Tricia said as she looked away. "He was pissed because I didn't tell him about the last time."

"Damn! I'm so sorry Tricia. I really messed up."

"No, don't you worry about it. It was my choice to keep that from him. He's pissed! I'm just going to give him his space for a little while," Tricia said.

"Trish, you know Tarik is going to hurt my husband right?" Melissa spoke slowly and slurred due to the pain.

"Yeah, I saw it all over his face. Please don't let this upset you."

"How am I supposed to feel? I didn't want Tarik to know about the last time because I was scared for Phil but I don't know how I feel right now. I wanna see my son," Melissa cried.

Tricia smiled, "how is little Christopher doing?"

"He's supposed to be coming home tomorrow. I assume he's doing fine. Can you please ask the doctor to bring my baby to me!"

"Ok you just Relax, I'll go find Mike and see if he can work something out for us." Tricia kissed Melissa on the forehead before she backed towards the door.

"Trish," Melissa mumbled, "come here for a minute."

Tricia sat on the bed with Melissa. "Thanks for not making me feel like the ugliest person in the world. I heard the staff saying that I was barely recognizable. How bad do I look?" she asked.

"Melissa, don't you worry about that. You concentrate on getting better for your son," Tricia smiled.

"That bad, huh? Trish, tell me what you see. I need to know how I look. I can't see out of my eye. Just tell me how I look."

Tricia looked at Melissa with sympathy. She didn't want to be the one to tell Melissa how she looked. She sat back in the chair and held Melissa's hand. "Ok sweetie, but just remember that you've just been through a terrible ordeal. The swelling hasn't gone down and this is temporary."

"Tell me Trish."

"Well, you have a black eye, your face is red and swollen with cuts all over. They had to cut some of your hair and your head is bandaged up. You don't look that bad. It's natural after this kind of attack."

Melissa was in tears. "Trish, please pass me the phone. I need to make a call."

"Not if you're getting ready to call Phil. I'm not doing it for you this time!" Tricia said.

"Please Trish? Help me make a call," Melissa pleaded.

Tricia sighed and opened up her cell phone, "what's the number?"

Melissa called out Tarik's cell number and asked for the phone. "Hello?" she said softly, "yeah, it's me. I'll be ok. Yes…but I wish you were here instead of there. Ok. Tarik? Kick his ass for me! Yep, I'll see you later." Melissa's face was filled with tears. She turned her head away from the phone as she handed it back to Tricia.

Tricia smiled and left the room. She dug in her pocket and found the card Mike gave her. She opened her phone and dialed the number. She explained the situation and asked him if he could help. Mike told her to sit tight and he was going to see what he can do. Tricia told him she'd be inside of Melissa's room and to meet her there.

She made another call to her mother to fill her in on the situation. She told her mother that they found Tarik and she could stop calling. She asked her mother to call Simone and let her know what happened. Mrs. Hobbs told her that she would come to the hospital as soon as she could.

Chapter 47

Tarik parked his car in Melissa's driveway. He turned off the ignition and waited. After he hung up the phone with Melissa, he was more focused on beating Phil's ass. He decided that he was going to sit there until Phil showed up at home. Tarik jumped up and realized that Phil may not pull into the driveway if he saw the truck. He parked his truck around the corner and called Tricia's cell phone.

"Trish, put Melissa on the phone! Lissa, where's your spare keys to the house? I don't have my keys on me. Ok got 'em, thanks. I'll be there as soon as I can." He hung up the phone and let himself into the house. He walked into the kitchen and looked around for any signs of Phil. He walked throughout the house and searched for Phil. He peeked inside every room. He came to their master bedroom and looked around. There was blood on the wall, broken glass on the floor and there were clothes hanging out of the armoire. He noticed the broken-empty Hennessy bottle on the floor. Tarik was livid. He ran downstairs with his fist balled up. He sat on the sofa and waited for Phil to walk into the house.

Tarik had dozed off. He looked up as he heard a lock click. He stood up and met Phil at the door. Phil walked into the house and saw Tarik.

"I knew I'd see you tonight," Phil said as he closed the door. "How dare you come into my house after you've been fucking my wife!"

Tarik was shocked. He tried not to let it show on his facial expression. He had no idea Phil knew about he and Melissa.

"How dare you hit on Melissa like she's a fuckin' punching bag," he mimicked Phil. "I'm getting ready to show

163

you how it feels to get beat the fuck up!" Tarik rushed Phil and swung a two-piece to the face. Phil tumbled back and came up swinging. He landed a right to Tarik's jaw. Tarik staggered back and punched Phil in the chest. He followed up and hit him in the chin. Phil doubled over and grabbed his chest. Tarik caught him with another two-piece and Phil fell to the floor. Tarik stood over Phil and frowned, *"You punk ass bitch! You wanna hit somebody? Get up and hit me! You ain't so tough now huh?"* Tarik lifted his foot and began to stomp Phil. He didn't stop. Phil was on his back covering his face.

Tarik slipped and Phil grabbed his foot. He flipped Tarik to the floor. He and Tarik got up at the same time. Phil put up his hands to defend himself.

"Yeah that's what's up. Fight me like a man. Come get some!" Tarik said. Phil rushed Tarik and backed him into the wall. Tarik hit the wall hard and fell to the floor. He moved as Phil was bringing his foot down towards his face. Phil punched Tarik in the arm as he tried to get off the floor. Tarik fell against the wall again and put his hands up to block the punches Phil threw his way.

Phil staggered back for a minute and Tarik rushed to his feet. Tarik swung at Phil and landed on his jaw. Phil stumbled back again and reached for the sofa to keep his balance. Tarik took advantage and swung Phil to the floor. Tarik stomped Phil's arms and legs. He was trying to break his legs. Phil yelled out in pain. Tarik continued to stomp all over his face and chest. *"You ain't so tough now huh? I'ma make sure you feel just like Melissa."* Phil grunted and tried to crawl to the door. Tarik dragged him away from the door and stood over him. He repeatedly punched Phil in the face. He noticed blood coming out of Phil's mouth.

Phil tried unsuccessfully to keep his face covered but he was in too much pain. *"Tarik stop! Just calm down!"* Phil managed to say. *"Is that what Melissa said? You son of a bitch! Did she beg you to stop?"* Tarik punched him in the mouth and jumped up when he saw blood coming from his own hand. He hit

Phil in the teeth and his finger was cut. He pushed away from Phil and went to the sofa.

"You...you're...that mu...much in lo...love with my...wife? I always...knew...y...you...had a...thing...for her," Phil said between breaths.

"You sick bastard! Melissa is my friend more like my sister! I sat back and watched you mistreat her for too long! I should have kicked your ass a long time ago!" Tarik said as he tried to clean his finger.

"She told...me about you two. She said... she...fucked you!" Phil said while trying to catch his breath.

Tarik looked at Phil with rage in his eyes. "Don't try to change the subject! You have no right to put yo fuckin hands on her! She's not yo child!" He yelled.

"Speaking of children, I know Christopher isn't my son. Are you the father?"

Tarik looked at Phil and shook his head. He couldn't believe that Phil was trying to take the heat off of him.

"Let me tell you something, Phil. I'm not the one! If you ever put yo fuckin' hands on Melissa again, I will kill you!" Tarik warned.

Phil was still on the floor. He couldn't use his left arm. He tried to pull himself up with the other arm but kept falling on the floor. "Tarik, I love Melissa! She's my wife. I never meant to hurt her. How is she?" he asked.

Tarik went over to Phil and kicked him in the stomach.

"You wanna know how she is? You left her here alone. Fuck you! Stay the fuck away from her. She don't need your kind of love!" Tarik kicked Phil to the side and stepped on his leg as he walked out of the door. Phil was in too much pain to move. He lay on the floor and watched Tarik walk out of the door.

Phil tried to get up but couldn't. He knew his arm was broke but he wasn't sure about his leg. He stopped trying to get off the floor and lay there in tears. He cried like a baby. He never intended to harm Melissa. He regretted everything that happened.

He loved Melissa so much. But he knew with Tarik on the rampage, it was going to be hard to win her back.

Chapter 48

D r. Carter turned around as he heard Tarik call his name. "What happened to you?" Dr. Carter asked.

"Nothing! I'm aiight. How is Melissa?" Tarik snapped.

Dr. Carter looked at him for a minute. Tarik shook his head and apologized, "my bad man I didn't mean to snap on you. I'm just a little pissed off that's all."

"I'm on my way to her room now. You can come with me," Dr. Carter said.

They walked into Melissa's room and saw Tricia sitting on the side of the bed holding her hand. Tricia's face was red from crying. She tried her best to keep it together while Melissa was asleep. She looked up and saw Tarik and Dr. Carter. Tarik went to his wife and hugged her. He looked down at Melissa and cringed. "Look at her! Phil's gonna think twice before he ever put his hands on her again!"

"You saw him?" Tricia asked.

"I saw his ass alright. The only thing he saw was the bottom of my boot!" Tarik said.

"Trish, how was she before she fell asleep?" Dr. Carter asked.

"She seemed ok. She kept talking about seeing Christopher before she dozed off. She tried her best to stay awake. She wanted you to wake her as soon as you got here."

Tarik sat in the chair and pulled Tricia on his lap. He squeezed her tight and kissed her on the neck. She hugged him tighter and returned his kiss.

Dr. Carter tapped Melissa on the shoulder to wake her. There was a bandage around her arm so he was extremely careful. Melissa opened her eyes and tried to smile. Tears covered her face from the pain. "Just relax Melissa. Don't try to speak," Dr. Carter insisted.

Tarik stood next to Dr. Carter and reached for Melissa's hand. He held it gently as Dr. Carter spoke.

"Melissa, I contacted Dr. Watters and she wouldn't allow Christopher to leave the nursery. I tried my best to convince her but she wasn't budging. She said she'll be here in the morning to talk to you about some test results."

"What kind of results?" Tarik asked.

"She didn't say. We all have to wait until tomorrow," Dr. Carter said.

"Tarik, did...did...you find...Phil?" Melissa stuttered.

"It's all taken care of, baby. I think he got the message," Tarik smiled.

Melissa squeezed his hand and smiled on the inside.

"It's time for Melissa to get some rest. You guys are going to have to leave now," Dr. Carter said.

"I'm not leaving, man. I'm gonna stay right here by her side."

Tricia pulled Tarik to the side. "Baby, I know this may not be a good time, but we need to talk. Please come home so that we can deal with this?" Tricia asked.

"We do need to talk. But I'm staying right here with Melissa. I wanna be here in case Phil decides to show his face. And I need to talk to Melissa about some things. I promise that we'll talk," he said.

"I love you," Tricia said.

"I love you too, Boo. Go on home and I'll see you in the morning. I'll call if there are any changes in Melissa's condition." He kissed Tricia on the lips then went over to Melissa.

Dr. Carter offered to walk Tricia to her car as he got the paperwork straight for Tarik to stay over. Tricia thanked him and went to kiss Melissa on the forehead. Dr. Carter said goodbye and led Tricia out of the room.

Tarik sat on the bed and looked at Melissa. He was furious that Phil put her in this situation. Melissa looked up at him with teary eyes. Tarik wiped her face very carefully.

"Lissa, we have got to get to the bottom of this whole thing. I need to know if I'm the father. I really need to know because if Christopher is my son, I do not want Phil near him let alone raising him!"

"Tarik, please don't do this. I can't talk about this right now. I don't know what's going to happen. I just need to get out of here. I am supposed to take him home tomorrow and I definitely can't do that while I'm in here," she slurred.

"Did you tell Phil about us?" Tarik asked.

"I didn't have a choice. I didn't want him to hurt me anymore. I had to tell him," she cried.

"Damn it! He asked me about Christopher. He told me that he can't be the father. Whatchu gonna do?"

"Tarik…I just can't."

"I know that this is hard for you but it's time to get this thing out in the open. I'ma talk to Tricia when I get home. Now that her secret is out, I have to tell her mine so we can work out our marriage."

"Tarik you can't do that!"

"Melissa, it's for the best. We can't keep pretending that it didn't happen or that the possibility of me being the father doesn't exist!" Tarik snapped.

"You can't tell her, Tarik. Tricia will never forgive me. I love her like a sister. Do you really think she's going to forgive or forget about what happened?" Melissa asked.

"I'm sorry baby. I gotta save my marriage," Tarik said.

"Wow! You went and made sure there was no way I can save my marriage now you wanna destroy my only friendship too? Have you ever thought about what would happen if you and Tricia got back together?"

"Melissa, you're jumping the gun a little bit. Anyway, if you had any sense, you wouldn't wanna try to save anything with Phil after the way he beat yo ass!" Tarik yelled, "it seems like every time I try to defend you, you find a way to make it seem like I did something wrong! That's it, if you ever get back with him, don't count on me to have yo back. Just let the muthafucka beat the shit out of you!" he said.

"That would probably be the case anyway sense Tricia and I will more than likely not be friends after she finds out what happened!" Melissa retorted.

Tarik stopped and stared at her. "Damn, I didn't even think about that."

"No because you're so fast! You're only thinking about yourself, what about my friendship with Tricia?"

"I'm only thinking about me? I just beat the shit outta yo husband! I didn't hesitate to do that for YOU! Never mind the fact that I could go to jail for assault. I beat his ass in his own house. But I'm only thinking about me?" Tarik walked to the other side of the room. "You got a lot of fucking nerves!" He looked at her as he walked towards the door. "Get some rest. I'll see you later. Better yet, I'll be here in the morning by the time Dr. Watters get here!"

"Tarik wait!" she pleaded. He walked out of the door without looking back. Melissa lay in the bed tired from exhaustion. It took so much out of her to have that conversation with Tarik.

Chapter 49

Kareem and Shelly walked inside of her apartment. Shelly turned on the lights and went into the kitchen. Kareem removed his coat and boots and went into the bedroom.

Shelly entered her bedroom and went to the dresser drawer and removed some items to take a shower. Kareem turned on the TV and pulled back the comforter. "Hurry up baby. You know I can't stay too long."

"I know. I won't be long. You wanna join me in the shower?" Shelly smiled.

"Nah, I'm tired as hell! That food gave me the ITIS. If you don't hurry up, I'ma be sleep," Kareem said.

"I don't have a problem waking you up," Shelly smiled. Kareem smiled as she went inside the bathroom.

Shelly stood in the bedroom doorway after she came from the shower. She was only wearing a black garter belt.

"Psst...psst," she whispered as Kareem watched the television set.

He looked over and smiled at Shelly, "damn baby, what you got planned for tonight?"

"I'm trying to make this little bit of time mean something. All you need to do is just go wit' the flow."

"So lets do this," he suggested.

Shelly danced her way to the bed and crawled towards Kareem. She pushed him back to make room for her show. Shelly got right in front of him and squeezed her breasts together. He reached out to her but she pushed his hands away. Shelly remained on her knees while she fingered herself. Kareem's soldier was standing at attention. He wanted to pin her on the bed and fuck her. He held restraint until Shelly was ready.

She lay back on the bed and opened her legs a little wider so that he could get a better look. Shelly slowly played with her clitoris and licked her fingers. She gently eased her hand inside of her, one finger at a time. Kareem moved closer to her and buried his face between her legs. She wrapped her legs around his neck while he licked her insides. Shelly moaned in pleasure. She reached underneath and tugged at Kareem's dick.

Kareem positioned himself on his knees so that Shelly could get a better grip. He moaned as loud as she. They made each other reach an orgasm almost simultaneously. Kareem removed Shelly's legs from around his neck and lay beside her. Shelly lay next to him trying to catch her breath.

After ten minutes, she sat up then leaned over Kareem and put her breasts in his face. He sucked her nipples hard and fast. Shelly sat on top of him and opened her legs so that he could see her insides. Kareem lifted her off of him and removed the garter. He sat on the edge of the bed and pulled her on top of him. Her back was to his face. He licked her neck and back as she rode him to the Promised Land. Shelly bounced up and down until Kareem reached his orgasm. She turned to face him and pushed him down on the bed. She jumped on him and rode ferociously until she reached her climax. She collapsed on top of him and they went to sleep in that position.

The ringing of Kareem's cell phone woke them up. He gently pushed Shelly to the side and went to retrieve his cell phone. He missed the call but noticed there was a voice message. He went into the living room and checked the voicemail. He listened to Simone tell him that she would be out all night because Tricia needed her to help deal with an emergency with Melissa. She told him that she'd call him later.

"Let me guess, you gotta go?" Shelly asked as Kareem put the phone back in his pocket.

"Why you sneakin' up on me like that?" he snarled.

"I wasn't sneaking up on you. I was on my way to get something to drink."

"Yeah right," he said.

"Kareem, I heard the phone ring just like you did. You missed the call so what could I hear anyway? Relax!" Shelly said as she brushed past him. "Why you always gotta start something every time we have a nice time? You can't never just chill afterwards," she whined.

"Cause I know you! You sneaky as hell!"

"Kareem, I'm not the one who's sneaky. I already know about Simone. I've always known about her. You act like she's a secret. I know she's your girl and I know you have to go home to her every night. I get it!" Shelly snapped.

"Why you all getting smart? You the one getting all serious," he said.

"Kareem lets just chill. I'm not trying to spend our time arguing and shit! I'm trying to look forward to round three," she smiled. Shelly went to him and kissed him on the lips. She let her hand brush against his dick as she made her way back to the bedroom.

He followed her to the room and pulled her to him. "You right baby, lets chill." They lay down and watched an x-rated movie that led to round three.

They fucked twice before they collapsed on top of each other. Shelly lay on her back while Kareem lay on her chest.

"I love you Kareem." She didn't mean to let her true feelings slip. She closed her eyes and pretended to be asleep. She was very still waiting for Kareem's wrath to her confession.

Kareem reached up and met her lips with his. "I love you too."

Shelly smiled on the inside and went to sleep.

Chapter 50

Mrs. Hobbs picked up her ringing phone just before she was about to walk out of her house. She smiled at hearing Marvin's voice. She told him that she would be at Tricia's place for a while. Marvin asked her if she would stop by his house after she was done. Maryanne told him that she wasn't sure what time she'd be home so she suggested that he come to her house whenever he finished his errands. Marvin agreed. Mrs. Hobbs hung up the phone with a smile.

She knocked on Tricia's door and waited for an answer. Tricia opened the door and hugged her mother.

Mrs. Hobbs removed her coat and took a seat on the sofa. Tricia went to the kitchen and grabbed two waters. Mrs. Hobbs opened hers and took a long swallow.

"So how is Melissa doing?" she asked.

"Momma, it's really bad. Phil beat her up so bad that we hardly recognized her. I held back while I was in her presence but as soon as I left, I broke down in tears. I feel so sorry for her. I wish I could have prevented all of this."

Tricia heard the knock and got up to open the door. Mrs. Hobbs smiled when she saw Simone. "Hey baby. How are you?"

"I'm fine Moms. I'm just taking it one day at a time."

Tricia handed Simone a water and sat down next to her mother.

"Simone, I was just telling Momma about the bad shape Melissa is in. She really took a beating."

"Who would beat her up like that? Was she being robbed or something?" Simone asked.

Tricia's eyes began to water. "Simone, Melissa's husband did this to her. And it's not the first time," Tricia looked from her mother to Simone, "he beat her up a few weeks before my wedding too."

"Oh my goodness! I didn't know they were having problems," Simone added.

"Well, it's something that she tried to keep from everyone. Phil drinks a lot and abuses her. He's been doing it since they got married. I know I shouldn't be telling you this but under the circumstances, I don't think she'd mind." Tricia paused to wipe the tears from her eyes. Mrs. Hobbs tried to comfort her daughter. "Tricia, don't go beating yourself up. There's no way you could have prevented this."

"That's not true Ma. I knew about the last time he beat her up and I promised her I wouldn't tell anyone. Tarik asked me to let him know if she was in trouble and I didn't say anything! He found out earlier that I knew and he went off! He's so pissed with me right now. I feel horrible because I know he would have done something if I would have said something," she blurted.

"Trish, you were trying to be a friend to Melissa. There's no way you could have known this would happen again," Simone said.

"Simone, I put Melissa before my husband. I never should have gotten in the middle of this whole thing."

"Trish, you and Melissa have gotten pretty close. But you need to realize that she is Tarik's friend. You met her through him. I'm not saying that she's not your friend too. I'm saying that their friendship is always going to come before your friendship with Melissa. You and Tarik have a different kind of relationship and you better watch your step. You can't go putting her requests before your husbands'," Mrs. Hobbs said.

"I know Momma. Melissa was so scared of what Tarik would do to Phil. She made me promise not to tell Tarik."

"So where's Phil now?" Simone asked.

"I don't know, but I'm pretty sure Tarik already beat his ass. He mentioned it at the hospital."

"Do you see what just happened? Tarik wound up defending Melissa anyway. Now he's pissed with you because you tried to stop him from doing just that! Was it worth it?" Mrs. Hobbs asked.

"Momma, I don't need you to do this right now. I feel bad enough. I don't know how to make it right with Tarik. We still need to work out our other issues," Tricia said.

"You two still haven't made up?" Mrs. Hobbs asked. Tricia looked at Simone before she spoke. "No, we haven't made up yet. But we're going to get together in the morning to talk. That's why I asked you and Simone to come over." Simone and Mrs. Hobbs looked at each other. Tricia turned to Simone. "I think its time to tell Momma what happened. Tarik already knows and it's bound to come out," Tricia said.

"Wait a minute Trish, Kareem doesn't know," Simone said hysterically.

"Simone, I'm sorry. I have to tell Momma. If Tarik wouldn't have overheard us, it'll still be a secret."

"Trish, that's not fair. I didn't mean for Tarik to hear us talking, why do we have to jeopardize my relationship too?" Simone said.

"I know I'm putting you in a messed up predicament but Momma has to know what our fight was about."

"Will one of you tell me what's going on?" Mrs. Hobbs asked.

"Simone, please. I wanted us to tell her together. I can't make you tell Kareem but weather you stay or not, I'm gonna tell Momma because I'd rather her hear it from me-well us," Tricia pleaded.

Simone dropped her head in defeat. She went to the kitchen and grabbed a paper towel to dry her face.

Tricia turned to her mother as Simone stood over the sofa. Tricia held her mother's hand and proceeded to tell her what happened between her and Simone. She wiped her tears from embarrassment. Simone sniffed and rubbed Tricia's shoulder. Simone sat next to Mrs. Hobbs and explained that it was all her fault. She wanted Mrs. Hobbs to understand that she was the one who made the advances.

Mrs. Hobbs looked at them both and took another sip from her water. She was speechless.

"Momma say something, anything," Tricia said.

"I don't know what to say."

Simone continued to wipe her face and blow her nose.

Mrs. Hobbs knew her well enough to know that she was embarrassed. She knew Simone was worried that she'd be judged by her actions. "Simone, I don't want you to think that I'm going to look at you any differently. I love you still."

"Momma, it's strange for you not to have a speech or something," Tricia said.

"Trish, I'm not going to judge you two. You both are grown women and have to suffer the consequences of your actions. No matter what they are. I love you regardless."

"I hope Tarik can be as understanding as you are," Tricia added.

"Well, I'm your mother not your husband. I'm going to always be here for you." She kissed Tricia on the cheek and went to the kitchen. She grabbed another water and drank half of it before she made it back to the living room. "Simone, that goes for you too. No matter what happens with you and Kareem, I love you too." Mrs. Hobbs sat on the sofa and the three ladies ordered pizza and talked.

Simone went to the kitchen and called her apartment. She got the voicemail and hung up. She tried Kareem's cell again and also got the voicemail. She didn't leave a message. She went back into the living room and joined in the conversation.

Chapter 51

P hil sat on the floor and sobbed. He thought about the events of last night and shook his head. Aside from a broken arm, he knew his right eye was swollen because he was barely able to see. His body was sore all over. He thought about Melissa. He couldn't believe that she'd betrayed him. He never suspected that Tarik would be the one who fathered Melissa's baby. Although Tarik avoided the questions about Christopher, Phil's gut told him that it was Tarik's baby.

Phil crawled to the sofa. It took some time but he pulled himself up on the sofa and sat upright. He picked up the phone and called the hospital to check on his wife. He was told that she was in stable condition.

He hung up the phone and limped into the kitchen. He used his right arm and reached in the pantry for a stash bottle of Hennessy. He sat in the kitchen chair and put the bottle between his legs to twist off the top. Once the top was removed, Phil put the bottle to his mouth and drank it down. He threw the bottle on the floor after it was empty.

Phil sat in the chair and cried. He was too embarrassed to go to a hospital. He knew he would have to go and get his arm and legs treated. He was worried about Melissa. He called her cell phone a few times in hopes that someone would answer to give him information about his wife. The phone went directly to the voicemail. He cursed under his breath.

The phone rang as Phil made his way back to the living room. He took his time to answer it. He sat on the sofa as he put the receiver to his ear. Phil was soaked in sweat and blood.

"Hel-lo?" he slurred, "who dis? Belinda?" Phil's eyes grew wide. He straightened up on the sofa and cleared his throat before he spoke into the phone. "How in the hell did you get my number?" He listened to what she had to say then slammed the phone down. He stared at the phone like he's just spoken to a dead person.

The phone rang five minutes later. Phil snatched it up and yelled into the receiver. No one answered him so he hung up the phone.

Phil lay on the sofa with his arm almost numb. He still refused to go to the hospital. He wanted something else to drink. He had drunk all of his liquor so he wouldn't feel any pain. Phil went up to the bedroom to change his shirt. He had to move on one leg so he stumbled onto the bed and fell directly on his arm. He yelled out in pain and never left that spot.

Chapter 52

Melissa tossed and turned all night. She was unable to get any sleep. She worried about Christopher and wondered about Tarik. She called Dr. Carter at his home just to talk. She asked him if he would be there when Dr. Watters came to talk to her about Christopher. Dr. Carter agreed and said he'd be there in an hour.

Melissa reached for the phone and called Tarik. Tricia answered the phone and told her that Tarik wasn't there. Melissa asked Tricia if she were coming with Tarik to the hospital. Tricia informed her that Tarik never came home last night. Melissa told her about their argument and asked Tricia to come to the hospital. She wanted her to be there when Dr. Watters came to talk about her son. Tricia told her that she was on her way.

Tarik tapped on Melissa's door and stepped inside. He went by the bed and stared at Melissa. His eyes were red from his fight with Phil. He wanted to protect Melissa from her husband. He bent down and kissed her on the forehead.

"How you feel?" he asked.

"I'm sore as hell. I'm trying to move around so that I can hold the baby," she tried to smile.

"Lissa' I wanna talk to you before Dr. Watters get here," he said seriously.

"Tarik, if it's about the baby, I don't wanna hear anymore of that."

"Melissa, I need to know if you're gonna take Phil back?"

Melissa looked at him. She closed her eyes before she spoke. "To be honest, I haven't really thought about it."

"Well, I'm asking you to think about it. How much more does he have to do to you in order for you to see that he doesn't love you!?" he shouted.

"Tarik, you don't know Phil like I do. I know he has his faults but he really does love me," she said through teary eyes.

Tarik looked at her with rage in his eyes. "Melissa, come on now! You can't be that stupid! He left you for dead! TWICE. And you're gonna sit here and tell me that you're not sure if you gonna go back to him?"

"Why is it always your way or no way?" she asked.

"You know what? That's it! I'm not even gonna go there with you. We'll find out if Christopher is my son and if he is, you or Phil won't have shit to do with him. You can have Phil's ass!"

Dr. Watters tapped on the door and waited for an answer. Tarik went to the door and snatched it open. Dr. Watters jumped back and grabbed her chest. "Is everything ok in here?"

"I didn't mean to scare you, Dr. Watters. We're good. Come on in." Tarik extended his arm.

"How are you today, Melissa?" she asked.

Melissa used the back of her hand to wipe away her tears. "I'm ok. How is Christopher?" she spoke through the pain, "why can't I see him?"

Tricia walked into the room with Dr. Carter as Dr. Watters was about to speak. Tricia greeted everyone and went by Melissa's side. She noticed Tarik was standing in a corner by the window. "Melissa, you ok?" she asked as she glanced over at Tarik.

"Dr. Watters was getting ready to tell us about Christopher. Please go on Dr. Watters," Melissa said.

"I ran some tests to see if the transfusion worked. It seems that the transfusion wasn't enough. Christopher still can't produce red blood cells. He's still anemic.

"What happens now?" Melissa asked as Tarik moved closer to the doctor.

"He has to have another transfusion right away," Dr. Watters said. Tricia squeezed Melissa's hand. She rubbed her shoulder as an attempt to comfort her.

"When can I give him the blood?" Melissa asked.

"Melissa, you can't give Christopher anymore blood," said Dr. Watters.

"Why not?" Tarik asked.

"Well, the blood she gave the first time was from a previous blood withdrawal. She lost a lot of blood before she was brought to the ER last night." She turned to Melissa. "I checked your chart and your body wouldn't withstand it even if you had the blood to give," she said sympathetically.

Melissa cried a little harder. She leaned on Tricia's arm and let the tears fall.

"It's ok, Lissa. Phil can just give the blood," Tricia said.

Tarik and Melissa stole a quick glance at each other. The look didn't go unnoticed by Tricia or Dr. Carter.

"What? The baby should have the same blood type as Phil, right?" Tricia asked.

"Well, it's a possibility. We need to run the tests on Phil immediately to be sure he's a match," Dr. Carter said.

"That's right. So can we get Dr. Monroe in here and start with the tests?" Dr. Watters asked.

"I'll call him now," Tricia said. She searched through her cell phone and dialed the number. She gave the phone to Melissa.

Tarik watched nervously. Dr. Carter and Dr. Watters stepped to the side for a discussion. Melissa closed the phone and looked at Tarik, "got the voicemail."

Tarik looked worried. He glanced at Tricia and shook his head.

"Tarik, would you please go to the house and see if he's there?"

"I'm not going nowhere near him!" Tarik exclaimed. Dr. Watters and Dr. Carter looked in Tarik's direction.

"Tarik, don't do this! I need you. This is for Christopher, not me."

"Melissa, we'll go by the house right now." Tricia grabbed Tarik's arm and pulled him out of the room.

Dr. Carter stared at Melissa as Dr. Watters discussed more possibilities with her.

Dr. Watters left the room and told Melissa to call her when Phil arrived.

Dr. Carter pulled a chair and sat next to Melissa. "You ok, Lissa'? You wanna talk about it?"

"Not really. It's so much going on right now. I'm beginning to feel pain in my leg and in my face."

"I'll order a higher dose of pain reliever," he said.

"Thanks Mike."

"No problem. Melissa, I'm worried about you. Why won't you talk to me anymore? I could have helped you prevent this if you would have just reached out."

"Mike, I already regret not reaching out to you or anyone else. I don't want to hear the I told you so's," she said. "Besides, there's nothing you could have done."

"We'll never know huh? As a doctor and your friend, I can't let you take that baby home to an abusive husband."

"Mike?"

"I'm sorry Melissa. I can no longer sit back and watch you let your husband destroy your life. There's a child involved now!"

"I can't deal with this right now! You are a great friend but please don't interfere, Mike," she pleaded.

Dr. Carter looked at her like she was crazy. He didn't seem to be getting through to her. He exhaled then pushed the chair back to the wall. "I'll check on you when we get the blood from your husband," he said as he walked out of the room. Melissa lay there with tear filled eyes.

Chapter 53

Tricia drove while Tarik sat in silence. His mind was filled with thoughts of Melissa and Christopher. On the inside he smiled at the thought of having a son. He was kind of excited. Tricia had made comments for years that she didn't want any children. He assumed that this would be his only child. He shook his head and tried to focus on the point at hand.

Tricia glanced over at him, "are you ok?"

"I'm ok. I just got a lot on my mind right now." He looked at her and realized that he would have to tell her the truth sooner than he thought. He reached for her right hand and squeezed it gently. She smiled at him and kept driving.

"Baby, I know we have a lot of issues to overcome. And I know we were supposed to have a sit down this morning to get everything out but then this thing with Melissa came up. I just want you to know that I really appreciate your understanding. I love you, Boo," Tarik said.

"You don't have to thank me baby. Melissa is my friend too and there's nothing I wouldn't do for her and that baby, our Godson," she smiled.

Tarik looked away nervously. He didn't have a response to her reply. He continued to squeeze her hand.

"Tarik, when we get inside, try to control yourself. I know Phil is the last person you need to see right now, but he is Christopher's father and we need him for the baby's sake."

"Trish, how about you go inside and I'll wait right here because I can't promise you that I'll be cool when I see him. That muthafucka put her in the hospital he don't give a fuck about her. He ain't even came up there to see how she or the baby are doing!"

"I know sweetie but you did just kick his ass. He definitely don't want to run into you again," she said as she pulled into the circular driveway. She parked behind Phil's Lexus jeep.

"Tricia, that's no reason for him to stay away. He claims he loves her so much, right? Then nothing or no one should be able to keep him from at least checking on her and Christopher!"

"Ok baby, calm down. You wait here and I'll be right back." She kissed her husband on the lips and got out of the car.

Tricia stood there waiting for Phil to answer the door. She waited for about two minutes. She looked back at Tarik and frowned. Then she twisted the doorknob and to her surprise, it was open. She walked inside of the house and left the door open. She glanced back at Tarik who was watching her every move. She went a little further into the house and saw dried blood stains all around the room. She backed out and ran to the car.

"Tarik, you have to come with me. It looks like a crime scene in there. What did you do to him?" she asked.

"I just showed him what it was like to be beat the hell up!"

Tricia reached for the car door to help Tarik out of the car. For the first time, she looked at his face and noticed the bruises and swelling. She put her hand to his face and shook her head. Baby, you need to get some ice on your face. It's swollen and puffy. Does it hurt?" she asked as she touched his cheek.

"Nah, I'm aiight. Lets go." He pulled her inside of the house. He walked in front and saw what she was talking about. He didn't realize that so much damage was done. He didn't care. They looked around the room and saw no signs of Phil. Tricia led Tarik into the kitchen and looked at the table. She picked up an empty Hennessy bottle and shook her head, "looks like he breezed past here."

They went back out to the living room and walked up the stairs. They peeked into different rooms until they spotted Phil lying across the bed fast asleep. His clothing was in array. There was a wine bottle next to him and dried blood all over his face.

"Damn, Tarik, he looks dead. I'm scared."

"Trish, relax, that bastard ain't dead. That would be too easy." Tarik approached the bed and got a closer look. Phil was in a deep sleep. "Besides, he's breathing."

Tricia got in Phil's face and backed away. "Damn! He smells like a freekin' bar! If we light a match to him, he's gonna blow," she said.

"Damn! Melissa won't be able to get blood from him in this condition. Shit! I should wake him up and kick his ass again," Tarik shouted. There was movement on the bed from Phil. He turned on his broken arm and yelled out in pain.

"Damn It! What the hell?" he stated as he tried to focus on the people in his bedroom.

"Phil, its Tricia, are you alright?" she asked.

Phil tried to open his eyes all the way but blood and eye cold made them stick together. When he tried to sit up Tarik backed away. He didn't want to lose control. Phil's head was pounding from a hangover. He reached out to ask for Tricia's help. Tricia looked back at Tarik, "what should we do?"

"We can get back to the hospital and see about Melissa and the baby. He's no use to us."

Phil recognized Tarik's voice. "Tricia, I need help. My arm is broken and my body is too sore to move. Please help me up."

"Oh, your bitch ass is in need of help, huh? Why should we help you after you left Melissa in here for dead?" Tarik yelled.

"Twice!" Tricia added.

"I know I was wrong, but I need to get to the hospital. My arm is broken and I don't want to make it worse. You don't know how much pain I'm in right now."

"You shouldn't feel anything the way it smells in here," Tricia said.

Phil reached out and Tricia pulled his arm to help him sit up. Tarik didn't budge. He refused to help Phil.

"Tarik, lets at least take him back to the emergency room on the way back to Melissa. We can't leave him here like this," Tricia pleaded.

"Oh yes we can! Let's go!"

"Tarik stop! Help me get him to the car," Tricia said.

"If you wanna help his punk ass, that's on you. I'm not doing shit to help! As a matter of fact, I'm waiting in the car." He left the room and ran down the steps two at a time.

Tricia helped Phil to his feet and ushered him down the steps. It was hard because Phil could hardly move.

She finally helped him in the back seat and jumped in the passenger's side. Tarik drove like a bat out of hell. He broke all the traffic laws to make it back to the hospital. Tricia went inside the emergency room and got a doctor to assist with Phil. The doctor grabbed a wheelchair and they rushed Phil inside. Tarik pulled the car into the parking lot while Tricia waited for him to return.

They left Phil in the emergency room to fend for himself while they went up to Melissa's room.

Chapter 54

Tarik opened the door to Melissa's room. She was staring at the window with tears in her eyes. He went to her and held her hand. "What's wrong?"

"Tarik, I can't believe I got myself in so much trouble!"

"Don't worry about any of that right now. I have to tell you something that's going to affect Christopher," he said.

"What? Tell me!" she said frantically.

Tricia walked into the room with Dr. Watters and Dr. Carter. They stood around the room while Tarik told them that Phil was drunk.

"Damn it! We can't test his blood if he's intoxicated," Dr. Carter said.

Dr. Watters exhaled. She really felt sorry for Melissa. She closed her eyes before she spoke. "Melissa, I'm sorry to tell you but if Christopher doesn't get a blood transfusion within the next three days, things will take a turn for the worse."

"Oh my goodness! What are we going to do?" Melissa shouted. "We have to save my baby. If I give more blood, what would happen to me?"

"I can't take anymore blood from you Melissa. I told you that you lost a lot of blood during childbirth and almost even more during your ordeal. There's no way I could even consider taking blood from you," she said with concern.

Dr. Carter looked at Melissa with tears in his own eyes. He really felt for his friend.

Tricia hugged Tarik and cried silently on his shoulder. He rubbed her back with one hand and squeezed Melissa's hand with the other. He pulled Tricia off of him and looked Trish straight in the eyes, "it's gonna be ok."

Tricia bent down to the side of the bed and hugged Melissa. "Don't worry sweetie, we'll figure something out."

Tarik looked at the two women then at the doctors. His eyes filled with tears as he looked back to Tricia. She was so supportive of Melissa but he needed to do what was right.

"Dr. Watters, can you test my blood?" Tarik asked just as Dr. Carter was getting ready to speak.

Everyone in the room became silent. Tricia stepped away from Melissa and looked at Tarik.

"Tarik, the parents are usually the best matches in an incident like this. The likelihood of a friend being a match is almost impossible," Dr. Carter said.

"Tarik, what are you doing?" Melissa asked through a painfully frowned face.

"Tarik, that's nice of you to offer, but like Dr. Carter said only the parents would have the best chance to match," Tricia said as she took his hand into hers and smiled.

Tarik looked at her and stroked her face. He turned to Dr. Watters and held his head down. He lifted it back up just before he spoke, "well, there's a chance that I am Christopher's father."

Tricia looked on nervously. "Baby, I know you wanna help but taking blood tests that aren't going to match is a waste of time," she smiled nervously.

"Trish, I'm so sorry but we've wasted enough time. There's a chance that Christopher is my son."

Dr. Watters and Dr. Carter looked at each other. Dr. Watters knew that they should excuse themselves but watching Melissa's life was like watching a soap opera. It was drama from the first time she met Melissa. She stepped back and pretended to write something in Melissa's chart.

Dr. Carter looked at Tarik for any signs of a joke. He looked at Melissa, who had her face in her hands crying like a baby.

"You're serious?" he asked.

"I'm serious Dr. Carter. Let's stop wasting time and get me tested," Tarik said.

"Tarik, what the hell are you talking about?" Tricia asked. She looked at Melissa who kept her face covered. "Are you saying that you and Melissa...?"

"Trish, I didn't mean for you to find out this way. I..."

"You and Melissa?" She turned to Melissa, "you bitch! I trusted you! You smiled in my face all this time knowing you were fucking my husband?" Tricia reached out and grabbed Melissa's neck. She was able to choke her for at least thirty seconds before she was pulled off. Tarik grabbed Tricia while Dr. Carter pried her hands from around Melissa's neck.

"Tricia, I'm sorry! It really wasn't like that. I didn't mean for any of this to happen." Melissa tried to apologize and grasp for air at the same time.

Tarik kept a tight grip on Tricia to ensure she didn't attacked again.

"After all I've done for you? This is how you thank me? I risked my relationship covering for you while Phil beat the shit outta you! You begged and pleaded that I didn't tell Tarik knowing that it would affect my relationship if he ever found out. As your friend, I agreed to deceive my husband and you go behind my back and not only fuck him but get pregnant by him too?" Tricia shook her head.

Dr. Watters slipped out of the room to get security. Although she wanted to see how it all played out, Melissa was still her patient and she couldn't see her in danger.

"Get the fuck off of me Tarik! You are no better than her! I wasn't enough woman for you? Is that it? You go behind my back and fuck someone who pretended to be my friend?"

"Tricia, I am your friend. You have to believe me when I say that it just happened. We didn't plan any of this," Melissa stuttered.

"I don't wanna hear shit from you. You fucking LIAR!" Tricia shouted.

The security officer came into the room with Dr. Watters. "I'm here to escort you out of the building ma'am," he pointed to Tricia.

"I'm not going anywhere until I get some fuckin' answers!" she demanded.

"Trish, please. Don't do this here?" Tarik begged.

"Fine, lets go home. We can do this there!" Trish yelled.

"Baby, you know I can't leave. We have to see if I'm a match for Christopher," he said.

"You're telling me that you're not coming with me?" she asked.

"Trish, I have to do what's right. I'm not going to let my son…"

"Your son?" she asked. It did something to her to hear her husband refer to Christopher as his son. She lifted her head and looked him in the eyes, "FUCK YOU!" She looked over at Melissa, "AND FUCK YOU TOO!" She pushed past Dr. Carter and ran out of the room.

Chapter 55

S imone used her key to Mom's house and unlocked the door. She was so upset when she got off the phone with Tricia. She rushed right over to find out what had her friend so upset. Simone walked into the house and called out to Moms and Tricia. She didn't get an answer so she picked up the phone and dialed Tricia's cell. She heard the ringing phone on the other side of the door and hung up the phone. She rushed to the door and swung it open.

Tricia stood there crying. Simone looked around to see if she was alone. She pulled Trish inside the house and locked the door. "What's up? What happened?" she asked.

Tricia reached out and hugged Simone. She cried until she couldn't breathe. Simone tried over and over to find out what was going on. It was an hour later when Tricia lifted her head from Simone's shoulder.

"Talk to me, Trish. Is everything ok?"

Tricia tried to speak but no words come out of her mouth. "You want some water or something?" Simone asked.

"I'll take something," Tricia said between sniffs. Simone went to the fridge and grabbed a bottle of wine. She returned to the living room and handed Tricia a glass and the wine. Tricia sat the glass on the table and twisted the top off the bottle. She put the bottle to her mouth and drank until half the bottle was gone.

"Whoa…gimme that." Simone grabbed the bottle. "Trish, talk to me. What's going on? Is Melissa ok?"

Tricia began to cry again at the mentioning of Melissa's name. Simone rubbed her back and handed her some tissues.

"Simone, I don't even know where to begin."

"Start from the part that got you this upset."

Tricia straightened herself up on the sofa. She looked at Simone and wiped her tears away. "Tarik is fucking Melissa!" she blurted.

"What? What are you talking about?" Simone inquired.

"And Christopher is his son," Tricia sang.

"WHAT!"

"Well, I don't know for sure if he's his son but there's a chance," Tricia said.

"Ok Trish, start from the beginning and tell me what happened," Simone said in a serious tone.

Tricia grabbed the wine bottle and drank what was left before she proceeded to tell Simone the entire story. She didn't leave out any detail. She cried through the entire story. Simone tried to calm her but she really didn't know the right words to say.

"So what are you gonna do?" Simone asked.

"I don't know. I do know that Melissa's ass is mine when she gets the fuck outta there!" Tricia yelled.

"Trish, I know you're upset but think about this for a minute. Tarik is your husband. You need to think about him."

"What about him? That muthafucka cheated on me! And now that I think about it, he fucked her before we were married. I don't know how long this has been going on! So FUCK Tarik!" she spat.

Simone looked at her friend and felt her pain. She knew how it felt to find out your man cheated. She let Tricia vent for the next half hour.

Simone picked up the ringing phone and raised her eyes as she heard Tarik's voice on the other end.

"Trish, its Tarik." Simone held the phone away as she spoke.

"Hang up on that bastard! I ain't got shit to say to him!" Tricia screamed.

Simone looked at the phone and took a deep breath. "Tarik, she really doesn't want to talk right now."

She listened to him and then put the phone back in its cradle.

Tricia went to the phone and dialed *60 to block his number from the phone. She sat on the sofa and heard her cell phone ringing. She looked at the number and flipped it open, "GO TO HELL TARIK!" She turned the phone off.

Mrs. Hobbs pulled up in front of her house driving Marv's car. She turned to him and displayed a disappointing look.

"What's wrong baby?" he asked.

"It looks like Tricia and Simone are here," she said as she looked at their cars. "Would you mind if I came by your house later tonight. I need to find out what's going on. They don't meet at my house unless there's a problem," she explained.

"Sure," he said in a defeated tone.

"Marv, I know this is a pain in the ass, but we agreed that it's for the best until the trial is over. And as you can see, my family is a little dysfunctional," Maryanne laughed.

"I can't wait until this trial starts." He kissed her on the lips then watched her get out of the car. She waited for him to get in the driver's seat and pull off before she walked into her house.

Maryanne stared at the two women and knew that they'd been crying. "Is everything ok? How is Melissa and the baby?" she asked.

Simone looked at Tricia and signaled for her to tell what happened. Tricia returned the look and started to cry. "I can't do this again. Simone please tell Moms what happened."

Mrs. Hobbs sat next to Tricia and hugged her. "What's wrong baby?" She looked at Simone for answers. Simone took a deep breath and told Moms what happened. She told the story exactly as Tricia did.

Mrs. Hobbs sat back and listened intently. She wanted to take Tricia's pain away but she knew this was only something time and communication would heal. She looked from the two of them and let a tear slip from her own eye. She quickly wiped it and lifted Tricia's head to meet her eyes.

"Aw Shit!" Mrs. Hobbs said. She didn't want to upset Trish any more. She held her daughter and let her cry in her arms.

Simone sat back and watched for a minute. She excused herself and went into the kitchen. She put on a pot of coffee and made sandwiches. She took the tray to the living room and went back to grab another bottle of wine. She gave Tricia a cup of coffee. And she poured two glasses of wine. She handed one to Moms and sat down. Tricia sipped the coffee and took a bite of the turkey and cheese sandwich. Simone heard her phone vibrate and took it out of her purse. She looked at the number and then at Tricia, "it's Tarik."

"Simone, I don't want to talk to him!" Tricia yelled.

Simone sent the call to voicemail then turned it off.

"Tricia, I know you're hurting, baby. But I can't see Tarik cheating on you. I think you should find out what he has to say," Moms said.

"Momma, I don't want to hear it right now! You know the worse part about all of this? Besides how I had to find out, Tarik had the nerve to stay there with Melissa while I had to leave!"

"Trish, you didn't expect him to walk out on a baby that may be his did you?" Mrs. Hobbs asked.

"I don't know. He could have at least asked me to stay with him while he gave the blood. He just let me walk out of there and didn't say anything," Tricia blurted.

"Trish, I think he was trying to calm the situation. You did say that you choked Melissa up," Moms said.

"Momma please don't sit here and defend him."

"Baby, I'm not defending him. I'm pissed with Tarik. There's no excuse for what he did. But you are his wife and that means for better or worse. I do know that he loves you. You need to at least ask yourself is this worth ending your marriage. And you can't do that unless you talk to him. Don't try to save face in front of us because you're the one who has to make a decision. Never mind what you think people are going to say about you. Besides, you made a mistake too," Mrs. Hobbs said.

Tricia stared at her mother. She couldn't believe her ears.

"Don't look at me like that. True love doesn't come around that often, don't let it slip away! You'll always be wondering what happened if you don't at least hear him out," Mrs. Hobbs said. She looked at Simone and sipped her glass of wine.

"Trish, maybe Moms have a point. It's no secret that Tarik loves you. You never know what you are willing to forgive unless you hear him out. Look at me and Kareem. I forgave him for what he's done to me and look at us now. We have never been better. I wish you would at least think about it. Tarik is your soul mate. Don't let him off the hook that easily," she said with an evil smirk.

Tricia thanked them both for being there with her. She told them that she wanted to lay down for a little while. She excused herself and went upstairs.

Chapter 56

Melissa sat in the chair next to her bed. She had been crying for hours. When Tarik told everyone that he may be Christopher's father, she wanted to run and hide. Seeing Tricia so upset made her hurt even more. The last thing she wanted was to hurt Trish.

Tarik walked into the room and sat on the bed.

"Tarik just leave me alone. I need to be by myself."

"Look Lissa, I'm sorry. You know I didn't want to hurt Tricia either but what other choice did I have? Christopher's life is at stake," he said.

"I don't want to hear it. You should have at least waited until the doctors were gone. Can you imagine how embarrassed Tricia felt standing here while you told everyone that we had an affair? You actually thought she wasn't going to snap?" Melissa asked through tears.

"I wasn't thinking about that at the time. I had to do something. You heard Dr. Watters say that Christopher needed to have the transfusion within the next few days."

"I heard her but you didn't give anyone a chance to respond!" She leaned on the bed and sobbed harder.

"I said I'm sorry. I don't know what else to say. You don't think I'm pissed either? You think I wanted my wife to know that I slept with my best friend? I didn't mean for her to find out like this! I can't even get her to talk to me. She won't return my calls! And I'm here with you and the baby, how do you think that makes me feel? I'm here because if I'm the father, this is where I should be! I don't like seeing her hurt like this, SHIT!" he cursed.

"Ok Tarik, lets stop pointing the finger at each other. We both knew that we messed up when we did it. I don't want us to fall out. I really wish that you and Tricia can work it out. I don't mean to sound selfish but I don't have anyone else. I really need you right now," Melissa said.

"Lissa' I know you need someone right now and I'm always going to be here for that baby. I need…"

"I'm not talking about as my baby's father. I mean as my friend," she said.

"Look, I told you before that I'm not going to let anything come between us again."

"Think about Tricia. She's not going to want you around me if you two work it out."

"Not *if* we work it out, *when* we work it out. Tricia has to forgive me because I didn't do anything she didn't do with Simone. We'll forgive each other and start fresh."

"I hope you're right. I don't want to be the cause of your marriage ending," Melissa said.

Dr. Carter tapped on the door and waited for Melissa to invite him inside. He opened the door and stood by the bed. "I stopped in for two reasons. First, I want to let you know that the blood tests won't come back until tomorrow. We'll know if we can use Tarik or not then. Second, I wanted to give you an update on your husband." Dr. Carter opened the chart he carried and read some notes to himself. "Mr. Monroe has severe injuries. His left arm is broken in two places. His eye is blackened with cuts underneath. He has a fractured leg and he has bruises all over his body. He was beat pretty bad but he'll recover."

Melissa stared at Dr. Carter. She noticed that he kept his attention in the chart and never once looked up at her. She glanced over at Tarik to see his expression. He was nonchalant and acted as if he didn't hear Dr. Carter.

"Thanks Mike. I appreciate the update. Will you be here in the morning for the transfusion?" she asked.

"Of course. You don't have to worry about that. I'll see you later," he said as he walked out of the room.

Melissa climbed back into bed. "You really did a number on him, huh?"

"Fuck him! He deserved it. Don't go getting all soft on me. You did tell me to kick his ass," Tarik said.

"I know. I meant it too. I took a look at my face and realized that this has to stop," she said.

"We gotta talk, Lissa."

"I know. We may as well get it over with while there's so much time to kill. You know waiting for the results and all."

Tarik positioned himself on the bed so that he was face to face with Melissa.

"Let me start by saying I'm sorry. I should have told you about Phil a long time ago. He never stopped hitting me. The last time he did it, I made Tricia promise not to tell you. I know you Tarik. I know you would have killed my husband. That was just something I wasn't willing to live with," she said.

"No, I'm not blaming you for anything. You know I love you Lissa. I just want you to be happy. I see the way Phil keeps you secluded. That's why I asked Tricia to keep an eye out for you. I knew once you started hanging around Trish that Phil was gonna start trippin'. So I don't blame you for her decision not to tell me. I understand why she kept it from me. But the most important person in this whole ordeal is Christopher. So I'm asking you what are you going to do?"

"I don't know Tarik. This is going to sound silly, maybe even stupid. But, I still love my husband." She looked away.

Tarik sighed before he spoke. "Well, I mean it when I say that if Christopher is my son I don't want him being raised by Phil. I also meant when I said that I'll seek custody so that you won't be around him either as long as you're with Phil. He won't get the chance to kill my son! You're grown and I can't tell you what to do..."

"I get it. But I still think you're jumping the gun. I still believe that Phil is Christopher's father."

"Didn't he tell you that there was no way he could be the father?" Tarik asked.

"I think Phil was just trying to see if I cheated on him."

"Why would he think you cheated? Unless he knew for a fact that he can't have kids."

Dr. Carter tapped on the door again. "Melissa, I'm sorry to disturb you but you have a visitor. He insisted that he see you tonight." Dr. Carter turned around and pushed the wheelchair into the room. Phil held his head towards Melissa and looked at her. He was disgusted by the way she looked. He hadn't realized that he'd beat her like that.

Tarik stood and walked towards Phil. "Nah, he gotta go!"

"Tarik wait! Let him stay," Melissa asked.

"I'm not leaving you alone with him. Are you crazy?" he asked.

"Then you stay as long as you keep it under control."

"I'll wait outside," Dr. Carter said.

"No Mike, will you stay too? I may need your assistance," Melissa said as she looked at Tarik.

Phil could hardly speak. His face was swollen and his lip was cut. "Lissa, I lo...love y...you. I'm so...sorry a bout what happened. I'm al so sorry a bout Chris...topher."

"Phil if you weren't so drunk, we could have had the transfusion today!" Melissa shouted through her pain.

"I told...you that I'm n...not the fa...ther." Phil took a deep breath and continued. "I had a vac..sec...tomy years a...go. I never wan...ted kids. I went to my doc...tor and tried to get it re versed so that we could try for a baby. He told me that it didn't work. I still can't have kids. I'm n...n...not the fa...ther. I wasn't lying about that. My blood type would not match Chris...to...pher's."

Melissa tried to control her crying but she couldn't. Tarik went to her side and hugged her. She looked at Dr. Carter and shook her head. "I can't believe this."

"Mr. Monroe, you need to get back into bed. I'm going to have to take you back." Dr. Carter pushed Phil out of the room.

"I love you Me...lis...sa." Phil mumbled as he got out of the door. Dr. Carter glanced back at Melissa and shook his head. He closed the door and returned Phil to his room. Melissa was

200

speechless and embarrassed. She didn't know what to say to Tarik. He held her as she cried herself to sleep.

Chapter 57

Kareem sat up from the sofa as Simone put the key in the door. He didn't want her to suspect anything so he ended Shelly's call like he was talking to one of the guys.

She sat next to him on the sofa and put her head on his shoulder. "Hey baby," she said as she snuggled under him.

"Hey, what up?" he asked.

"I just had the worst day. I was with Tricia and Moms all day." She proceeded to tell him what happened. He hugged her and told her he'd run her a nice bubble bath.

"You just sit here and wait. I'll get everything together while you just sit here and relax," Kareem said.

"Thanks baby. I really appreciate this," Simone said.

Kareem went to the bathroom and ran a bath. He then went into the bedroom to get toiletries. He gently shook Simone and guided her to the bath. He undressed her and helped her to the tub.

Kareem pampered her inside of the tub. He sat on the side and scrubbed her back. He took the bar of soap and rubbed it over her breasts until they were rock hard. He took the washcloth and squeezed water over her breasts. Kareem got on his knees and began to suck her nipples. Simone sat back and enjoyed the sensation she was feeling. She moaned in pleasure as he made her feel good. She grabbed the back of his head and kissed him hard on the mouth. She tried to pull him inside the tub. He broke from her grip and made her stand up.

He took the towel and dried her from head to toe. She slid her feet inside of her slippers. Kareem dressed her in the nightie he chose for her to wear. She smiled and kissed the back of his neck. He carried her to the bedroom where there was a jazz cd playing in the background. The lights were dimmed as he placed her on the bed. Kareem went to the kitchen and grabbed two wine glasses and a bottle of wine. He took them to the bedroom and filled both glasses halfway. He and Simone toasted to a new beginning and took a sip of wine. He reached over and grabbed her glass. He pushed her back on the bed and pushed up her nightie. Kareem poured the remainder of his wine down Simone's body. He pulled her to the edge of the bed while he got down on his knees. He licked the wine from her body in slow motion. He made sure to spend a little extra time in her special areas. He did this until there were no traces of wine left.

Simone enjoyed the special treatment. She didn't realize that she was so horny. Kareem made up for lost time. He took his time and made love to her. She enjoyed every minute.

Once they finished, she lay in his arms and smiled.

"Whatchu thinkin' about?" he asked.

"I'm thinking how much I'll miss this if we don't win this case. I'm not sure if I'll be able to make it in jail."

"Hey, stop worrying about that. We are not going to jail. At least you ain't going to jail. And if I do get locked up, I'm not gonna get more than a year."

"A year? That's a long time for us to be apart. I'm not sure I can handle it," Simone said.

"Baby, Mr. Woodsby said that we'll be ok. Let's just trust him and see what happens. We have the rest of the week to prepare. Let's not spend this time with negative thoughts." Kareem kissed her on the cheek and she smiled.

She went to sleep with a smile on her face.

Kareem was wide awake. For some reason, he couldn't get Shelly off his mind. He needed to find a way to end their relationship before the trial. He didn't want to be involved with her if he was sent to jail. Simone deserved to have him all to herself. He thought about how to get out of the bed he made for himself to sleep in.

Chapter 58

Tricia opened the door to her apartment and saw Tarik with his head on the kitchen table. He jumped up when he heard the door open.

"Hey Boo," he said as he ran to her.

She brushed past him and went to the bathroom. She closed and locked the door behind her. After ten minutes, Tarik knocked on the door. "Trish, come out here, we need to talk."

"Tarik, I don't have anything to say to you. Go AWAY!" she yelled.

"I'm not leaving until we talk. At least tell me to my face that you don't want to be bothered."

Tricia remained in the bathroom and turned on the shower. She stepped into the hot water and let it wash her tears away. She tried to wash off every spot that Tarik had touched. She scrubbed until her skin was raw. The water started to burn. She turned it off and snatched a towel from the rack.

"Trish, please just talk to me. I'm not leaving until we talk," he begged.

Tricia wrapped the towel around her body and unlocked the door. She stepped out of the bathroom and went to the bedroom. Tarik followed close behind. Tricia went to her drawer and removed a pair of underwear. When she bent down to slip them on, her towel fell to the floor.

"Boo, what happened to you?" Tarik asked as he saw the rawness of her skin. He walked towards her to try to feel her back.

"Ouch! Don't touch me. It hurts," she said.

"Why did you do this to yourself?" he asked.

"I didn't do anything, you did this to me. You wanted to make me hurt? I'm hurt," she said through teary eyes.

"Tricia, you know that I never meant to hurt you. I love you Boo," he pleaded.

"Don't do that! Don't say you love me. You made a fuckin' fool outta me! How could you fuck Melissa? Of all the people in the world, why her?"

"Baby just listen to me. It was a mistake. I'm sorry you had to find out like that but you gotta believe me. We were drunk and we were talking then things got a little out of control...we just..."

"You expect me to buy that? Why is this so different from what I told you about me and Simone?" she hissed.

Tarik was dumbfounded. He didn't know what to say.

"You want me to forgive you for fucking your best friend but I told you the same thing about my best friend and you tried to make me out to be a cheating slut! And all the while you had fucked Melissa? And to make matters worse, you may have gotten her pregnant! That's love, huh?" Tricia said as she made her way to the closet. She snatched a pair of jeans off a hanger and sat on the bed to put them on.

Tarik looked at her and shook his head. He really didn't know how to defend himself. He knew that Tricia was absolutely right. "Trish, please. I wanna work this out. Let's just forgive each other for what we did and save our marriage."

Tricia looked like she'd seen a ghost. She couldn't believe what she was hearing. Tarik sounded so sincere. He said all the things that she needed to hear at that moment. But she didn't know how to begin to forgive Tarik for him and Melissa. She looked at him and shook her head.

"Trish, you're being hypocritical. You begged me to forgive you and now you won't even consider the same thing. That's selfish!"

"Uh uh. Don't you dare try to flip the script on me! The last time we talked, you told me that you didn't know if you can get past that. So don't come in here trying to make me out to be the bad guy. We both fucked up! I trusted Melissa. I asked you from day one if there was a chance that you and her were more than friends! You assured me that you had no feelings for her like that. She even assured me that you two were platonic friends!"

"And I still have no feelings for her. I love Melissa like a sister; Nothing more!"

"Tarik now is not the time for you to try and insult my intelligence. You fucked her with no protection! What if you are that baby's father?" she paused, "oh my goodness! How could she ask me to be the godmother of a child that may be my stepson?"

"Trish, Melissa doesn't really believe that I'm the father. That was the last thing on her mind when she asked you to be the godmother," Tarik said. He didn't want to tell her about Phil's confession.

"Don't you dare stand here and defend her!! Are you outta ya mind?" Tricia said as she got in his face.

He grabbed her hands and sat her back down on the bed. He saw the conversation taking a turn for the worse. He really didn't want to rub her the wrong way. He knew she was upset and needed to vent but he also knew that Tricia would haul off and hit his ass if she was mad enough. "Baby, lets just take this thing slow. Why don't you come back to the hospital with me and we can find out together if Christopher is my son," he urged.

"You think you slick. You just wanna get back to Melissa. I know you are worried about her and that baby but, you need to be more concerned about our marriage and if there's a chance in hell that we'll be able to repair it!" She eased back on the bed and tried to calm herself. She loved Tarik more than anything. She wanted to take him in her arms and forget about both of their indiscretions. She sat on the edge of the bed and cried. She hung her head low and shook her head.

Tarik grabbed her and hugged her. He put her head on his shoulder. He gently caressed her back and played with her hair. She accepted his hug and cried on his shoulder.

After another three hours of talking, screaming and yelling, Tricia agreed to go with him to the hospital to see if he was Christopher's father.

Tarik showered and got dressed. He grabbed a few things then grabbed Tricia's hand.

"Wait a minute. I wanna call Simone and ask her to meet me there," she said.

"Why? I'm going to be there with you."

"No, you're gonna be there for Melissa. And if you're the father, you're gonna be there for the baby to give the transfusion. And while you're in the operating room, I'm going to need someone to talk me out of whooping Melissa's ass!" She picked up the phone and quickly put it back down. "Tarik, I can't do this. I don't need to be around Melissa right now. You just go and call me with the results. I'm too close to her and the baby. It hurts so much knowing you slept with her. I can't even look at her right now!" Tricia said.

"Baby, don't do this. I need you by my side. I want you to be right there when I hear the news. Please Boo! I need you," he pleaded.

Tricia looked at her husband and shook her head no.

"Baby, let me ask you something. You forgave Simone for what she did, how come you won't forgive Melissa?"

"How could you ask me something like that? You know how long it took for me to even look at Simone, let alone talk to her. And it's different with Melissa. She smiled in my face for months knowing she fucked you. That's just trifling! Don't ever use what happened with me and Simone to try and rectify this situation! I can't believe you asked that!" She was furious all over again.

"I'm sorry baby. I didn't mean it like that. I'm just trying to get you to understand that Melissa is just as sorry as I am. She's just as hurt as we are about the whole situation but I need to be at the hospital. I really want you to be right by my side. If the baby is mine, I need you to be there before I go to give the blood."

Tricia exhaled. She was confused. She wanted to be there for her husband but she didn't know how. She was not the type of person who could just switch off her emotions. Even when she and Simone were on bad terms, she thought about her well-being. Even with all the drama, she didn't wish any bad luck to Melissa and the baby. "Tarik, I can't. I'll stay here. Call me later."

"No, I need my wife by my side. If you'll feel better with Simone there, then call her from the car." Tarik pulled Tricia by the hand and locked the apartment door behind them.

Once they were inside of the car Tricia turned to her husband. "I have one question for you: You said that Melissa doesn't believe that Christopher is your son but do you believe it?"

"Yes. I think he's my son. We all know that Phil doesn't believe he's the father." He kept his focus on the road. He couldn't bear to look at the hurt on Tricia's face.

Chapter 59

Maryanne Hobbs put the phone back in its cradle and looked over at Marvin. He was rubbing her lower back.

"I tell you Marv, if it ain't one thing, it's another. Tricia is really going through something right now and it's killing me that I can't do a damn thing to help."

"Sweetie, I'm sure everything will work out. The one thing you don't have to worry about is the trial. Things are beginning to fall into place. I am ready to defend my clients," he said while shaking his head up and down.

"What's going on? Is there something I need to know about the trial? The last thing I need is another surprise. I've had too many of those this week alone," she said.

"Well you know it's not ethical for me to discuss the details with you, but I don't want you to worry about Simone or Kareem. They'll be fine." He assured her as he rolled over.

"Where are you going?" Maryanne asked.

"I have to get to the office. I just remembered that I asked some clients to meet me there to tie up a few loose ends. I'll see you later?" he asked as he headed to the shower.

"You sure will because I'm staying here all day. I really don't feel like being bothered with anyone today. I'm hiding out."

"That's fine with me. I'd love for you to be here when I get back," he smiled.

Maryanne was watching TV when Marvin walked into the bedroom wearing a towel. She noticed his soldier standing at attention. She eased her way to him as he sat down to put on his socks. She slipped her hand between his legs as an attempt to put the soldier at ease.

Marvin rolled his head back and moaned. He was enjoying the attention. Maryanne used her hand and aroused his penis. If Marvin didn't know better, he'd have thought she was using her mouth. He positioned himself on the bed and pulled her hair. This brought out the freak in Maryanne.

She slid down to the floor and got on her knees. She covered his penis with her mouth. She slowly bobbed her head up and down until Marvin was about to explode. He moved her head and used his hand to catch his thick cream. Maryanne watched with excitement. She swung her hair and continued where she'd left off. She looked up at him as she took him in her mouth. She watched his facial expressions and smiled on the inside.

Marvin looked down and their eyes met. He gently guided her head up and down his shaft. She watched him the entire time while his body shook and jerked with excitement. When he could no longer take it, he got on the floor behind her and rode her doggystyle.

His slow pumps quickly turned into a race. He grabbed her hair and leaned forward on her back. Maryanne grabbed his penis and forced it in and out of her while she watched his face. Marvin opened his eyes and saw her watching. He lost control and exploded all over her ass cheeks. Maryanne smiled and continued to massage him. She turned and faced him and kissed him on the neck.

Marvin's breathing finally slowed as he walked back to the bathroom. He came out wearing boxers this time. Maryanne was on her way to sleep when he sat next to her on the bed. He continued to get dressed. When he was ready to go, he kissed her on the forehead. He looked at her and smiled. He thought, *Not too many women is gonna watch while she's giving her man some head.* That separates the women from the girls. He took his smile and walked out the door.

Marvin arrived at his office the same time as Brian Castro and Belinda Chaste. Brian held the door open for everyone then followed them inside of Marvin's office.

"Would anyone like some coffee or tea?" Marvin asked.

"Not for me," Brian said.

"I'll have tea please," Belinda smiled.

Marvin buzzed the receptionist and asked her to bring the tea. "Now let's get down to business. You have something to tell me Brian?"

"As a matter of fact, I do. I just found out that Dr. Phil Monroe was rushed to the emergency room a couple of nights ago."

"What happened to him?" Belinda asked in a slightly alarmed manner.

"He was beaten up pretty good. He's been admitted," Brian said.

"Who did it? Will he be available for court next week?" Marvin asked.

"That's all I know right now. You'll know something as soon as I do."

Belinda accepted the tea from the receptionist and dropped two packets of sugar inside. She stirred the tea and sipped it slowly. She tried not to look worried but she was sure it was all over her face.

"Ok, just make sure to keep me informed. I need him to be ready for cross examination," Marvin said.

"No problem," he said and turned to Belinda. "The movie is starting soon so we'd better be leaving if we want to catch the early showing."

Belinda smiled and placed the tea on a coaster while she put on her coat. "Mr. Woodsby, when do you think you'll be needing my services?" she asked.

"If all goes according to plan, I'll have you back on a plane in no time. You won't even have to appear in court. I'll let you know by day two of the trial. Brian, I need you to be there from the beginning," Marvin smiled.

"Thanks," she said dryly. She walked ahead of Brian and waited by the reception desk.

"Is she ok? She didn't change her mind did she?" Marvin asked Brian.

"She'll be fine. She just really wants to get this over with," Brian assured. "I think you should use her testimony as soon as possible though." Brian closed the door as he walked out of the office.

Chapter 60

Tricia waited in the waiting area while Tarik went to visit Melissa. He tried his best to get her to come with him but she insisted that she wait for Simone in the wait area.

He walked into the room and found Melissa sleeping. She looked so peaceful and tired at the same time. He sat next to her on the bed and held her hand. She tossed and pulled her hand away.

Tarik backed away from the bed so he wouldn't wake her. He knew that she was tired and needed her rest.

Dr. Carter and Dr. Watters entered the room. "We have the results." Dr. Watters announced.

Tarik gently shook Melissa to wake her. She sat up and spoke to everyone in the room. "They have the results Lissa. I just need to run out and grab Trish," he said.

"She's here?" Melissa asked.

"Yeah, she's in the waiting room. I'll be right back. Just sit tight for a minute." He walked out of the room.

Dr. Watters asked Melissa how she was feeling. Melissa told her that she was feeling ok but she was worried about her son. She also told the Dr. that her face was hurting. Dr. Watters held her hand as a means of comfort. She told Melissa that her face was sore due to the amount of talking she'd been doing the past couple of days.

Tarik stepped into the room with Tricia in tow.

"Hello Tricia," Dr. Carter spoke.

"Hi Dr. Carter, Dr. Watters." She nodded her head towards them.

Melissa looked at Tricia who wouldn't even look her way. She lowered her head to cover her shame. Dr. Carter walked to the bed and held Melissa's hand.

"Well, let's get started. Is my blood compatible for the transfusion?" Tarik asked as he squeezed Tricia's hand.

"Tarik, we're not going to be able to use you for the transfusion. Christopher is not your son," Dr. Watters stated calmly.

"What!" Tarik exclaimed. "How is that possible, Lissa?"

Melissa hung her head low and cried out loud. She sobbed and wiped her eyes continuously. Dr. Watters excused herself and left the room. Dr. Carter gently hugged her and soothed her lower back.

Tarik stood there in shock. He didn't know what to say. He looked at Tricia who stood with her mouth hung open. Melissa covered her face and apologized to Tarik over and over again.

"I'm sorry too," Tricia whispered in Tarik's ear. She looked at Melissa and couldn't help feeling sorry for her. She stood next to the bed. "I hope everything works out Melissa." She squeezed her arm and hurried out of the room when she felt her own eyes fill with water. Tarik followed his wife.

Tarik walked Tricia to the waiting room. He asked to have a few minutes alone. Tricia rubbed his back and went to talk with Simone.

He paced the floor back and forth. He didn't know what else to do. He kept his head hung low. He was positive that he was Christopher's father. He also felt some sort of relief that he wasn't. At least he could try to reconcile with his wife. He'd thought all night about Tricia's feelings towards his having a son with Melissa. At least now Tricia wouldn't have to resent a child for his mistake.

Tarik walked over to Tricia and pulled her to the side.

"Baby, I know this may seem awkward or even unfair but I really need to talk to Melissa alone for a few minutes. I just can't abandon her. She needs a friend now more than ever. Do you mind?"

"Tarik, you can't be serious! You're really upset about not being the father? I thought you would be relieved but I see I was wrong. Do what you wanna do I'm out!" She walked away with Simone chasing behind her.

"Damn!" Tarik shouted. He didn't know what to do. He wanted to go after his wife but he knew that she had Simone. Melissa was in her room all alone stressed about the news. He looked in the direction Tricia ran then at the direction of Melissa. He ran after his wife but she and Simone were nowhere in sight.

Tarik walked back to Melissa's room shaking his head.

He entered the room and saw Melissa crying on Dr. Carter's shoulder. She was obviously upset. Her skin was beginning to regain its normal color but the swelling was still noticeable. Dr. Carter patted her back and reassured her that everything would be ok. He saw Tarik standing in the doorway and nodded the manly nod. He pulled back from Melissa and stared at her. She wouldn't lift her face to look him in the eye.

"Hey, everything will be ok. Let me go check a few things and I'll get back to you in a couple of hours. Promise me that you'll try to relax and get some rest." He shook Tarik's hand and walked out of the room.

Tarik sat on the bed next to Melissa. She edged off and limped into the bathroom. Tarik could hear her sobs over the running water. He just sat on the bed and gave her some time. The water stopped running after about ten minutes. He stood by the door to help her to the bed but she didn't come out of the bathroom.

"Melissa, come on out here."

"Tarik, I'm sorry. I'm really, really sorry."

"Don't worry about that right now, just come on out." Melissa unlocked the door and stepped out of the bathroom. She was welcomed by Tarik's open arms. He hugged her and led her back to the bed. "Just sit here." He opened his phone and called Tricia. He begged her to come back to the hospital. He told her that he really needed her to be by his side. She rejected a few times but he finally talked her into coming.

Chapter 61

Tricia and Simone were only in the lobby so they caught the elevator back up to Melissa's room. She asked Simone to go inside the room with her. She was going to be with Tarik but she also needed a friend by her side.

They walked into the room and saw Tarik consoling Melissa. Melissa pulled back when she felt the icy glare from Tricia's eyes. Tarik turned around and saw his wife. He stood up and greeted her with a hug and kiss. Tricia didn't show any emotion. She didn't even return his affection.

Simone stepped around Tricia and spoke to Tarik as she walked passed him. She went to Melissa and hugged her. "How are you holding up sweetie?" Simone asked.

"I'm ok I guess. It's good to see you," Melissa said as she wiped her eyes with the back of her hand.

Simone kissed Melissa on the forehead and gave her a sympathetic pat on the arm. She walked to the other side of the room. She knew Melissa was beat up but it was hard looking at someone that was once so beautiful. The swelling was still horrible.

"Trish, I wanted you here while Melissa and I talked." He looked over at Simone. "I was wondering if you could leave us alone," he said.

"No, she stays or I leave!" Tricia said.

"It's okay Tarik, Simone can stay. I'm ready to get all of this out in the open anyway. She's still a friend, right?" Melissa asked as she looked at Simone.

"Of course," Simone smiled.

Tricia pulled a chair by the window and sat down. Simone remained standing and Tarik sat on the bed next to Melissa.

Melissa held her head up. "Trish, I'm sorry. You have to believe that I didn't mean for any of this to happen."

"Melissa, please don't say anything to me. I'm only here because *my* husband insisted. I don't have anything to say to you right now!"

"Trish, hold up." Tarik looked around the room. "Please just calm down. There's no need to be rude."

"I agreed to come Tarik, but don't tell me how I should feel or act. I don't want *your* friend talking to me!"

Melissa held her head down. The thought of Tricia not considering her a friend anymore was humiliating. She understood that Tricia was upset and had every right to be. "It's okay Tarik, I understand how she feels."

The tap on the door made everyone turn to see who was entering the room. Phil slowly rolled himself into the room. Simone and Tricia looked at him and cringed. Tarik really did a number on him. Phil looked around the room and nodded to everyone. "Melissa, can we talk? Alone?"

"I'm glad you're here. You may as well be here while we all get everything out in the open," Melissa said.

Tarik was getting ready to object until he met Tricia's stare. He didn't want her to become upset again.

"Melissa, I heard about the blood tests and I'm sorry. What's going to happen now?" Phil slurred. He was in no condition to talk without cringing from pain.

"I'm not sure, Mike told me to sit tight and he's going to let me know my options."

Dr. Carter opened the door and was surprised to see everyone crowded in Melissa's room. "Uhm...I just came back with some news for you Melissa," he said.

"It's okay Mike. You can talk in front of everyone here. How is Christopher?" Melissa asked.

"That's why I'm here. He needs to have that transfusion. Dr. Watters wanted to test donated blood and see if we could get a match."

"That's good news right?" Tarik asked.

"If we got a match we'd still have to run the tests to make sure the blood is safe to use."

"So have you started the process?" Phil asked.

"Well," Dr. Carter hesitated.

"Well what?" Melissa asked.

"I've began the process of testing blood that matched. It's safer to have blood from a relative." Dr. Carter looked at Melissa.

She looked him in the eye and shook her head up and down.

"What does that mean?" Tarik asked.

"Go on Mike," Melissa urged.

"The blood I've had tested is my blood. I'm Christopher's father."

"What! Ouch!" Phil yelled and grabbed his face.

"I'm sorry that it had to come out like this." Dr. Carter turned to Melissa. "I wasn't going to interfere. I was going to let you do it your way but under the circumstances, I had to come forward."

Melissa just sat there numb. She was almost shocked. Although she'd slept with Mike twice, she didn't believe that he was Christopher's father. She was too ashamed to look at anyone in the room.

"Melissa? How could you?" Phil slurred and shook his head. "Who else were you fucking behind my back? I guess you weren't so lonely after all, huh?" He turned his wheelchair towards the door. Tarik moved towards Phil but Trish grabbed his arm.

"Wait Phil, it's not what you think. I'm…I just…It happened but…" Melissa couldn't find the words to say. She saw the hurt on her husband's face and lowered her head.

"Don't bother trying to explain. I know we haven't had the best marriage, but cheating?" He rolled himself out of the room.

"Damn Melissa!" Tricia said while Simone looked on with her mouth hung open. "I guess you put on a front for all of us. Tarik, did you know that she was out there like that?"

Dr. Carter told Melissa he'd be back when the results were done. He apologized to her again and left the room.

"Alright, let's all just sit down and talk this thing out," Tarik said.

"What is there to talk about? We know who the father is now. I'm leaving!" Tricia said.

"Tricia, please stay. I really want to get this off my chest. I'll make it quick," Melissa pleaded.

Tarik held Melissa's hand and tried to make her feel better. Tricia stood and walked towards her husband. "Tarik, I'm not going to stand here and watch you two sit here and make intimate passes at each other!"

"Intimate passes? What are you talking about?" Melissa asked.

"I'm talking about Tarik rubbing and touching you every chance he gets. Tarik, you're sitting here holding her hand rubbing her back and kissing her forehead like I'm not even sitting in the room!"

"Trish, I'm just consoling Melissa. You acting like we sitting here fucking," Tarik yelled.

"No, you've already done that! How do you think I feel sitting here watching all of this after finding out that you two fucked?" Tricia yelled.

"Baby, it's not like that," he said as he hugged her. He put her head on his shoulders while she let out her frustrations. "Please just sit and listen. I think we both owe it to ourselves to get to the bottom of this," he begged. He pulled her down and sat her on his lap. He squeezed her tight and kissed the back of her neck. Tricia got up and stood next to Tarik. "No! Let's get this over with," she mumbled.

Melissa took a deep breath then looked around the room Trish, do you remember the night I called you right after the three of us had dinner for the first time? I asked you if you wanted to bump our plans up to that night but you said you were meeting Simone for drinks. I was so lonely that night. I just wanted to be with someone and my husband wasn't around. Anyway, when you said you were busy, I called Mike. He and I went out and that was our first time together." Melissa controlled her emotions as she recalled and explained her night with Tarik.

Tricia expressed hurt and anger. She backed away from Tarik as he and Melissa told about their affair. Afterwards, she ran out of the room.

Chapter 62

Kareem sat on Shelly's sofa and waited for her to enter the apartment. She had called and told him that she was on her way upstairs. He'd called her earlier and told her that they needed to talk.

"Hey baby, what's up? You alright?" Shelly asked as she entered the apartment.

"I need to holla at you real quick. I been doing a lot of thinking about the trial."

Shelly sat down next to him. She removed her jacket and took a swallow from his beer can. "I know. I've been thinking about that too. It's hard to believe that it's going to happen in two days."

"Yeah, me and Simone was talking last night and I told her not to worry about nothing. I keep telling her that she won't do no jail time but I'm not so sure. I told the lawyer that I am going to take the blame for everything."

"What if you go to jail?" Shelly asked.

"Better me than her. I can't have my girl sitting up in no jail," he frowned.

"So where does that leave us if you go to jail?"

"Come on Shells, you know how I feel about you."

"But?"

"But you know that Simone and me are trying to work it out. I don't want to hurt you this time. I figure we could talk like two adults."

Shelly was furious. She really believed that Kareem would choose her this time. She never stopped loving Kareem and she wanted him all to herself. She had to do the only thing that she thought would work.

She sat next to him and pouted. She folded her arms like a child. She suddenly began to cry. Kareem leaned over and put his arms around her. He was hoping her little escapade would only last a few minutes. He needed to get back home to Simone. He'd spent every night at home with her all week. He didn't want to break the pattern.

Shelly pulled away from his embrace. She wiped her eyes and tried to smile at him. "I guess I always knew that I didn't stand a chance at having you."

Kareem looked at her with raised eyes. She was talking crazy. "Yo, whatchu talking about? I told you before that I wasn't leaving Simone for you or anybody else!"

"I know you said that but I just knew once you found out about her and Tricia, you would be out," Shelly said.

"What about her and Tricia?" he asked.

"What? You mean you don't know?" Shelly asked in an innocent voice.

"Stop playin' games and tell me Shelly!" he yelled.

"You don't have to yell. I…I…just thought you knew. Simone told me about what happened and I assumed that's why you two were having problems."

"What problems? It's all good with us. We ain't having no problems! So tell me about Trish!" He was getting upset.

"Well Simone told me that they were drinking one night and she pushed up on Trish."

"The fuck is you talkin' bout, pushed up?"

"She said that's why they had the fight. They were having sex and Tricia called out her boyfriend's name and Simone got mad. Tricia woke up and realized that it was Simone and went off!" Shelly told the entire story as Simone told it to her one night after sex.

"They did what?" Kareem yelled. "Nah, you trippin'"

"I really didn't want to tell you that. I'm sorry to be the one to break the news. Simone told me that a while ago. I thought that was when you two started having problems again."

Kareem felt like a fool. He didn't want to believe Shelly but the thought of it all being true made sense to him.

"Damn!" You better not be lying Shelly!" he warned.

"I told you before, I have no reason to lie. So does that mean that you and I can continue to see each other?" she asked.

"You must be outta yo mind! Just because you tell me some bullshit like this doesn't mean that I wanna be with you! Come on now, you gotta come better than that with this bullshit." He walked towards the door.

"Kareem wait." She realized that it didn't work. She had to take it to the next level. "Did Simone tell you why or how we became friends?" Shelly asked.

"You call yourself her friend? What kind of shit is that?" he hissed.

"No, we're not close friends anymore. Ever since you suggested that she and I can't be friends, she cut me off. I couldn't understand why she wanted you back after she saw our relationship for what it really was."

"Shelly, are you crazy? What the fuck is wrong with you yo?"

"I just wanted to see what was so good about Simone." Shelly said in a daze. It was like she forgot Kareem was standing in her apartment. She was in a zone. "I had to know why you would never leave her. When she made a pass at me, I didn't fight back. I went all the way to see what it was about her that you couldn't let go of."

Kareem went to Shelly and shook her. He knew she was making up that story. "What the fuck man? You can't be serious. You'll do anything to keep me in your life, huh?"

"Kareem, will you listen to me! At this point, I don't care if you walked out of here and never came back. I'm just telling you what happened. Me and her were fucking way before I popped up at that wedding. It was all a set up. She was supposed to dump your ass so we could be together. She told me she was done with your lying ass! I should have known that she was too in love with you to leave. Hell, I was just as in love with your lying ass! Why else would I go through all of this to be with you?"

"Yo, Shelly stop..." he interrupted.

"No, let me finish! You may not believe me but I can prove that I'm not lying. Think about it, Kareem. How else did I get to the wedding? I don't know Tricia or Tarik. Simone invited me. She even brought the dress I wore. I was going to be your surprise after the wedding. She was planning to reveal that you and her fucked the same woman! I didn't know what to expect so I brought a gun for protection. When I told Simone I had a gun, she snatched it out of my bag."

"Shut the fuck up you lying BITCH! I should knock you the fuck out!" he yelled, "I don't believe that bullshit! Anyway, Simone told me it was her gun!"

"She was protecting me from you. I told her that I was scared at what you would do if you found out I brought a gun. I can prove it to you," Shelly stated.

"Yeah, how?" he asked thinking that she was still running game.

"I'll call her right now while you listen on the other end. That way you can hear it from her mouth."

Kareem went to Shelly and pushed her on the sofa. "You fucking Bitch! Call her right now. I wanna see if this shit is true!"

"I'll call her but you can't say anything. Just listen and hear what she says. You have to promise me that you'll leave me out of it!"

"Bitch, you already in it. If what you're saying is true, she dragged your ass in it." He pulled her to the phone.

"Kareem, I didn't mean for you to find out this way. You are dumping me again and Simone dumped me a few weeks ago. I can't take this shit! After I call her, I don't wanna have anything else to do with neither one of you assholes!" Shelly stated.

"Just do it! I can't believe that you pulled some shit like that anyway. But you sittin' up here saying you love somebody. That's why you by yo damn self! You play too many games! Make the call!" He warned as he threw the cordless phone to her.

Kareem went into the bedroom and picked up the phone as soon as Shelly dialed Simone's cell number.

"Hello?" Simone asked.

"Hey Simone. What's up?" Shelly asked.

"Not much, I'm just sitting here waiting for Kareem to come home."

"Like I really wanna hear that," Shelly said.

"Look, my bad. Why are you calling me? Is everything ok?" Simone asked.

"No! I miss you like crazy. I wanna see you."

"Shelly, I told you that it's best if we didn't see each other any more. Besides, I have so much going on with the trial and everything. I don't have the time."

"Simone please? Let's make each other feel good one last time. There's no telling what could happen after the trial."

"Come on Shelly don't do that. We agreed that the last time was the last time. I'm working it out with my man. I don't need anymore drama. It was fun while it lasted but I'm gonna hafta pass. I'm sorry," Simone said.

"I'm sorry too. I thought we were still friends even though we can't be lovers anymore," Shelly said.

"We can't be friends if I'm trying to make it work with Kareem. I love him Shelly and I'm not going to risk it again. I must have been crazy to think that I could fuck someone that my man cheated with and be ok with it." Simone was clearly frustrated.

"Don't say I didn't tell you that he ain't shit! He'll be right back with the next woman who gives him the time. Bye Simone!" Shelly slammed the phone down. Kareem hung up too and came out to the living room. He looked at Shelly and shook his head. He couldn't believe that it was true. He couldn't think of anything to say.

Shelly watched him put his head in his hands and smiled to herself. Her mission was accomplished. She told Kareem the truth. She knew that Kareem would never consider being with her after he found out the truth but she didn't care. All she wanted was for Simone and Kareem to split. If she was going to be lonely, she wanted to make sure they were too.

Kareem's ego was shot to hell. He was hurt as well as embarrassed. "Look Shells, I…"

"Just leave Kareem. And don't come back!" She walked to the door and turned the knob. Kareem grabbed his keys and walked out the door. Shelly slammed the door and sat on the couch. She vowed that to be the last time she cried over Kareem or any man.

Kareem sat in his car and stared out of the window. He took his time and really thought about his relationship with Simone. He started the car and drove home. He parked outside their window and cleared his mind. Although he was hurt at what Simone did, he was in love with her. He decided that it was all his fault. If he would have been able to keep his dick inside his pants, she wouldn't have had to go to the extreme to get his attention. He wanted to be with her and promised himself that he'd be faithful from this point forward.

He thought he was playing Shelly when all the while, she got the last laugh. He felt like a fool. He decided right then and there that he wouldn't let Simone know that he knew about her and Trish or her and Shelly. He would just let it go. He owed her that much, especially after all the shit he put her through.

Chapter 63

Maryanne Hobbs gathered her things for a shower. She took Marvin's suit out of the closet and hung it on the back of the bedroom door. Today was the first day of the trial.

Marvin smiled as he walked into the bathroom with Maryanne.

"What's got you in a good mood?" she asked.

"I'm excited about this trial. I have a good feeling about this. I can't wait to get into the courtroom. "Do you mind if I join you in the shower?" he asked.

"Not at all." She removed her robe and stepped into the shower. Marvin removed his robe and stepped in as well. They showered and got dressed.

"Marvin, I'm going to leave a little early because I need to stop by my house for something," she said.

"Okay baby. But you are coming back over tonight aren't you?" he asked.

"I don't see why not. I'm going to be at the courthouse, if something comes up, I'll let you know then." She kissed him on the lips and wiped away the traces of her lipstick, "good luck today baby."

"Thank you sweetheart. I'll see you later," he replied.

* * *

Tricia and Tarik were both exhausted. They were up most of the night trying to come to terms with their marriage. Tarik wanted so desperately to salvage the marriage while Trish was unsure if she would be able to deal with his indiscretion. She loved Tarik more than anything but she also knew that a relationship couldn't survive without trust. She wasn't sure if she could forgive. She knew that she would never forget.

Tarik slept on the sofa bed upon Tricia's request. She told him that she needed time. He didn't push. He was willing to give her all the space she needed. He was in the shower while Tricia stood in the kitchen ironing her clothes. He walked into the kitchen wearing nothing but a towel. He opened the fridge and removed the orange juice.

"Good morning," he said.

"Morning," she responded dryly. Tarik walked up to her and kissed her on the neck. "Tarik please don't do that. I'm having a hard time just looking at you, I can't have you touching me right now."

Tarik's feelings were clearly hurt. He wanted to grab his wife and wrap her in his arms until the pain went away. She kept her back to him and asked him if he needed her to leave the iron plugged.

"No, I ironed last night. Are you sure you want to go to court today?" he asked.

"Of course I'm sure. Simone is my best friend. Why would I not want to be there?" she said sarcastically and walked into the bedroom. She gathered her things and brushed past Tarik and went into the bathroom. It took her about twenty minutes to shower and come out of the bathroom. She walked into the bedroom and heard Tarik on the phone with Melissa. She shook her head when he finally turned around and noticed her standing there. "We're taking separate cars," she said and walked out of the room.

* * *

Simone and Kareem had just finished making love.

"I love you Simone. No matter what happens today, that won't ever change." He kissed her on the mouth.

"I love you too, baby. I just want to thank you in advance for everything. If you wanna reconsider about taking the wrap for everything, I'll understand. Don't feel obligated to protect me. I

228

made this mess and I'm ready to accept whatever punishment that comes my way," Simone smiled.

"Stop talking like that. I told you before that it's all good. We'll be ok. Let's not count our chickens before they hatch." He kissed her again passionately on the lips. They climbed out of bed and began to get ready for their day in court. He didn't have the heart to make her realize that he couldn't take the wrap for everything since she was being charged with separate offenses. He just assumed that Simone was so stressed it slipped her mind.

Kareem held Simone's hand as they left their apartment to see what the future had in store for them.

* * *

Phil was waiting for on orderly to escort him to the lobby. The prosecutor wanted to make sure that their star witness was on time. She made sure there was a car service to pick him up. Phil was the only guest at the wedding who was willing to testify that Simone caused a disturbance during the ceremony. His testimony would prove that Simone intentionally shot Melissa and it would collaborate the most serious charge of attempted murder.

Chapter 64

The judge entered the courtroom and the bailiff asked everyone to rise. A few seconds later, he announced The Honorable Judge Janice Watkins. She sat and slammed her gravel and then asked everyone to be seated.

She looked at the prosecutor's table and asked them to begin with opening arguments. Ms. Stykes stood and adjusted her beige Donna Karen suit jacket. She looked at the jury. She started her opening argument with the charges Simone and Kareem were facing. She ended by promising to prove that the defendants attempted to murder Mrs. Melissa Monroe.

"Now we'll hear from the defense," Judge Watkins said.

Marvin Woodsby stood and buttoned his suit jacket. He turned to the jury and smiled. He looked at the prosecutor and shook his head. "Ladies and gentleman of the jury, I intend to prove that my clients neither conspired nor attempted to murder anyone. The prosecutor says she'll prove differently. As long as I've been an officer of the court, I've yet to see any prosecutor prove a case without a victim. The alleged victim has not come forward to testify. In fact, she doesn't know who shot her. Yes, my clients were on the scene when she was shot. But you won't hear testimony from anyone stating they saw either of my clients shoot anyone." He walked back towards the defense table.

"Objection, your honor!" Ms. Stykes yelled.

"Approach!" The judge ordered.

"Mr. Woodsby, you have a copy of the prosecution's witness list. I'm sure that your copy reads the same as mine. You can clearly see that Dr. Phil Monroe is the state's witness. You know he is here to prove that there was intent."

"Your honor, if you would allow a ten minute recess, I can prove that Mr. Monroe is not a credible witness," Mr. Woodsby stated.

"You'll have your chance to prove that in your cross examination. Be seated! "The jury will disregard the last statement from the defense's opening argument. Court is adjourned until tomorrow at 9am!"

Marvin approached Ms. Stykes. "Cheap shot," she stated.

"You're right. But I would really like to save you some embarrassment Paula. Just give me ten minutes of your time and I guarantee that you'll thank me."

"Marvin, what are you talking about? I offered your clients a deal but you declined. That deal is off the table!"

"Paula, you can take a chance with your witness or you can hear me out now. We can end this trial sooner than expected. Meet us in the big conference room on this floor in ten minutes." Mr. Woodsby walked away and turned around. "Oh, and bring your witness."

Paula Stykes sat at the table and gathered her things. She put her folders inside her briefcase and asked her co-counsel to push Phil to the conference room.

Kareem, Simone, Melissa and Brian Castro were already seated. Marvin opened the door and let the prosecution's team into the room.

"Ok, what's going on?" Ms. Stykes asked.

"Paula, I'd like to introduce you to someone." Marvin gave Brian the cue and he left the room. He returned seconds later with Ms. Belinda Chaste. All eyes were on her as she sashayed towards Phil.

"Hi daddy," she smiled as she adjusted the belt on her leather coat. She pulled her hat from her head and revealed a face that was identical to Phil's'.

Melissa was frozen in her seat. Ms. Stykes threw her pen on the table and exhaled.

"What is this? Why is Mr. Monroe's daughter here?" Ms. Stykes asked. She knew this was a surprise but she had to try and save face.

"Daughter? Phil...wh...what's going on?" Melissa asked.

"Oh, let me guess, daddy didn't mention me?" Belinda asked.

"Ms. Stykes, once the jury learns that Mr. Monroe has a twenty three year old daughter that his wife knew nothing of, how much credibility do you think he will hold? They won't believe anything that he has to say. Are you sure you want to go through with this trial? He is your only witness," Marvin smiled.

Ms. Stykes looked at Phil and shook her head. "I don't believe this." She sat there for a few minutes while Kareem and Simone looked at her with surprised facial expressions.

"I guess we can downgrade the attempted murder charge but I'm not dropping the lesser charges. I'll send you the paperwork this afternoon for a plea."

"My clients aren't interested in a plea, Ms. Stykes."

"Excuse me?"

"We'll see you in court." Mr. Woodsby smiled.

Ms. Stykes and her colleague walked out of the room.

Kareem and Simone kissed each other. Kareem stood and shook Mr. Woodsby's hand. "Why didn't you take the plea?" he asked.

"Relax son, let me do my job. Trust me."

Simone put her head on the table and closed her eyes. She didn't believe what just happened.

Melissa stared at her husband waiting for an explanation. She looked at Belinda and knew that this wasn't a made up story. Belinda was identical to Phil. He couldn't deny her if he wanted.

"Ms. Chaste, would you please come with me?" Melissa asked as she pushed Phil out of the room.

Belinda looked at Brian for approval and he gave her an *'it's up to you'* look.

"Sure, it is a family affair, right?" She followed Melissa and a courtroom bailiff.

Once outside the conference room, Melissa ignored the stares and questions from everyone. Her face was hard and emotionless. Tarik stepped in front of her with Tricia in tow. "You ok? You want us to come with you?" he asked.

"No, I'm fine!" she said in a stern voice. The bailiff led them to an empty room and closed the door.

Chapter 65

O nce inside the room, Belinda removed her coat and took a seat. Melissa was still in pain from her wounds. She limped over to a seat next to Phil. "Okay, let's hear it Phil?" she demanded.

"Melissa, I don't even know where to begin," Phil said.

"Try the beginning!" she yelled.

"Yeah, why don't you tell her how you walked out on my mother and never claimed me!" Belinda said.

"Please, Belinda. I know you're upset but let me explain. I was in love with your mother but she knew I didn't want kids."

"So you abandoned me? It wasn't my fault I was born!"

"Phil, why didn't you tell me you had a daughter?" Melissa didn't want to turn this into a fight between Phil and his daughter.

"Are you even listening? He didn't want me. He ran off and didn't look back. Ole daddy here thought he could just buy us off by sending money every month!"

"I don't understand Phil...how...wha?" Melissa said.

"I had a vasectomy. It was a few months after Belinda was born. I wanted to make sure I didn't have anymore children. But I loved you so much. I knew how much you wanted children so I attempted to reverse the operation to make you happy. I tried to do something good for us and our marriage for a change."

"Wow! That makes me feel so much better! You didn't want me but you had a baby by your wife? What, did you get a son this time?" Belinda was irate.

"No Belinda, it's not like that. I don't have anymore kids. You are my only child," Phil said as he looked at Melissa.

"I don't understand. You just said that you had the operation reversed. She has a baby and..."

"It's a little complicated. Your dad and I have been having some problems…"

"Yeah, I can see that. What happened to you anyway? Did dear ole dad give you a beat down too?"

Phil looked surprised. He attempted to say something but Belinda cut him off. "Yeah, Mommy told me all about it. I know about each time you hit her. I even know about the time you tried to beat me out of her," Belinda said in a shaky voice.

"Baby, that was so long ago. I was young and…"

"Stop, Phil! Don't even think about trying to lie your way out of this," Melissa said as she turned to Belinda. "Your father did this to me and a friend of mines did that to him. We are having problems right now and we're both patients in the hospital. Phil, I can't believe that you would keep something like this from me. A child you never claimed? Just when I thought you couldn't get any lower." She looked him directly in the eyes. "I'm tired Phil. I told you before that if you ever put your hands on me again, I would leave. You've taken me for granted for too many years. I'm going to take my son and leave. I must have been a fool to even consider making this marriage work. I want a divorce!"

"Melissa! No, we're not getting a divorce. I love you. I…"

"You don't know how to love. Look at what it took in order for me to realize that. Belinda, I'm sorry we had to meet under these circumstances. I wish you well." Melissa turned to walk out of the room with Belinda close behind.

"Melissa Get back here, NOW! Don't make me come after you!" Phil yelled. Melissa and Belinda turned around simultaneously.

"Look at you. You're not capable of change," Belinda said. "You just sat here and claimed to love her and in the same breath, you're threatening her. And I thought I missed out on having you in my life. I guess I should thank you for staying away. Goodbye Daddy."

Both women walked out of the room. Melissa asked an officer to make sure Phil got back to the hospital. She turned to Belinda and apologized for blowing up in her presence. She told her that it was inevitable. Belinda said she understood and gently hugged Melissa. "You seem like a really nice woman. I'm sorry for what he put you through."

"Thank you. I wish you all the best," Melissa said.

Belinda went up to Brian and hugged him. "Get me the hell out of here," she whispered.

* * *

Melissa sat in the waiting room of the children's ward along with Tarik, Tricia, Simone, Kareem and Mrs. Hobbs. While she waited for Dr. Carter, she brought everyone up to date. She told them all about Belinda while Simone told about what charges were dropped.

"You know it's not going to be easy going through a divorce. You can call me if you need anything," Mrs. Hobbs said.

"Yeah, you know you can count on me," Tarik smiled. Tricia looked at him with daggers in her eyes. She stood and walked towards the elevator. Tarik followed and attempted to say something in her ear. She pushed him away. "Just leave me alone Tarik. I need to get out of here."

When the elevator doors opened, she bumped into Marvin Woodsby.

"I have news," he blurted. Tricia stopped and listened. "Is it ok that I speak in front of everyone?" he asked.

"If you all don't mind, we'll go someplace private," Kareem suggested.

"How about you two meet me in my office first thing in the morning? This can wait until then," Mr. Woodsby said.

"That'll work," Kareem said.

Marvin turned to Maryanne and kissed her on the mouth. "I'll see you at the house tonight?"

Everyone stood there with their mouths hanging open. "Ma, what's going on?" Tricia asked.

Mrs. Hobbs smiled and put her arms through Marvin's. "Marv and I have been seeing each other for months now. We wanted to keep it a secret until after the trial." She turned to Marvin, "It is over right?"

"You better believe it. So I'll see you tonight?"

"You sure will." She kissed him on the cheek. Marvin jumped on the elevator.

"Oh Moms, that's wonderful. I wish you two the best." Simone smiled.

"I can't believe you didn't tell me, Momma. Now I see why you're never at your house." Tricia raised her eyes. "Good for you. As long as you're happy, I'm happy for you." She kissed her mother on the cheek.

Mrs. Hobbs blushed and walked over to Melissa. "I have to go baby, call me if you need anything. And don't worry, everything will work out fine." She kissed Melissa on the cheek and headed towards the elevator.

"If you all would excuse me, I have to go too," Tricia said. Simone and Kareem said goodbye then followed her.

"Trish, would you please stay here with me? I...well Melissa..." Tarik stuttered.

"Tarik, you stay here with your friend. I have to go. I'll call you later."

"What time would you be home?" he asked.

"Most likely, before you," she said as they stepped onto the elevator. Tarik stood with his hands in his pockets and shook his head.

Chapter 66

Tarik sat opposite Melissa as she thanked him repeatedly for being such a great friend. She kept talking to waste time. Dr. Watters had come out earlier to let her know that Christopher was out of surgery. That was two hours ago. She told them that the next few hours were crucial. They had to make sure Christopher's body didn't reject the blood.

"Tarik, I'm so glad that I have you here by my side but you need to go home to Tricia if you ever want to get back together."

"I don't wanna leave you here alone. I want to make sure the baby is going to be fine," he said.

"I'll call you and let you know the results. Your place is with your wife right now," Melissa insisted.

"You sure you'll be okay here alone?" Tarik asked.

"Yeah. I've been doing a lot of thinking. You and I are platonic friends but Tricia just found out that we had an affair and she needs to be reassured that it was a mistake. I would love to have you stay here with me all night but I know how Tricia must feel. You can't let our friendship get in the way of your marriage. She needs you to be there with her. I don't want to hurt her anymore than I already have. Go home and make it right," Melissa said.

"I don't know if I can make this right. I think that's why I've been avoiding spending time with her. Tricia's a very giving person. She'll give you the clothes off her back but when she feels like you've crossed her, there's not much you can do to change her mind."

"You owe it to her and yourself to try. I made this mess I'm in. I'll deal with it."

"You're right. I should be with my wife. I just want to tell you one thing before I leave. I don't think any less of you because you were cheating on Phil. He never deserved you. I'm not disappointed that I'm not Christopher's father but I am shocked! Why didn't you just tell me that there was someone else? I'm glad that you were getting some on the side. Fuck Phil!" he laughed. "You and Mike huh?"

"It really wasn't like that. Mike and I slipped up twice. I really didn't think anyone but Phil could be my son's father. I didn't even suspect you until you said something." She looked away.

"Don't be shy Melissa. At least you won't let Phil raise that baby. And you have the courage to finally leave."

"Well, I didn't really have a choice. Mike already threatened to take Christopher and expose my marriage if I even considered going back to Phil. And truth be told, I was going to go back to him until I found out about Belinda. Christopher is my pride and joy. I can't imagine Phil not claiming him as his own son. He would have thrown that up in my face every chance he got. He wouldn't have been able to get past that. Now you get out of here! NOW!" she smiled.

Tarik kissed her on the forehead and walked backwards to the door. "Call me," he said as he walked out of the room.

* * *

Melissa had fallen asleep in one of the chairs in the waiting area. She was awakened by a tap on the shoulder. She looked up and saw Dr. Watters standing over her.

"Is everything alright?" Melissa rushed her words.

"It went very well, Melissa. Christopher is going to be fine. His body is doing exactly what it needs to do."

"Oh thank you Dr. Watters. Can I see him now?"

"Yeah, you can go on back. I have to leave now. My children have been paging me since I got off two hours ago."

"Thank you for staying. I really appreciate that." Melissa grabbed the railing and walked to the back to see her son.

She walked towards the incubator and saw Mike sitting in a chair staring at their son. "What are you doing here? You should be resting. He's amazing isn't he?" she smiled.

"No one could keep me away. Yes he is amazing. I was just thinking about how strong he is. He deserves the best Melissa. Not what your husband gives to you," Mike said.

"We need to talk, Mike. I just need to sit with Christopher for a few minutes alone then can you meet me back in my room?"

"Sure." Mike smiled at his son then left the ward.

Melissa sat in the nursery and watched her son. He was in the incubator with tubes and IV's running through his little body. She felt so helpless. She wished there were something she could do for her him. She talked with him for about half an hour. She was hoping he'd awaken while she sat by his side.

The nurse came and changed his diaper and changed the medicine in his IV bag. Melissa told him she'd be back soon and wished him a speedy recovery. She kissed her fingers and placed them on the incubator as she exited the nursery.

Chapter 67

D r. Carter sat in a chair by the window. He'd had a nurse's assistant to come and change the linens on Melissa's bed. He also requested fresh ice water and juice. He looked out of the window and smiled. It finally registered that he was a father.

Melissa walked in and interrupted his thoughts. She was nervous and didn't know where to begin the conversation. She went to her water pitcher and poured a cup of water. Mike smiled at her and shook his head up and down. "It went well. He's going to be fine. That was one of my main concerns."

"Yeah. I'm so glad that this is all over. Dr. Watters told me that he should be fine," she smiled.

Melissa glanced at Mike and decided to break the uneasiness. "How long have you known that you were Christopher's father?"

"I just went ahead and did a paternity test when we realized that Tarik wasn't the father and with Phil's announcement, I just had this gut feeling. You're not mad at me are you?" Mike asked.

"No. If you wouldn't have done that, we'd still be waiting on the blood transfusion." She looked in his eyes before she spoke again. "Mike, I'm so sorry. I really didn't know. I honestly thought that Phil was his dad," she said.

"Don't worry about that, I'm not upset about that. I'm concerned about you though."

"No, don't be worried. I'm fine," Melissa insisted.

"Look at you Lissa. He intended to kill you this time. You were unrecognizable when they brought you here. It's not just a black eye to cover up," he explained.

"Before you get started about my marriage, I want to let you know that I'm getting a divorce. I already told Phil and I'm going to see a lawyer as soon as I can. My first concern is Christopher right now."

"He's my concern too," he smiled. "I'm really excited about this. I gotta tell you Melissa, it was pretty rough listening to Tarik confess that he's Christopher's father. When did you two become an item?" he asked.

"I know how this seems but it's really not like that. Tarik and I are friends. We are not an item. It just sort of happened one night," she explained.

"Just like us?" Mike asked.

"No, it wasn't like us. I could never consider being with Tarik. He and I have been friends forever, he's like my brother. That's why I blocked it out of my mind. I feel like it was incest. You and I have a very different relationship. When you and I happened, both times I wanted it to happen. I was overwhelmed with my husband and I needed you to comfort me the way that you did. I don't have any regrets about us." Mike tried to interject but she cut him off. "And I hope that you don't either."

"Melissa, I've never hid the way I feel about you. I tried to show respect towards your marriage but we did get weak. I don't have any regrets but I would like to know if you'd consider giving me a chance to make you happy. I love you and I always have," he confessed.

"Mike, I don't know what to say. I care for you and you know that. It's just too soon for me to think about getting involved with someone. I have so much to deal with right now. I know Phil is going to fight the divorce to the bitter end."

"Well let me be there for you this time. I'm not going to sit back and let Phil do anymore harm to you. Christopher needs you." He lifted her face and looked her in the eyes. "I need you."

"I...Mike I just...I don't know. I wouldn't want to put you in the middle of all of my drama. And as you can see, I've had more skeletons fall out of my closet than a little bit. I've made a mess of things and probably lost some good friends. I need to handle my business for a change," she said.

"I hear you. I understand that you have a lot going on so I'm not going to put any pressure on you. You'll be getting out of here in a few days, where are you and Christopher going to be staying?"

Melissa looked towards the door. She closed her eyes and then opened them. "Gosh, I haven't thought about that. I'm sure that we can stay in my house. I can't see Phil being that unfair."

"You can't really believe that he's going to let you stay there do you? Melissa, the man just tried to kill you. He left you for dead. He's not thinking about you or my son!"

"Mike, please. Phil's not going to have a problem with it. This is the least he could do after all he's put me through."

"Fine! If you believe it's ok for *you* to go there, then go. Christopher is not going back to that house! He can stay with me until you are completely finished with Phil."

"Are you kidding me? My son is staying with ME! How could you think I would let him out of my sight?"

"You're welcome to stay with me too. As a matter of fact, I'll feel much better knowing that the two of you are safe," Mike said.

"I told you that I can't get into anything right now, Mike."

"I'm not asking you to. I just have my son's safety at heart. We are his parents and we need to protect him from danger. Whether you want to believe it or not, Phil is a threat to our child. He's not going back there! I will take this to the next level if you try to take him there. You just think about it. I'll come by later to check on you." Dr. Carter walked out before Melissa had the chance to respond.

She stared at the door as he walked out of the room.

Chapter 68

K areem opened the door to Mr. Woodsby's office and let Simone enter before him. Marvin greeted them and asked them to have a seat.

"I'm going to start by saying congratulations. Neither of you are going to be charged with attempted or first degree murder." Both Kareem and Simone smiled. They sat eager to hear the rest of the news. "I tried my best to get the weight off of Simone like we discussed, but she already knew that Simone had the gun."

"Wait a minute…" Kareem said.

"Hold on son, let me finish. Simone, you are being charged with Aggravated assault, Possession of a weapon for unlawful purpose, Possession of a handgun without a permit, and Possession with intent to cause bodily harm along with other misdemeanors."

"How is she being charged with all of that? Intent to cause bodily harm? She is friends with Melissa. Everyone knows that she didn't intend to harm her," Kareem yelled.

"They have investigators just like I do. Simone's being charged for intent to harm Tricia."

"But who says that she wanted to harm Tricia?"

"Well, there were over one hundred people at that church. She pulled out a gun and it doesn't matter who, if anyone, she intended to harm. Especially when the prosecutor has proof that Simone and Tricia weren't on good terms. Anyway, Ms. Sykes are dropping all charges against you. Although Phil was not a credible witness on the stand, we know that he's not lying. There were many people questioned at the scene and every one of them mentioned that you were trying to control the commotion. We're getting off lucky and I'm not going to push it. Someone will have to pay for this and unfortunately, it will be Simone."

244

Simone stared at the wall. She couldn't believe what she'd just heard. Mr. Woodsby continued to talk for another few minutes when suddenly, Simone let out a high-pitched scream. She grabbed her hair and pulled like a crazy woman. Kareem grabbed her hands and pried them from her hair. He hugged her tight. She cried on his shoulder while he rubbed her back and told her it was going to be ok.

"I can't go to jail. What am I going to do in jail?" she cried.

"Baby calm down we'll be fine, I promise. Mr. Woodsby, we shoulda took that deal!" Kareem tried to sooth Simone.

Mr. Woodsby was sympathetic to their situation. He sat back and let Simone vent for a few more minutes.

He cleared his throat and rubbed his forehead. "Simone, I'm going to do all I can to keep you out of prison. I have to be honest. These are serious charges and the judge may not be so lenient. But like I said, I'm going to do everything I can. The judge already set a date for sentencing. We have to be in court in two weeks," Marvin took a deep breath. "Now listen to me. We didn't take that deal because I wanted to ensure that neither of you are charged with this crime again. As long as we had a trial, and by that I mean as long as a jury was selected and sworn in, the double jeopardy law is in effect. And by taking a deal, Simone was guaranteed to do jail time, much more time than she'll probably get if any at all. The prosecutor is dropping those charges because of lack of evidence." Mr. Woodsby cleared his throat. "I am advising you both to keep this information to yourselves."

Kareem shook his hand and thanked him for the work that he provided. Simone was still in tears. She looked at Mr. Woodsby with pleading eyes. "I can't go to jail. Please help me." She begged. Kareem almost dragged her out of the office.

Kareem drove to their apartment while Simone sat in silence. She tried to accept the fact that she may go to prison. She never expected to be charged with anything. When Kareem told her he'd take the fall, she assumed it would work. She just shook her head and looked out of the window the entire ride home.

Simone unlocked the door and went straight to the bathroom. She bent over the toilet and let out her nerves. She cried so hard that she lost control of her breathing. Kareem wanted to give her the space she needed but when he heard her choking, he kicked in the door and went to her rescue.

"Baby, just relax. It's not as bad as it sounds. Stop stressing yourself about it," he said.

"That's easy for you to say. You're not the one in danger of going to jail. What am I gonna do?" she wailed.

"Don't worry, we'll figure something out. But this ain't it. Come on let's go." He pulled her up from the floor and turned on the shower. He undressed her and then told her to get into the tub. Simone did as she was instructed. She tried to wash away her tears. She scrubbed for a few minutes then turned off the shower.

Kareem walked into the bathroom and wrapped her in a towel as she stepped out of the shower. He led her to the bedroom and handed her underwear and a night gown. She dressed as he pulled the covers back. He laid her in the bed and rocked her to sleep.

As Simone slept, he thought about her going to prison. He thought about Tricia and then Shelly. Simone had already experienced a sexual relationship with them both. He knew she would probably have no problems adjusting in prison. He just didn't want to lose her to anyone else, especially another woman.

Kareem closed his eyes and thought about how much he really loved Simone. He was saddened by the fact that he couldn't do anything to help her situation.

Chapter 69

It had been a week since the trial. Tricia and Tarik were trying to move forward in their marriage. Tricia agreed that they would both stay at the apartment together.

Tarik apologized constantly for the affair with Melissa. He tried everything he could to get Tricia to understand that it was a mistake. He just couldn't answer that one question she kept asking. She wanted to know why, after all these years, did they decide to get together. Each time Tricia asked that question, he froze. He didn't know how to respond. He couldn't possibly tell her that he'd always secretly lusted for Melissa. He knew it was out of his system but Tricia wasn't trying to hear it.

Tarik sat on the sofa after Tricia stepped out of the shower. She was wearing a robe as she walked into the bedroom and closed the door behind her. Tarik moved about trying to keep himself from standing at attention. He couldn't hide his erection. He went to the bedroom door and knocked before he twisted the doorknob. Tricia looked up from putting lotion on her legs.

"What do you want Tarik?" she asked as she continued to apply lotion to her body.

"Trish, we can't go on like this. You're not trying to get past this. We need to communicate. Every time I try, you back away."

"What do we need to talk about? You cheated on me! I need to decide if I want to be with you!" she yelled.

"Trish, you gotta know by now if there's any hope for our marriage. I love you and I want to be with you. I need you to meet me in the middle. Just tell me what you're thinking." Tarik said as he sat on the bed.

Tricia stopped what she was doing. She looked at her husband and shook her head. "Tarik, I love you. I've been doing a lot of thinking about us. I asked you if there was anything between you and Melissa. You swore to me that you two were only friends. I…"

"Trish, I didn't lie to you." He cut her off.

"You did lie to me! This is the reason I asked you to choose. I welcomed Melissa into my life and I loved her like a sister. I could never trust that BITCH again. You are my husband! The betrayal from you hurts more than anything." The tears began to roll down her cheeks. "How could you?"

Tarik went to Tricia and tried to hug her but she backed away. "No, I don't want your sympathy. I've been thinking about us while you've been consoling Melissa. You showed more concern for her than for us. How could you think I was ok with that?" Tricia asked as she wiped her eyes.

Tarik stood next to the bed, slipped his hands in his pocket and clenched his jaw. "Tricia, please? Let me make it up to you. I know we can get past this. Whatever I need to do to gain your trust again, I'll do it," he said.

"Tarik, it ain't shit you can do to make me forget about this!"

He went to her and grabbed her tight. He hugged her while she struggled to get out of his grip. "Let me go Tarik!" He squeezed her until she stopped struggling. Tricia let all of her weight fall on her husband. He sat on the bed and held his wife.

"Trish, it's going to be ok. We'll get through this." Tricia was tired. She stopped fighting and just lay in his arms. There was no question about her love for Tarik. They lay back and went to sleep in each other's arms.

Tarik was the first to awaken the next morning. He got up and went to the bathroom. Tricia sat up as soon as she heard the bathroom door close. She went to the dresser and pulled out a pair of pajamas.

"Good morning," Tarik said as he entered the room.

"Hi." Tricia said.

"Baby, I need to know wh…"

"Tarik?" Tricia interrupted. "I really want to work this out. We've both made mistakes. I'm willing to try and move forward."

"That's great baby!" he smiled.

"Wait a minute, I figured out the only way that I can begin to trust you," she said.

"What is it?" he asked.

"This time around, there will be no Melissa in our lives," she stated.

Tarik stared at her in disbelief as he frowned his face. "You can't be serious?" he asked.

"Oh, I'm serious. That's the only way we'll be able to work this out," she said.

"That's not fair! I'm not asking you to stop being friends with Simone."

"Whoa! How dare you? That's a totally different situation! You and Meli..."

"No it's not! Simone is your best friend. I would never ask you to kick her to the curb. Tricia, don't do this. There's gotta be another way for us to handle this."

"No, this is it! Either she's out or I'm out!" Tricia warned. Tarik stood there and shook his head. He closed his eyes and hoped that he was dreaming.

"What is there to think about? I'm your wife! This should be easy." she said as she went to her closet and pulled out a pair of jeans.

"It's about as easy as me accepting you and Simone."

"Why you keep throwing Simone in this?"

"Because it's the same fuckin' thing! You fucked her and I accept that it was a mistake. How come you can make a mistake and I can't!" he yelled.

"This is not up for debate. But I can see that you've made your choice."

"What you mean I made my choice? You didn't..."

"Because you're still trying to defend her! Instead of you working on us, you wanna make sure you'll always have her," she screamed as she walked into the living room grabbing her belongings.

"I can't believe you. I almost forgot just how selfish you are!" he said.

Tricia left out of the apartment and slammed the door behind her.

Chapter 70

Melissa zipped her duffle bag. She walked over to the mirror and looked at her reflection. She stared in disbelief. She couldn't believe the scars and the bruises were still noticeable. She stepped back from the mirror and examined the rest of her body. She was still a little sore in certain areas but for the most part, she was much better. Her ribs was bruised and bandaged. She knew that time would heal that wound. At least her skin tone was almost normal again. The black and blue bruises turned into plain red bruises.

She headed out the door towards the nursery to see Christopher. She looked up and saw Phil coming towards her on crutches. She stopped dead in her tracks. She hadn't seen or heard from Phil since she told him she wanted a divorce.

"Melissa, can I talk to you for a minute? Please?" he asked as he noticed her hesitation.

"Right now? I was on my way to see Christopher."

"It'll only take a minute. Can we go back in your room?" he asked.

She turned around and he followed her in the room. She pulled a chair for him to sit while she stood a few feet away by the door. Phil put his crutches on the floor and looked around the room. "You're leaving?" he asked.

"Yes, we're going home today. I'm waiting for all of the necessary paperwork to be completed." She paused then spoke a little louder. "You know the police came to see me the other day. They wanted to know what happened to me," Melissa said.

"I know. They came and asked me some questions about what happened to me."

"Phil, I'm not going to press charges if you won't press charges against Tarik," she said.

"That's fair. I hadn't planned on doing anything like that. I'm ready to move on."

"Thanks," Melissa said.

"How is Christopher?"

Melissa smiled and looked at Phil, "oh he's great. I can't wait to get him home."

"Speaking of home, I'll arrange for a car service to come and get the two of you to bring you back to the house."

"Uhm…Phil…I…I mean we…," she exhaled, "It's not a good idea for us to stay at the house. We're not…"

"Wait." He put his hands up for her to stop speaking. "That's not necessary. You and the baby can stay at the house. I've already moved into an apartment. I want you to stay in the house. I'm not going to be there," he urged.

"I can't Phil. Mike wants his son to be with him so we're going to move in with him for a little while. Just so that Christopher can know his dad," Melissa said.

"What! Are you out of your mind?" he yelled.

Melissa jumped and backed up. She didn't want to be within his reach in case he tried to hit her. "Phil, this isn't necessary. I've already made up my mind. I'm not bringing my son back to the place where his mother was left to die!"

"I'm sorry about that Melissa. It may not mean much to you, but I still haven't forgiven myself for what I did to you. Not just this time but through all of these years. I love you and I always have. Hurting you was never my intention."

"Phil, I have to go. I need to see my son."

"So you're just going to walk out without giving us another chance? I told you I was staying in a different place to give you time to heal. I'm your husband! You better remember that!" he yelled.

"Not for long. I'm filing for divorce, remember?" she yelled back.

"We'll see about that!" He retrieved his crutches and left the room.

* * *

Dr. Carter grabbed Christopher's baby bag and put it in the car. Melissa sat in the back seat next to her son's car seat. She didn't want him to be alone back there. She strapped on her seatbelt and leaned against the seat. She closed her eyes and waited to start over without Phil.

Mike pulled in front of his house and got out of the car. He grabbed the bags and took them inside. He made three trips before he tapped a sleeping Melissa. She looked up and smiled. She turned and undid the car seat.

"I'll get him. You get out and stretch. Just grab his bag from the front seat. I've taken everything else inside." Melissa picked up the bag and locked the doors once Mike was out of the car. She closed the doors and followed him inside the house.

Mike placed the car seat on the sofa and removed his coat. Melissa stood and looked around the room.

"Melissa, I'll give you a tour in a few minutes."

She removed Christopher's outer garments and picked him up. She wrapped him up in a blanket just as the nurse taught her. "We're ready," she said to Mike.

Mike grabbed her hand and took her to the kitchen. He pointed out everything. He took her up to the second level of the house and showed her a bedroom. "This is the master bedroom but it's your now," he said.

"No Mike, I don't want to put you out. You stay in your room," she begged.

"Nonsense! Follow me," he instructed. Mike opened the door to the second bedroom and surprised Melissa with a Looney Tunes nursery for Christopher. There were countless stuffed animals and pictures of Daffy Duck, Tweety Bird, and Bugs Bunny throughout the room. She was in awe. She looked around and smiled as she pointed out different things in the room. "Mike this is wonderful. When did you do this?" she asked.

"I had the baby store come in and set it all up. I told them what I wanted and they did it. I'm glad you like it," he smiled.

"Yea, I love it," she smiled and looked at Christopher sleeping in her arms. "I think Chris likes it too."

Mike smiled and pulled her towards the bathroom. "Here is the bathroom on this floor. There's another on the first level and a half bathroom in the basement."

"Wait, we can put Chris and me in the same room so that you can keep yours," she said.

"Melissa, I told you that it's now your room. For as long as you want, I'll be fine. I'm going to move downstairs in the basement."

"No! I insist that you keep your room," she said.

"It's all settled. I'm not having it. You two will be fine up here. I'm hardly here because of work so you stay and make yourself comfortable. Anything you need, just help yourself. If you can't find something, just ask. I know it's not as much as you're used to but my home is your home." He led her back to the first level.

"Mike, its fine. I don't need much. That big house was Phil's idea. He wanted to make sure I had everything I needed so I wouldn't need a reason to go out."

Once they were settled, Mike asked her if she was hungry. "I'm going out to grab a sandwich, do you want anything?" he asked. "Food is the one thing I don't have. When you want to go shopping, let me know. I'll take you and buy whatever you need."

"Mike, I don't want to be your charity case. I'm not broke just because Phil and I are splitting. I do work, remember? Phil took really good care of me but I have more than enough saved to take care of myself. I'm ok. And once I get my car in a few days, I'll be even better," she smiled.

"I didn't mean to insinuate…"

"That's ok. I know you're only trying to help. I really appreciate everything you're doing for me," Melissa said.

"So do you want a sandwich?"

"Yes please. I'll have a turkey and cheese on wheat with the works. Also, I'll take a bottle of lemonade."

"Ok. See ya in a few. I have my cell in case you need me before I get back."

"Ok." Melissa removed her shoes and began putting Christopher's belongings in his room. She placed him inside the crib and put the baby monitor in her pocket as she emptied her own bags.

It took her half an hour to get things just the way she wanted. She picked up her son and brought him into her new bedroom. She laid him in the bed next to her as her body shut down from exhaustion.

Chapter 71

Simone had been sitting in the diner for ten minutes staring into space. She didn't even notice when Tricia pulled out a chair and sat next to her. It wasn't until the waitress asked to take their orders before she realized that she wasn't alone.

"Give us a few more minutes please?" Tricia looked at the waitress. "Simone what's going on? Are you okay?"

"I'm good," she replied.

"You don't look so well. Are you sure everything's alright?" Tricia asked.

"Yes. We're here to talk about you not me. So what's going on?" Simone inquired.

Tricia removed her coat and exhaled. She looked like a ghost with the dark circles around her eyes. It was obvious that she'd been crying. Not only was her eyes red but her face was twice its normal size. "It's Tarik. He done gone and lost his mind! You know that we've been trying to work on our marriage right?"

"Yeah," Simone said.

"Well I told him that it's either Melissa or me."

Simone was shocked. "Trish, you asked him to choose again?"

"Hell yeah! I made a bad decision the last time. Melissa and I had gotten so close. She betrayed me in a way that I can never forgive. My husband and I can not work this out of she's still in his life."

"What did he say?" Simone asked.

"He had to think about it. That tells me that he'd rather have her in his life than me. Simone, I can't be with Tarik under those circumstances." Tricia wiped an escaped tear from her eye.

"Trish, maybe you're jumping to conclusions. He made a mistake. I'm sure that he wouldn't be trying to work it out with you if there were something going on with Melissa."

"No Simone, that's how I got into this mess the last time. You and Momma told me to trust her and I listened. Look what it got me."

"Hold up! Don't you dare try to blame this on us. I stand by my opinion. I would give you the same advice again."

"No, I didn't mean it like that. I'm not blaming anyone. But, you know how it goes. Fool me once, shame on you. Fool me twice, shame on me. I'm not going to look or feel like a fool again."

"I can't even imagine how you feel. I'm so sorry that this is happening to you. I do have one thing to say though."

"What's that?" Tricia asked.

"Tarik loves you. I honestly believe that Melissa was a mistake." Simone stared at her friend. "Just like us."

Tricia looked at Simone with a blank expression. The waitress returned and took their orders.

They ate their food while Simone tried to make her friend feel better. After a two-minute silence, Simone cleared her throat and tried to smile.

"What is it Simone? And don't tell me nothing because I know you too well," Tricia said.

"I don't know how to say it." She paused. "Trish, we found out the other day that I may have to go to jail."

"What! Oh no. Why? I thought we beat the case."

Simone looked around and tried to hush Tricia. She covered her face and drank from her glass of water. "The major charges were dropped but Mr. Woodsby said that I'm still being charged with a few minor charges and that means that I could get jail time." Simone's face was wet but she continued to talk as if nothing was wrong. "But I'm prepared to take responsibility for my actions." Tricia reached across the table and squeezed Simone's hands. She then reached in her purse and paid the bill. She grabbed Simone and they walked outside.

"Follow me," Tricia ordered.

"Where?" Simone asked.

"To Mom's house. Call Kareem and have him meet us there."

"Only if you call Tarik," Simone said.

Tricia gave her the evil eye before she agreed. They jumped in their cars and drove off.

Chapter 72

Maryanne Hobbs was preparing lunch when she received a telephone call from Tricia. She listened intently and asked a few questions. Tricia told her mother that they were all on their way to her house. Mrs. Hobbs said it was ok then hung up the telephone.

"Marv?" she yelled upstairs.

"Yeah?" he hollered back.

"Are you decent? We are getting ready to have company. That was Trish on the phone. She said that she needed to talk to me about Simone and it was urgent."

Marvin tied a knot in the belt to his robe. He walked down the stairs and kissed Maryanne on the cheek. "What's going on?" Did she say what about Simone?"

"No, but she was all upset and carrying on."

"I think I may know what it's about," he said.

"What? Tell me!" she begged.

"No, I'm going to let them tell you and if you all need me, I'll be right here," he said. "I'm going to throw on something before they get here. Are you making enough or should we order a pizza or something?"

"I'm setting up a tray for cold cuts. They can have sandwiches. Simone and Tricia used to love it when I did that for them in high school," she smiled.

Marvin kissed her on the lips then disappeared up the stairs.

Tricia looked into the window of her mother's house. She didn't see anyone so she unlocked the door. She entered the house and her mother walked out from the kitchen. "Hi baby. What's wrong?" She asked as she saw Tricia's face.

"You name it. My life is a mess and now this thing with Simone," she said.

"Come on and sit down. You just going through a rough period right now, things will surely work out." Mrs. Hobbs patted Tricia on the back.

Marvin came down the stairs and startled Tricia.

"Oh Momma, I didn't know you had company. I'm sorry. I wouldn't have just barged in without ringing the doorbell. Hello Mr. Woodsby." Tricia said as she used the inside of her fingers to wipe her face.

"Call me Marvin," he said.

"Please, if you were interrupting, I would have told you on the phone. Where is everybody?" Mrs. Hobbs asked.

"They should be here any minute. Simone was right behind me," she said as she peeked out of the window. She went to the kitchen and grabbed the tray of cold cuts and the bread. She placed them on the table while Simone and Kareem were being greeted by Mrs. Hobbs.

"Simone, what's wrong?" Mrs. Hobbs asked as Kareem hugged Simone.

"She's just a little upset, she'll be ok in a few," Kareem said.

Tricia hugged Simone and Kareem and then disappeared downstairs to the bathroom in the basement. She couldn't look at Simone. She felt sorry for her and hated to see her so hurt. She still believed that if she'd talked to Simone before the wedding, all of this nonsense could have been prevented. She splashed cold water on her face and dried it with a towel. She returned upstairs and saw Tarik shaking hands with Mr. Woodsby.

"I called everyone here to just hang out. Simone have some news and I thought we should all be together to hear it at the same time." Tricia shook her head and held it down.

Simone stepped up and led Tricia to the sofa. "It's ok Trish. I'll tell them." Simone looked around the room and tried to smile. She wiped her face with a tissue and exhaled. "I found out that I may have to spend time in jail." She controlled her tears as she continued. She told them about the charges in which she was still being faced.

Mrs. Hobbs looked at Marvin who held his head down. "Is this true Marv? There ain't nothing you can do? We can't let this baby go to jail?" she cried.

"It's ok Moms. I'm ready to face whatever is coming to me," Simone said.

"Look everyone, like I told Simone, it's a possibility that she'll do minimum jail time. It's really up to the judge. I only know that Simone is still being charged and those charges could be accompanied with jail time."

"Oh my goodness," Mrs. Hobbs cried. She smothered Simone in her bosom and rubbed her back while Simone let the tears fall.

Tarik went to Kareem and started a side conversation. They talked for about ten minutes while everyone in the house sat in their own thoughts. Tricia looked at Tarik who was staring in her face. He went to her and hugged her. She didn't reject his touch. She cried on Tarik's shoulder.

After about twenty minutes of condolences, Simone cleared her throat. "I need you all to do me a favor."

"Anything," Tricia said.

"Please stop feeling sorry for me. I'm going to be ok. I'm scared but I know I need to pay for what happened to Melissa."

Tarik looked at Simone and nodded in agreement.

"I can only pray that she really knows that I never meant to hurt her."

"She knows. Stop worrying about that. We all know that it was an accident," Tarik said.

"What about you Trish?" Simone asked.

"Of course I know," she said.

"I mean do you know that I never intended to hurt you either? I'm facing these charges because they believe that I intended to hurt you." Simone said as Kareem squeezed her hand for support.

"Don't you even think about that, I know better," Tricia said.

WITH FRIENDS LIKE THAT

They spent the next few hours just enjoying each other's company. Tricia remained civil towards Tarik. No one could tell that they were having problems. She didn't want to do anything to upset Simone. The purpose of the get together was so that they could all spend quality time together one last time in case Simone went to prison tomorrow.

Chapter 73

Phil got dressed and went by his house. He had been staying at an apartment since his release from the hospital. He still wasn't able to drive so he called a car service to pick him up and drop him off.

He'd been in the house for half an hour looking through things. He went through Melissa's drawers and threw the clothing about the bedroom. He sat on the bed and thought about Melissa. He couldn't understand why she refused to stay in the house.

Phil went to the baby's room and walked over to the crib. He viciously pushed it over and repeatedly kicked it with his good leg. He tore the wallpaper off the wall. Phil went to a guestroom and returned with a screwdriver. He stuck the teddy bears and ripped them to shreds. He stuck the screwdriver in the walls and the baby furniture. The room was trashed by the time Phil finished. He looked back on his way to the kitchen.

He went to the bottom cupboard and reached for a bottle of Hennessey. He was glad he had the driver stop at a store to reload last week when he dropped by. He drank straight from the bottle until it was half empty. Phil went down to the basement to see if there were any traces of Melissa. He went to the laundry room and ripped the clothes that were in the hampers.

Dr. Mike Carter pulled up in front of Melissa's house. He volunteered to take her to get a few of her and the baby's belongings.

"Why don't you and Chris wait here, I'll only be a few minutes. There's no need to take him out of the car when I'm coming right back," Melissa suggested.

"I think we should all go. It'll take less time if I'm helping," Mike said.

"No, I know where everything is and I'll be right back. Just sit here with the baby."

"Ok, if you insist. Hurry back," Mike smiled.

Melissa walked into the house and went directly upstairs to the bedroom. She looked around the room and gasped. She went to the dresser and picked up a few of her shredded clothing. She tripped over a pile of shoes that were in the middle of the floor. She looked down and picked up one of her shoes and saw that the heel was broken off. "What the hell?" she whispered.

She backed out of the room and went to Christopher's room. She saw the condition of the room and began to shake uncontrollably. She was nervous and scared. Her instinct was to run out of the house. But as she turned out of the room, she bumped directly into Phil.

"Hi honey. Surprised to see me?" he slurred.

"Phil what happened? I thought you were staying in an apartment." She backed further into the room to get out of his face.

"What? A man can't come to his own house? I offered you the house but you refused."

"No, I didn't want the house. As a matter of fact, I'm just going to leave. I see that you're in one of your moods," she said nervously.

"Melissa, please reconsider this divorce. I want to make it right with you," Phil said.

"Phil, we've already discussed this. I'm not getting into this with you right now. I have to leave. Now would you please let me pass?" Melissa asked.

Phil walked towards her and backed her into a corner. She had nowhere to go. He got up in her face and grabbed her head. He forced a kiss from her. Melissa yelled for him to stop. Phil pushed her and knocked her on the floor. Melissa tried to get up but she couldn't grab onto anything for support. Phil was in bad shape. He was still limping because of the beat down from Tarik. His leg prevented him from kicking her. She slid back and winced in pain. She too was still bruised from her last meeting with Phil. She was able to use one of the shoes on the floor and hit Phil in the leg. He bent down in pain and Melissa hit him in the face with the shoe. Phil fell to the floor and Melissa staggered down the stairs. She ran to the car screaming.

Mike got out of the car and welcomed her into his arms. "What's the matter?" he questioned.

"Phil is in there." She pointed to the house. "He destroyed most of our things and tried to attack me again," she cried.

"I've had it with this guy. I'll be right back!" Mike walked towards the house.

"No. Mike please. Let's just get Christopher out of here," she begged.

Mike tried to convince her to let him go and see Phil. Melissa knew better and insisted that they let it go. She said she wanted to get her son as far away from Phil as possible. Mike reluctantly agreed and jumped back into the car once Melissa was strapped in her seatbelt. He took another look at the house and drove off.

Melissa sat in the backseat with her son and cried silent tears. She couldn't believe that she'd let her marriage get so out of control. She stared at her son and shook her head.

"You remember what we talked about?" Mike asked as he looked at her through the mirror.

"I know. But…"

"There's no but Melissa! You have to do it. He's not going to go away. He's going to fight the divorce with everything he has."

Melissa stared back at Mike and wiped her face. She couldn't believe that she had to put a restraint order against her husband. "I'll do it in the morning," she said.

"Think again. We're right around the corner from the police station."

Chapter 74

Tricia called Simone as soon as she woke. She called to wish her good luck in the courtroom. She hung up the phone and went to the shower. Once she finished, she went to her bedroom and tapped on the door. She agreed to stay in the apartment with Tarik so that they can be there for Simone and Kareem. But she still refused to sleep in the same bed.

"It's open," Tarik shouted.

Tricia walked into the room and went directly to the closet. She tightened her robe and bent down to get a pair of shoes. Tarik tried not to stare but her robe barely covered her ass. She wasn't wearing underwear and her freshly shaven private area peeped through the robe.

He adjusted himself and walked out of the room. He didn't want to push her about their marriage at the moment. He knew she was stressed and upset about Simone's sentencing. He decided to get through court and then bring up their marital situation later.

The telephone rang as Tarik walked into the living room. He picked up the phone and heard Melissa on the other end. He walked back into the bedroom and sat down. He was almost in a trance. He listened in silence as Tricia walked towards him. She saw her husband's face go from calm to rage in a matter of seconds. She sat down beside him and tapped his shoulder. "Tarik, what is it? What happened?"

"That son of a Bitch! Ok. Tricia and I are heading to the courthouse now. I'll call you as soon as we're done there." He pushed the off button on the cordless phone.

"What happened?" Tricia asked.

"Mike took Melissa to her house to pick up a few things and Phil was there. She said that he had shredded most of her clothes and completely destroyed the baby's room. He tried to attack her again," he explained.

"Damn." That was all Tricia said. She continued to gather her clothing. Tarik looked over at her and shook his head.

They were both dressed and ready to walk out of the door. Tarik grabbed Tricia's hand and pulled her towards him. "Baby, I think we should take my car. I'll drive because if the worse happens, I don't want you out there trying to drive yourself anywhere."

Tricia thought about what he said and then agreed. They walked out of the apartment and she locked the door.

* * *

In the courthouse, Kareem and Mrs. Hobbs were seated directly behind Simone and Marvin Woodsby. Tricia and Tarik walked in and joined them. Tricia hugged Simone and told her that everything was going to be alright. Moms went to Simone and told her that she loved her and wished her luck.

"Would everyone please rise for the Honorable Judge Janice Watkins," the bailiff announced.

"Please be seated," said Judge Watkins. "Good morning all. It seems that we're here today for the sentencing of one Ms. Simone Benson. The charges are possession of a firearm with a purpose to use it against a person, possession of a handgun without a permit, and possession of a weapon for unlawful purpose and last but not least, endangering the welfare of children. Before we proceed, would anyone like to say a few words?" she asked.

Paula Styles rose to her feet and announced that Tricia Hammond wanted to say a few words.

"Please come forward Mrs. Hammond," the judge ordered.

"Thanks your honor. I would just like to say that I'm the woman whose wedding was interrupted by this incident. Simone and I are as close as sisters. I know that she didn't intend to hurt me and I forgive her. Please don't punish her for attempting to hurt me. She would never do anything to harm me or Melissa."

"Thank you Mrs. Hammond. Please be seated."

"Your Honor, if it pleases the court, I'd like to read a letter written by the victim, Mrs. Melissa Monroe. She is unable to attend but agreed to this sworn statement."

"You may do so," said the judge.

Mr. Woodsby proceeded to read the letter and then he place it back into a vanilla folder. "My client would also like to say a few words if it pleases the court."

"Please rise Ms Benson," Judge Watkins said.

Everyone in the courtroom was shocked. No one knew of Simone's plans to speak on her own behalf. She stood and adjusted her suit jacket.

"Thank you your honor. I would like to apologize to everyone who was harmed by this incident. I never intended to hurt anyone. I hope that with time, I can be forgiven." Simone took her seat.

"Thank you Ms. Benson. Will the defendant please rise. The court has considered the facts in this case. I have taken in consideration your remorse for your actions and the fact that the victim and you are friends."

Simone folded her hands together and looked the judge in the eyes with tears rolling down her own face.

"However Ms. Benson, a woman and her unborn child were harmed due to your recklessness. I have no choice but to sentence you to six months in prison in a facility named by the department of corrections."

The judge banged her gravel on the desk and looked at the bailiff to escort Simone into a holding cell.

Simone stood frozen to the floor. She literally could not move. Kareem went to her and hugged her tight. He kissed her and told her he loves her. Simone stood motionless. Tricia pushed past Kareem and hugged her sister-friend. "Simone, I am so sorry. I love you girl. Call me as soon as you get a chance," she sobbed.

The court officers had come to take Simone into custody but Tricia wouldn't let go. Tarik had to pry her arms from around Simone's neck. Simone had the most pitiful expression on her face. She waived goodbye to everyone as she was taken behind the closed doors.

"Marv do something!" Mr. Hobbs cried.

He pulled Maryanne into his arms and hugged her tight. "Maryanne, you know I've done all I could. She has to do the jail time. Six months is a gift," he said as she sobbed on his shoulder.

Tricia had sat back down. She was still surprised at the judge's decision. "How could she send her to jail? I'm the so called intended victim. Why would she let me speak if she weren't going to listen to me?" she wined.

"Believe it or not Trish, I think you did make a difference. She only gave Simone six months. She would have given anyone else anywhere up to two years for either one of those charges.

"Come on baby. Let's go home," Tarik urged. He pulled Tricia by the arm and walked to the back of the courthouse.

"Moms, we'll give you a call a little later. I just want to get her calm and cool," Tarik said.

Everyone said goodbye while Kareem went back to his seat. Mr. Woodsby tried to talk to him but he didn't want to hear anything. Moms sat beside him and convinced him to let her and Marv follow him home. Kareem finally agreed. They all walked out of the courthouse together.

Chapter 75

Tricia slept in her husband's arms. She tossed and turned all night. Tarik tried his best to keep her calm. But she kept waking up throughout the night. She rolled over and looked Tarik in his face. "Are you sleeping?" she asked.

"Nah, I couldn't sleep. How are you feeling?"

"I don't know. I keep having nightmares. I'm so scared for Simone."

"Baby, she's going to be fine. These six months are gonna fly by. You'll see."

"I hope so." Tricia lay on his chest and inhaled his scent. She missed Tarik so much. She wanted things to go back to the way they were a year ago when she couldn't be happier. Tarik caressed her arm and kissed her on the forehead. He held her as long as he could without touching her. He was as horny as she.

"Trish, I miss you baby."

"I miss you too."

"I want you." He said as he pulled her up to meet his face. He kissed her on the lips. Tricia's heart melted at the touch of his mouth on hers. "Can I have you baby? It's killing me that we are going through this."

"Tarik," she said through heavy breathing, "baby don't talk just make me feel good."

Tarik climbed on top of his wife and initiated the foreplay. He licked her breasts and massaged between her legs. Tricia grabbed his dick and made it come to a full erection. Tarik kissed her neck and worked his way down to her stomach. He turned her on her stomach just as she prepared to feel his tongue between her legs. He placed a pillow under her stomach so that her ass was protruding in the air. Tarik spread her legs apart and began to kiss Tricia's ass cheeks. He licked her inner thighs and worked his way to her kitten. Tricia's body jerked as she moaned in pleasure. Tarik grabbed her hips to keep her still. He buried his head in her wetness. Tricia squirmed until she was directly in his mouth. Tarik sucked and slurped up all the wetness that escaped her body. She began to sex his tongue. Tarik stuck it out as far as it would go and let her have her way.

After about fifteen minutes of that, Tarik climbed on top of his wife. She stuck her ass out as much as she could. Tarik pumped in and out as his eyes rolled all around his head. He grabbed Tricia's right leg and placed it on his shoulder. She pumped him and got him to moan out loud.

She looked back and saw that her husband was on cloud nine. She missed seeing his face when they made love. She wanted that moment to last forever but Tarik had other plans. He pumped faster and faster. She stopped him and made him lay on his back. She hopped on top of him and rode him until they exploded together. Afterwards, she jumped off and went to the bathroom.

"Are you ok?" he called out.

"I'm ok. I'll be right back," she shouted back.

Tarik lay in bed with a smile on his face. He looked forward to him and Tricia getting back on the right track.

Tricia got back into bed wearing a pair of underwear and t-shirt. She resumed her position in her husband's arms.

"I love you Tarik."

"I love you too, Boo. Now maybe you can get some rest," he said as he kissed her on the lips.

Tarik woke bright and early. He remembered that he never returned Melissa's call. He went out to the living room and grabbed the cordless phone. He dialed her cell number and she picked up. They engaged in conversation where she explained the entire situation. He told her he was going to pay Phil another visit but she told him about the restraint order. He sat back and exhaled. Tarik asked about Christopher. Melissa told him that the baby was wonderful. She doted about how Mike was a great father. She seemed to be at ease with her current living arrangements. He told her about Simone and the sentencing. She expressed her apologies and condolences. She asked how Tricia was doing. Tarik explained that Tricia was trying to cope with everything. Melissa asked Tarik if he could stop by Mike's place sometime during that day. He thought about it before he answered. "I really need to be with Tricia today. I'll see if I can get out for a minute though. I'll call you and let you know. Tell Mike I said hey and I'll talk to you later." He put the phone in the charger.

Tricia walked into the living room wearing a sweat suit. "Tarik, there's something I should tell you," she said as she sat next to him on the sofa.

"What's up Boo?" he asked as he took her hand and kissed the back of it.

"Well, I know that you're waiting for me to say that everything is cool and we can go back to normal. I can't sit here and pretend that I don't know what I want. I love you with all of my heart. But there's no way I can be a part of this marriage," she said.

"What are you talking about? We are ju…"

"Tarik let me finish. Melissa is always going to be a part of your life. I can't deal with that. I'm not going to commit to a marriage where I can't trust you. I asked myself over and over if I can get past this and I can't. Melissa betrayed me in the most unforgivable way and there's no way I can overlook that. It seems to me like you've already chosen her. I'm going to file for an annulment," she said.

"Tricia, think about what you're saying. I love you baby. I don't want to lose you. Melissa and I made a mistake. You don't have to worry about that ever happening again."

"You say that but my intuition is telling me different. I went against my better judgment the first time around and now I'm hurt. I'm not going to put myself through this again."

"Trish, please don't do this. We can find a way to work it out."

"No we can't. You're not going to agree to my terms and I'm not sure I want you to. Melissa doesn't have anyone else.

She needs you to be there for her like you always have," Tricia said.

Tarik sat on the sofa with his head in his hands. He didn't want this to be the end of his relationship with Tricia.

"Trish, we have too much invested to end like this. Don't do this," he begged.

Trish stood and Tarik pulled her back into his arms. He hugged her tight and kissed her on the cheek.

"Tarik, I'm going to stay at Momma's, you can stay here. There's no need for us to give up this apartment."

"Trish, this is not what I want. Why don't you just take some time to yourself and think about it?"

"I have thought about it and it won't work. I walked out here and heard you on the phone with Melissa. You told her that you would try to get away. I don't want you to sneak away from me to be with your friend," Trish said.

"I don't understand?" Tarik said.

"You'll never understand. I was betrayed by a friend. I loved Melissa just like I do Simone. You two crossed a line that you can't undo. It's better if we just cut our losses now. I should go."

Tarik shook his head in disagreement. He didn't know what to do or say. Tricia went into the bedroom and grabbed a suit case. She filled it with a few of her belongings and returned to the living room wearing her coat.

"I guess this is goodbye." She looked at her husband.

"I'm not gonna just let you walk out of here."

"Tarik please let's not make this a long drawn out thing. You know just like I do that this is the way it has to be. I'll be contacting a lawyer as soon as possible," she said.

"Stop talking like that. Don't do anything just yet. Give yourself a little more time. Please? Do it for me?" Tarik begged.

Tricia bent down and kissed her husband on the lips. She stood up and looked him in the eyes, "Tarik, I'm really sorry for what I put you through with Simone and me. I should have told you about us as soon as it happened. And since you don't understand how I can forgive her, I'll tell you this-Simone never lied to me. Goodbye Tarik." She walked towards the door. She didn't even look back as Tarik called her name.

Chapter 76

Tarik remained on the sofa for hours. He ignored the ringing phone and stared at his and Tricia's wedding photo. He didn't realize how big of a mistake he made. He never thought that Tricia would leave him, especially after he overlooked her indiscretion with Simone.

He looked at the clock on the wall and picked up the phone. He dialed the eleven numbers and mumbled to himself. *'I should've done this a long time ago.'*

He spoke to the person on the other end and explained about the past year. He managed to convince the person that it was time for a fresh start.

* * *

Kareem lay in bed and wondered how he was going to get through six months without Simone. He'd stop seeing all of the women he had on the side. The only woman he wanted was Simone.

He glanced at the clock and realized that he had to work in the morning. He couldn't sleep. He did not want to be in the bed alone. The phone rang as he closed his eyes and thought about Simone.

"Hello?" he asked.

"Hi baby." It was Simone.

"How you doing? Are they treating you right?" he asked.

"Kareem, I'm fine. I just really needed to hear your voice tonight. One of the guards let me make a call before I went to my cell. I love you baby," she said.

"I love you too. I'm going to be down to see you as soon as you can have a visit."

"I can get visits in ten days. I'm looking forward to seeing you. Goodnight baby."

"Goodnight," Kareem smiled. He was like a kid in a candy store. He was finally able to get some sleep after he heard Simone's voice. He didn't know how he was going to make it every night but this was a start. He thought to himself, *funny how when Simone was home I cheated like crazy and now there's no way of getting caught, I realize that she's the love of my life.*

Chapter 77

It had been two weeks since Tricia left Tarik. She'd been staying at her mother's house. Maryanne was barely there since she spent most of her time with Marvin.

It was Saturday and Tricia decided to go to the mall. She showered and fixed herself something to eat. As she cleared the dishes, her mother walked in the front door.

"Momma?" she yelled.

"Yeah where are you?" Mrs. Hobbs called out.

"I'm in the kitchen."

Mrs. Hobbs walked into the kitchen and smiled at the sight of Tricia. "I'm glad to see you're up and about today."

"Yeah, I'm tired of lying around being miserable. I'm going to the mall this afternoon. I need to get spring clothes. I'm going back to work and I need a new wardrobe. What are you doing here? I hardly ever see you anymore. I guess you and Marv are pretty serious huh?"

Mrs. Hobbs smiled, "you can say that again, he's wonderful. That's what I wanted to talk to you about."

"What is it Momma?"

"He proposed to me last night," she blushed.

"Wow! That's great Momma. Let me see the ring," Tricia said excitedly.

"I couldn't accept his ring Trish."

"Why not? You are in love with him right?" Trish asked.

"Yeah but it's not that simple."

Tricia looked confused. "What do you mean?"

"Let me see if I can explain it. You are still in love with Tarik right?"

"Yes but..."

"And for your own reasons, you can't take him back right? That's how I feel. For my own reasons, I don't want to get married again. I'm happy the way things are."

"What did he say about it?" Tricia asked.

"He couldn't understand it at first but by the time I finished talking, he saw it my way. If it ain't broke then don't try to fix it," Mrs. Hobbs said.

"Well I guess you have your reasons but I think you should go for it. He makes you glow. I haven't seen you this happy since daddy."

Mrs. Hobbs smiled at the thought of her late husband. She shook her head at some memories. "I haven't been this happy since your father. How are you holding up about Tarik?"

"I'm still coping. I miss him so much Momma."

"Are you really gonna throw your man away? I know you're hurting honey, but don't try to act tough when you're really not. He's still your husband and if you want him then go get him before it's too late."

"Momma, please don't lecture me. I'm really not in the mood."

"I'm not here to lecture you. I would be less than a mother if I didn't tell you how I feel. I support your every decision. It's just something for you to think about. I have to get moving, Marvin and I are going away this week. We leave on Tuesday."

Tricia sat at the kitchen table and thought about what her mother said.

Chapter 78

Melissa went to Christopher's room and put his clothes in the laundry basket. She decided that she could get some laundry washed while he slept. She moved about the room and then went to her bedroom. She grabbed her belongings and put them in a separate basket.

Melissa stopped to answer the door on her way to the basement. She looked through the peephole and almost fell to the floor. She opened the door and saw Dr. and Mrs. Evans standing on the front step.

"Mommy, daddy?" she asked.

"Hello Melissa." Mrs. Evans hugged her daughter.

"How did you know where to find…"

"Tarik called us. He thought we should know what's been going on with you," Dr. Evans said. "Why didn't you call?" he asked.

Melissa led them to the sofa. "Where's my grandson?" Mrs. Evans asked.

Melissa smiled, "he's upstairs sleeping. I just put him down for a nap."

"Well he's about to get awaken. Where is he?" she asked.

Melissa took her parents to Christopher's room and turned on the light. Her parents went to the crib and smiled. Mrs. Evans picked him up and woke him out of his sleep. She played with him and handed him to her husband who politely waited his turn to hold his grandson.

The Evans' followed their daughter back downstairs to the living room. They all took a seat while she offered them something to drink. Dr. Evans declined and cleared his throat.

"Lissa' we're here to take you back to Maryland. I can not believe that Phil is behaving in this manner. I do not want you or this child anywhere near him. Tarik filled us in on everything. And if I get my hands on Phil, he's finished," Dr. Evans said sternly.

"Daddy, you can't just come and take me away. I can't just take Christopher away from Mike. What about my friends?" she said.

"The way I see it, you don't have any friends. Tarik is the only friend you have and he seems to think the best thing for you is to come back home with us," Mrs. Evans said.

"Well that's not his decision to make! I'm not leaving!" Melissa said. She took Christopher from her father and rocked him back to sleep then lay him in the cradle next to the sofa.

"Melissa just hear us out. We love you and we're not going to sit back and watch you go through this with Phil. You can just come on back home for a little while until this is all over. We want to be a part of you and Christopher's lives. We're so sorry that we parted on the terms in which we did," Mrs. Evans said.

"And we're sorry that we forced you to choose between us and the man you loved," Dr. Evans said.

"Oh daddy I love you and I'm sorry too." She hugged her parents and they sat back and talked until they heard Mike put his key in the door.

"Lissa?" He called out as soon as he walked through the door.

"Mike, I'm here," Melissa said.

"Oh, I'm sorry. I saw an unfamiliar car out here and thought you may be in trouble." He locked the doors behind him.

"Mike, I'd like you to meet my parents. This is my mother, Mrs. Rosa Evans and my father Dr. Maurice Evans."

Dr. Evans stood and shook Dr. Carter's hand. "Nice to meet you."

"Likewise," Mike said. He went to Mrs. Evans and shook her hand also. "This is a pleasant surprise," he said.

"Mike, my parents are here to take me back home."

"Back home? You are home," he said confused.

"Tarik called them and told them about my situation and they want me and the baby to go back to Maryland until this whole thing blows over."

Mike sat down and frowned at Melissa. They all sat around and discussed the situation. After going back and forth for a few hours, Mike went to the kitchen and ordered a Pizza. It was sure to be a long night.

By the time it was over, Melissa had her and Christopher's belongings packed.

Six months later..............

Chapter 79

Kareem moved around the apartment and prepared for Simone's surprise welcome home party. He told Simone that he couldn't get off work to pick her up but Trish was coming to get her.

Mrs. Hobbs and Marvin were the first to arrive at the apartment. Mrs. Hobbs made sure the food was just right. She quickly prepared a platter of cheese and crackers and put a bottle of wine on ice.

Tarik rang the doorbell and Kareem let him inside. They gave each other the brotherly hug and engaged in small talk. Mrs. Hobbs saw Tarik and went to give him a hug. She kissed him on the cheek and told him to help himself to anything.

Kareem sat on the sofa and waited nervously. He couldn't wait to see Simone. They spent so many nights on the phone. He recalled every conversation they had. He even memorized her letters. He wanted this night to be perfect.

He was happy that Tricia didn't object when she was told that Tarik would attend the party.

"Ok everyone, I see them getting out of the car. Be quiet," Marvin said as he stood by the window.

Mrs. Hobbs turned off the lights and everyone waited for them to enter the apartment.

"Here, Kareem gave me your key so you could get in," Trish said to Simone.

Simone stood in front of the door. She turned to Tricia and smiled, "I'm so glad to be home."

She hugged Tricia then unlocked the door. They entered the apartment and Simone turned on the light switch.

"*SURPRISE*!" Everyone yelled in unison.

"Oh my gosh!" Simone cried, "Trish, why didn't you tell me?"

"I couldn't spoil the surprise," she laughed.

Kareem walked up to Simone and lifted her off her feet. He kissed her and hugged her until she lost control of her breathing.

"Kareem let the girl breathe!" Mrs. Hobbs said as she walked over and hugged Simone. "How are you baby?"

"I'm much better now that I'm home."

Marvin walked over and shook Simone's hand. He welcomed her home with a drink. She accepted the drink then Kareem interrupted.

"Wait. I wanna make a toast." Everyone gathered in a circle and waited for Kareem to make his toast. He stood in front of Simone. He kissed her on the lips and smiled. She blushed and grabbed his hand. "Simone, welcome home. I know you just got here but I really need to ask you a favor."

"Anything," she smiled.

"Will you marry me?" he smiled.

Everyone applauded. Simone wiped a tear from the corner of her eye as she shook her head yes. Kareem slipped the diamond ring on her finger and everyone stood in line to congratulate her.

Kareem managed to hear the doorbell through all of the noise. He walked to the door and swung it open. Shelly stood there and smiled. Simone saw Kareem at the door and went to see who was there.

"Hello lovebirds," Shelly said. She had a baby wrapped in blankets and put the child in Kareem's hand. "Here, her name is Sabrina and she's your daughter."

Simone looked at Shelly then at Kareem with rage in her eyes before she spoke. "What are you doing, Shelly? Kareem, what's gong on?"

"I'm giving Kareem his child because I'm not ready to be a mother." Shelly caught a glimpse of Simone's ring. "I guess you can make your family complete now. Take care of my baby." She handed Simone a diaper bag and a folder containing Sabrina's personal legal information. "Welcome home," she said as she rushed away from the door.

Simone pulled Kareem inside the apartment and shut the door.

Tricia turned off the music and walked up to them. "What's going on? Who's baby?"

Kareem sat on the sofa while Simone took the baby from his arms. Everyone gathered around to find out what was going on. Simone looked at Kareem for answers. He knew he owed Simone an explanation. He didn't want to discuss their business in front of everyone.

Mrs. Hobbs came over and took the baby from Simone.

"Moms, can you hold her for a minute? We'll be right back." Kareem ushered Simone into the bedroom. He went to the window as soon as he walked inside. He saw Shelly get into a car and kiss a very attractive woman on the lips.

"Simone, it's not what you think," he began.

"I think you've been cheating on me with Shelly!"

"No, me and Shelly is over! We been over," he tried to explain.

"How the hell can she pop up here and say that you have a daughter with her? I've only been gone for six months. That baby is at least two months old!"

"Simone, I'm not gonna lie to you. I was seeing Shelly before you went away. I broke it off with her just before the trial started. I didn't even know that she was pregnant."

"Kareem, how could you? You told me that you were through with all of that. How are we supposed to start a life together when you're still out there fucking everything that moves?" she yelled.

"Baby, I have changed. You're all the woman I need. If I didn't mean that, I wouldn't have asked you to marry me," he pleaded.

"I don't believe this," she said.

"We will work this out. I promise that it will all be ok. Just bear with me baby." He kissed her with passion.

Simone relaxed in Kareem's arms. She believed that he was sincere. She wasn't sure if Shelly mentioned their affair or not. Since Kareem didn't mention it, she knew she owed it to him and to herself to work out their situation. Simone sat on the bed and shook her head. She asked Kareem to give her a few minutes. He closed the bedroom door as he went back into the living room.

She thought about the past six months. She wanted to marry Kareem. After all, that had been her dream since she was a kid. After she broke it off with a woman she'd sexed a few times behind bars, she decided that it was out of her system. She did some serious soul searching and realized that it was her man- not those women- that made her happy. She would live her life with Kareem in a monogamous-hetero-sexual relationship. She was a little pissed that Shelly was fucking Kareem while they were trying to repair their relationship. But she smiled, '*I still got the last laugh.*'

She entered the living room and sat on the sofa, held Kareem's hands and explained Sabrina to everyone. Mrs. Hobbs adored little Sabrina. She held her the entire time Kareem and Simone were in the bedroom.

Tricia refilled everyone's glass and asked them to rise for a toast.

"I just wanna welcome my girl Simone back home. I also want to congratulate you and Kareem on your engagement. I think Sabrina was sent here with a purpose. She's the missing link in your life. Be happy! Congratulations on it all!" She clicked her glass with everyone's and took a sip from her wine.

Tarik walked up to Tricia and asked if they could talk. She walked with him to a corner of the room. "How have you been?" he asked.

"I'm ok, and you?"

"I'm miserable without you," Tarik admitted.

"Tarik, please don't. We're here to celebrate Simone and Kareem," she said.

"I know. I just want to ask you something. I know you couldn't move on with our marriage because of my friendship with Melissa. I just want to let you know that she's gone."

"Gone, what happened?" Trish inquired.

"She moved back to Maryland with her parents. They asked her to move back home until her divorce is final. Mike left a few weeks ago to be with her and Christopher."

"Oh, I see," she said confused.

"I'm telling you this because I want you to reconsider us."

Tricia exhaled. She looked at Tarik and closed her eyes before she spoke. "Tarik, I'm sorry. We can't stay married. I don't forgive you for what you've done. I'll never be able to trust you again. I'm sorry." She walked away and went into the bathroom.

Tarik made his way around the room saying goodbye to everyone. He hugged and kissed Simone and congratulated her again. He slipped out of the door before Tricia came out of the bathroom. He didn't want anyone to see the hurt on his face.

Tricia walked out of the bathroom and looked around for Tarik. When she realized that he'd left, she went back inside the bathroom and cried. She couldn't believe she'd actually given up the only man she'd ever loved. She wasn't sure if she'd made the right decision and she definitely wasn't prepared to live with it. But it was too late now. Or was it?

The End

Now...... wasn't this worth the wait? ☺